QUEEN OF MISFORTUNE

A DARK, MAFIA ROMANCE

SHADOWS OF REDEMPTION

AJME WILLIAMS

Copyright © 2024 by Ajme Williams

All rights reserved.

No part of this book may be reproduced in any form or by any electronic or mechanical means, including information storage and retrieval systems, without written permission from the author, except for the use of brief quotations in a book review.

This is a work of fiction. Names, characters, businesses, places, events and incidents are either the products of authors imagination or used in a fictitious manner. Any resemblance to actual persons, living or dead, or actual events is purely coincidental. The following story contains mature themes, strong language and sexual situations. It is intended for mature readers only.

All characters are 18+ years of age and all sexual acts are consensual.

ABOUT THE AUTHOR

Ajme Williams writes emotional, angsty contemporary romance. All her books can be enjoyed as full length, standalone romances and are FREE to read in Kindle Unlimited .

Shadows of Redemption Series

Soldier of Death | Queen of Misfortune | Prince of Darkness

High Stakes
Bet On It | A Friendly Wager | Triple or Nothing | Press Your Luck

Heart of Hope Series
Our Last Chance | An Irish Affair | So Wrong | Imperfect Love | Eight Long Years | Friends to Lovers | The One and Only | Best Friend's Brother | Maybe It's Fate | Gone Too Far | Christmas with Brother's Best Friend | Fighting for US | Against All Odds | Hoping to Score | Thankful for Us | The Vegas Bluff | 365 Days | Meant to Be | Mile High Baby | Silver Fox's Secret Baby | Snowed In with Best Friend's Dad | Secret Triplets for Christmas | Off-Limits Daddy

The Why Choose Haremland (Reverse Harem Series)
Protecting Their Princess | Protecting Her Secret | Unwrapping their Christmas Present | Cupid Strikes... 3 Times | Their Easter Bunny | SEAL Daddies Next Door | Naughty Lessons | See Me After Class

Billionaire Secrets
Twin Secrets | Just A Sham | Let's Start Over | The Baby Contract | Too Complicated

Dominant Bosses
His Rules | His Desires | His Needs | His Punishments | His Secret

Strong Brothers
Say Yes to Love | Giving In to Love | Wrong to Love You | Hate to Love You

Fake Marriage Series
Accidental Love | Accidental Baby | Accidental Affair | Accidental Meeting

Irresistible Billionaires
Admit You Miss Me | Admit You Love Me | Admit You Want Me | Admit You Need Me

Check out Ajme's full Amazon catalogue here.

Join her VIP NL here.

DESCRIPTION

3 rules I follow no matter what:
Never marry into the mafia.
Never trust a man again.
Never fall in love with a mobster.

But Donovan Ricci isn't taking no for an answer.

When I was younger, my father married me off so I'd stop causing trouble for him. But now, years later, my husband is dead, and there's another dangerous man who wants me.

Donovan is obsessed with me from the moment we meet. But because of everything I went through, I made a vow to myself one I won't break, not even for him.

I only care about reuniting with my sister. Some older mafia boss won't catch my attention, no matter his desperate attempts. But when my father threatens my safety, Donovan proposes an irrefusable deal: *marry him, and he'll protect me...*

At the cost of sharing a bed with the most handsome mafia kingpin in the city.

DONOVAN (1 HOUR AGO)

"Kill them both."

Fucking hell. Are those the last words I'm ever going to hear? Don Giovanni Fiori telling his men to kill me and my Boss, Don Niko Leone?

I'm pissed off about that and that Niko and I were duped into thinking we had a lead on Fiori when, in fact, the asshole who was supposed to lead us to Fiori led Fiori to us in one of Niko's old warehouses.

After a short firefight, where Niko and I killed four or five of those motherfuckers, Fiori corners us. I wonder where our men are as Niko and I stare down the barrel of Fiori's gun. A sound distracts Niko, and I see it in Fiori's eyes. He's ready to rid this earth of Niko. I'm moving before the gun goes off, putting myself in front of Niko. It isn't just that it's my job to protect him. Niko is my friend. My brother. The life I have is all due to him. Sure, my father worked in the Family, but Niko was the one who saw my potential. I also just learned that the woman he's with, who I'm pretty sure he's in love with even if he doesn't say so, is pregnant. If that's not a reason for him to live, I don't know what is.

The bullet pierces my chest. Already off balance from moving to protect Niko, I'm jerked back, losing my balance and falling on Niko. He's not moving under me, which means either the bullet went through me or that thud I heard was his head hitting the concrete.

That's where I am now as Fiori gives the order for his men to kill us both.

It's quite possible that the bullet hole in my chest will do the trick. But it hasn't yet. I know because my chest feels like it's on fire. They say your life flashes before your eyes when you're about to die. That's not the case. At least not for me. Right now, regrets and disappointment are filling my thoughts. Why didn't I check Ugly Eddie for a tracker myself when we took him to interrogate him on where Fiori could be found? How did I not consider that Ugly Eddie's walking into one of Niko's clubs was part of a setup? Why didn't I tell Niko how much he meant to me and how I hoped that he was in love with Elena, who in a fucking weird turn of events is Fiori's daughter? And why did I have to die before getting to know Lucia, or Lucy as I call her, Elena's sister? From the moment I nabbed her at the airport, I've been enamored. Yes, she's beautiful and has a body made for fucking. But her mouth, the shit she spews... God, the woman has balls bigger than most men I know. Oh, how I wanted to tame her.

As I lie waiting for the kill shot, I'm reminded that Lucy is married. To another Don, no less. Of course, Don Giuseppe Conti is a million years old. He's also in Italy while Lucy is here.

Thoughts and images in my mind are fading. Maybe I'll bleed out before Fiori's men take me out. But damn, what I would give to have lived long enough to drown in Lucy's dark eyes, lose myself in her sweet body. The last image I hold is of her, defiant, mouthy, sexy.

1

LUCIA

It's turning out to be a very bad night. But that's what life is like in my world. There were many nights my mother waited up late for my father to return, concerned that he'd been killed. Of course, I secretly hoped he had been killed. Maybe Elena and I would be able to get away from the Mafia and live like regular people.

I'd come so close to leaving years ago. I'd met a man who wasn't in our world and fell in love. Dylan knew who I was, or more accurately, who my father was, and he still promised to take me away. Sometimes, I think about him and what would have happened had my father not found out about him. The night my father made him kneel in front of me and shot him in the head is seared into my brain. I didn't have time to grieve as my father called me a whore and put me on a plane heading to Italy to marry Don Giuseppe Conti. I was terrified, forced away from my sister, sent to a family I'd never met, speaking a language I didn't know that well.

Luckily for me, Giuseppe, while he could be lethal, was kind to me. In some ways, Niko reminds me of him, except that Giuseppe was ill for all of our marriage. Earlier tonight, I received a call to tell me Giuseppe's illness finally caught up with him and he died. I'm sad about that. He was good to me, and I feel fortunate that his son, Luca, is as well.

Despite my loss, I'm more worried about my sister, Elena. She's fallen for the man who kidnapped her and is pregnant with his twins. In the real world, this might be good news. In our world, it could be the death of her. Because of that, I'm glad that Luca has suggested that I stay in New York while he deals with the power plays about to come due to his father's death.

It's late, past midnight, but I find Elena sitting in the living room, wallowing in her sadness that Niko doesn't want the babies and is planning to send her away.

"You should rest," I say, sitting next to her on the couch. We've had a long day, her worse than me after a car accident set up by my father, his men kidnapping us and in her case, my father handing her over to Romeo Abate, the man my father gave her as payment for a debt. I don't know how she did it, but she killed Romeo. I know that has to weigh on her. Elena is a sweet, innocent young woman who shouldn't have to have killed anyone.

"I can't."

I hate how sad she is. "If he succeeds, maybe he'll change his mind." I hold her hand, trying to comfort her.

"I don't want to talk about it." She leans on my shoulder. "I should be asking about you. How are you holding up?"

I know she's asking about Giuseppe. "I'm okay. I mean, I'm sad. I'll miss him. But I know now that one of the reasons he let me come here, insisted I come when you didn't show up like you said you would, was that he knew his time was coming. He didn't want me to see him like that. He'd want me to remember the good times."

"Good times? I was so worried when Dad sent you away. I was afraid he'd be mean to you. I'm so glad it turned out to be the opposite."

It's one of those situations in which I could call my dad and say, "suck it!" since Giuseppe was kind. My life was infinitely better in Italy than it would have been had I stayed home.

"I was lucky. Giuseppe never asked for more than my company. He's definitely a rarity in our world."

"When do you have to go back to Italy?"

I turn to face her. "Luca wants me to stay here in New York. It's... unsettled times when a Don dies."

"Luca? That's Giuseppe's son, right? Is he kicking you out of the Family?"

"He says I'm still family, that I can return if I choose to." I squeeze her hand gently. "He said I could bring you with me. He'll protect us. I think he's grateful for all I did for his father." Another reason to be grateful to the Contis. Luca still sees me as family and is willing to take Elena. It's not wise, but Luca is like his father, lethal and yet loving, and willing to do whatever it takes to protect those in the Family.

"Does he know about the babies? About their being Niko's?" She knows, as I and Luca do, that it could be problematic for her to leave while pregnant with Niko's kids. Any other Don would worry about Niko's response.

"Yes. He has no problem with that."

"Niko wants me to get a new identity," she says, her voice so small it makes me want to punch Niko in the throat.

"What Niko wants doesn't matter once he decides he doesn't want you or the babies."

We sit in silence. Decisions need to be made, but not at this moment.

The quiet is disrupted by a commotion at the front door to Niko's penthouse.

"In here!"

Elena and I startle, jumping up from the couch.

Three of Niko's men storm in, their faces etched with lines of urgency.

"What's wrong?" Elena's voice is full of worry.

"We need to go. You have five minutes to pack. Both of you," one says.

"Where?" I demand. I don't know Niko's men well enough to be sure these three actually work for him. Considering just that morning, the car Elena and I were in was driven off the road and we were kidnapped by my father, it isn't too much to consider the possibility that he'd breached Niko's penthouse.

"Why? What happened?" Elena asks.

"Giovanni set a trap. We need to take you to the compound. Now."

I grip Elena's hand, knowing this could mean Niko is in trouble. And if he's in trouble, then his right-hand man, Donovan, is too. God, what an annoying human being he is. Not that I want him dead, because I don't. I know he's important in Niko's business, which means he's important to keeping my sister safe if she convinces Niko to let her stay. It has nothing to do with the way he looks at me like I'm an Italian feast he wants to consume.

"Where is Niko?" she asks.

"We don't have time for this. Pack so we can go!"

"No." Elena steps forward with a bravado I didn't realize she has. My little sister was more sheltered, more coddled even as my parents tried to mold her into a subservient Mafia wife. That sort of woman didn't stand up to her husband or his men. And yet, Elena is doing just that.

"I demand to know what's going on," she insists.

I worry that this could be a problem. Depending on Niko's orders, they could drag us out of here, or worse, kill us. "If they're moving us, Niko is probably fine."

Elena swings around to me. "But you don't know that, do you?" She whirls back toward the men. "Tell me everything."

The man looks to the other two as if he isn't sure how to proceed. It's odd that they appear unsure of what to do. Elena seems to have more sway in Niko's family than I realized.

"We have orders to take you both to the compound in Long Island immediately."

"Who ordered? Niko? Where is he?" she asks.

"It's protocol," one of the other men says. "Your safety is our priority." I'm sure he's trying to reassure her, but it's not working.

"Is he hurt?" she pushes. "I'm not stepping one foot outside this place until I know exactly what's happened to him!"

"We really must insist." The third man, younger, with unease clouding his eyes, makes a move as if to usher us out.

"Insist all you want, but I'm not moving!"

"Boss would want you safe—"

"Then he can come and tell me himself!" The defiance surges, fierce and powerful within her.

Go, baby sister, is all I can think. I decide to take a stand with her. I arch a brow at them, expecting them to follow her orders.

"Please," the first man implores again.

"Tell me where he is. Now. Is he hurt?" Her voice is getting stronger, and I'm so proud of her.

The first man sighs. "It's complicated."

"Just because I'm a woman, doesn't mean I'm stupid or ignorant. I'm the daughter of a Don. Do you think I don't know what goes on?"

"We're not at liberty—"

"And I say you are. Niko isn't here, and that means I'm in charge."

The three men glance at each other, clearly uncertain of the truth of that.

"The woman of a don is to be held up, respected," I inform them. She's not married to Niko, and it's clear that he'd told her he didn't intend to make her his wife, but maybe his men don't know that.

"They're not married—"

"That's inconsequential. Do you think Don Leone would want to see you bullying the woman he sleeps next to?" I continue.

"We're not bullying. We have orders to keep you safe."

"I'm safe here. Now, tell me, where is Niko?"

Movement across the room has us all looking, tensing as if my father's men had breached Niko's sanctuary.

Liam, Niko's *consigliere*, strides in. "Are you supposed to be taking her to the compound?"

"You weren't with them?" Elena asks.

Liam is FBI, so while I'm sure he helps Niko in some areas, it seems unlikely he'd be involved in the more nefarious, violent tasks.

"No. I was preparing your documents and travel plans." He turns to the men. "Why aren't they on the way to the compound?"

"Because I'm not leaving without answers," Elena says firmly. "Answers you're going to help me get."

Liam's gaze sharpens as he looks at her. I hold a breath because I know that Liam has more power than the three men sent here to pack us up and take us to the compound.

I glance at Elena, who arches a brow, challenging him.

He sinks his teeth into his lower lip as he turns to the men. "Well? What's the hold-up?"

"Orders are to take them to the safehouse," the younger man says, almost apologetically.

"The mistress of the house has other plans." Liam's words are clipped, authoritative. "Elena, what do you need?"

Inwardly, I'm shouting, *Yes! Liam is going to support her.*

"Information. Confirmation. Assurance that Niko is not on death's doorstep." She sounds strong, but I can hear the undercurrent of panic.

"We don't know where he is or how he is," one man finally says. "All we know is that Giovanni ambushed him."

Liam turns to Elena. "That's all I've heard too. But" —he puts his hand on her arm— "there is a protocol. We'll know soon. In the meantime—"

"In the meantime, we secure this place. If he is okay, he'll come back here, right? This is his most secure location in the city."

Liam nods. "Right."

Elena turns to the three men. "Station men outside the garage and at the elevator. At least two men should be in the hall and one at the stairwell outside the penthouse. No one, except Niko or his known men, go in or out without my say-so. And you" —she turns back to Liam— "get on the phone. Find out everything you can about Niko's location and condition."

"What about Donovan?" I ask. "Niko doesn't seem to go anywhere without him." God, why do I care what happens to that giant Toady?

Liam nods. "I'll get on it." He turns to the other men. "You have your orders."

"Are you sure that's wise?" the man challenges, more out of worry than defiance.

"You are asking Elena, right?" Liam says.

Another inward shout of *Yes!*

The men spring into motion, a testament to Liam's influence, or maybe just the realization that Elena's determination is unbreakable.

"If Dad killed him…" She doesn't finish the sentence.

"Don't think of that." I rub her back.

One of the men approaches. "We're following your orders, but the compound is truly the safest place."

"The last time I was on the road between the compound and here, I was driven off the road and kidnapped by the very man you say has ambushed Niko. I'm staying here."

I nod next to my sister. I'm so pleased she has found her voice. I just hope it doesn't get her killed.

The door crashes open, and Niko strides in. He looks fierce. He's pissed and ready to kill someone. Maybe he already did because his shirt is covered in blood. Unless it's his blood.

Elena rushes toward him, relief evident. But she stops short when Niko barks out to his men, "Why are they still here?"

Liam steps up to him. "They've been taking charge."

I look beyond Niko, wondering about Donovan.

"Taking charge? What the fuck, Liam?" Niko stabs him with his forefinger. "You're in charge in situations like this."

He shrugs. "Elena had it under control. She's the mistress—"

"She's leaving, remember? I gave you an order—"

"Yeah, well, that was before you walked into Giovanni's ambush."

I'm finding it shocking that my father was able to pull this off. Yes, my father is a Don, but as far as I can tell, he has significant weaknesses. Weaknesses that require him to partner with other families, such as Don Tiberius Abate. Although, I believe that Niko killed Tiberius earlier tonight. That means my father is acting on his own and found a way to lure Niko to him. Could it be that my sister has distracted Niko enough to make that possible?

And what happened to Donovan?

"Where's Donovan?" I ask.

"I want them gone," Niko says, ignoring me. "Now."

"I'm not going." Elena lifts her chin in defiance. It's a potentially deadly move.

His jaw clenches, a muscle ticking in his cheek. He moves closer to her, and I'm ready to step in and hope it doesn't end up bad for both of us.

"What do you hope to gain by staying?" he sneers.

Elena is unable to answer.

"Whatever." He turns away. "I'm going upstairs to clean up. We meet in my office in fifteen, then we go end that motherfucker and burn his business down."

Niko turns to leave, and as he does, the door opens and two men enter, dragging a moaning Donovan inside. Blood seeps through his shirt over his chest.

Oh, God. Panic shoots through me.

"Get him to a room now. Not his. He'll bloody it up. The empty servant room. Where's Doc?" Niko's command slices through the tension, and yet, the crack of fear is clear in his voice. His friend, his brother in arms, is injured. Seriously injured, judging by the amount of blood.

I gasp and rush to Donovan.

Just as I'm about to reach him, one of the men helping him pushes me back. "Hey!"

Donovan grips the man's arm. "If you ever put your hands on her again, I'll rip your throat out!" Then he passes out.

2

LUCIA

"Take care of him," Niko orders. He turns to head upstairs, and it seems cold of him to leave Donovan like this, but I see the worry in his eyes. And the anger. He now has another reason to seek vengeance.

Elena follows Niko upstairs, and my first instinct is to go with her. Niko is in a state, and I want to protect her, especially if he rejects her again. But I recall how Elena has acted tonight. She was assertive. Determined. A leader. She doesn't need me.

So I turn my attention to Donovan. I elbow my way through the sea of bodies. "Move. Put him down here so I can check him."

There, in the center of their circle, lies Donovan. They've propped him against a wall, his face waxen. I'm shocked at the amount of blood. It's everywhere, soaked into his shirt.

My fingers find Donovan's pulse, a thready beat telling me he's alive, but for how long? Panic nips at my nerves, but I squash it down. He should be at the emergency room, but I know why he's not. Why he won't. Too many questions. Too much risk. No, Mafia families have their own medical personnel to avoid hospitals.

"Where's the doctor?"

"Stuck in traffic. He won't make it for a while." The response comes from one of Niko's men, his face pinched with worry.

Memories flood back of all the times I nursed Giuseppe. It wasn't due to gunshot wounds, but he'd had a few falls near the end that required bandaging. Something needs to be done for Donovan, and it appears I'm the only one remotely suited to taking care of it.

"Fine. We'll start without him. First, we need to move him. Somewhere flat, somewhere I can work."

"Are you sure?" Liam's voice is filled with doubt.

I ignore him. "Get me alcohol, towels, bandages, a knife, and tweezers."

"She's one of them," one of the men grumbles. "Giovanni shot him and she's—"

"She's not." Liam's voice is stern.

The man appears hesitant and yet compelled to press on. "She's a Fiori."

I step into the man's space. His eyes narrow, and I'm sure he'll have no problem breaking my neck. "Maybe you should march upstairs to tell that to Elena. She's a Fiori too. I'm sure Niko would love the reminder."

The man's face scrunches in disgust.

"Well? What's the problem? Or how about I go do it for you?" I turn to go upstairs. Why was I worried about Donovan, anyway? Elena and Niko have been upstairs long enough.

"Please, Lucia." Liam puts his hand on my arm. "Lou is just being protective."

"Giovanni is a dead man," Lou says.

"If you were better at your job, he'd already be dead." I glare at him, daring him to challenge me even though I don't much want to be punched or choked.

He bares his teeth but steps aside.

"Let's get him into another room," I say.

The men shift, discomfort in their stances, but no one moves.

"Did you not hear me?" Do they want Donovan to die?

"Go! Now!" Liam barks.

Finally, they scatter, a flurry of activity to get what I need and move Donovan.

"Where can we take him?" I ask.

"There's a room over here. It's for servants, but Niko uses it for visitors." Liam leads the way, and two of Niko's men carefully scoop up Donovan's limp form. I follow behind as they bring Donovan into the room.

Once he's settled on the bed, I open Donovan's shirt to inspect the wound. I'm no expert, but the entrance appears to be right of center. That's good, I think. I mean, it didn't hit his heart. But there is a great deal of blood. That is a concern.

My fingers probe the wound gently, searching for the bullet.

"Here are the supplies." One of Niko's men places alcohol, towels, and bandages on the side table.

"Okay, Toady, let's see about keeping you alive." I take a breath to steady my shaky hands. I start by pouring alcohol onto a towel to clean the wound.

"Always did like a woman who takes charge," Donovan's weak voice murmurs.

I glance down, catching the ghost of Donovan's infamous smirk before it fades into a grimace of pain.

"Idiot," I mutter, even as my heart stutters. "You'll owe me for saving you from being six feet under."

"Counting on it." His eyes flutter closed once more.

With the tweezers, I press down on the area around the bullet wound. His chest rises and falls steadily under my touch, which reassures me that I'm not making anything worse.

As I prod gently, seeking the bullet lodged within him, the memory of first meeting him flashes in my mind.

I'D JUST ARRIVED in New York with the goal of finding Elena and bringing her back to Italy with me. She'd made a plan to escape a forced marriage, but when she didn't arrive, I knew something had gone wrong. Then she called to say Niko Leone had kidnapped her off the altar. Terror struck deep at the idea that *Il Soldato della Morte* had kidnapped her. Still, I was determined to save and protect her.

I'd ordered a ride, pleased it was waiting once I exited the airport.

"Welcome to New York," he'd said, voice smooth as silk.

But we hadn't driven very far before I realized this was no ordinary ride. He'd pulled off into a secluded area and zip-tied me. Perhaps I should have considered him a serial killer, but given the world I grew up in, I knew he was Mafia. The question was whether he was with my father, in which case I was dead, or the Abates or Leones.

"Who are you? What do you want?" I demanded, my pulse hammering in my ears from fear.

"Donovan. I don't want anything. My Boss, on the other hand—"

"Who's your Boss? Do you know who I am? My husband is Don Conti."

Donovan smirked at me through the rearview mirror. "How do you think I knew to pick you up? Of course I know who you are."

"Jerk. Who is your Boss?"

"You sure are loud. Are you like this with Conti? Why does he put up with it?"

"Because he's a real man, not a Toady like you."

He laughed. He actually laughed. It made me hate him more. How dare he be amused by me when I was being serious?

Once in the city, he pulled into an alley. He got out of the SUV and opened the back door with that stupid grin.

"Behave."

"No. Why should I? You're just going to kill me anyway. Why make it easy for you?"

"There's no plan to kill you at this time."

"Then why am I here? Who is—"

"You're here for your sister, right? Well, if you want any chance to see her, first talk to Don Leone."

"Why does he have my sister? Is this all some ploy to get my father?"

"You know, if you'd shut up and behave, you'd have these answers."

I shook my head. "I'm just another pawn in your stupid games."

For a moment, he studied me. "Nah. I see a fierce woman who'll do anything for her sister." His words stopped me cold. I wasn't sure why except I felt seen. It was a stupid feeling, but there it was.

Of course, most of my encounters with him have been acrimonious. Like a few nights ago when Elena insisted we had to be respectful to Don Leone and show up for dinner. He had us locked up in his compound, but we needed to show respect?

But when we got to the dining room, Donovan was the one eating steak at the table.

"Don Leone lets his dog eat at the table?" I said before I could think better of it.

"Luce!" Elena gaped at me.

Donovan smirked at me. "Can you eat with that mouth or just spew garbage?"

"Surely, we can eat in your room," I said to Elena.

Donovan shook his head. "Have a seat, Ladies."

Once seated, he said, "I have to tell you, Princess, I'm surprised I'm not out back digging a hole in Niko's mother's garden."

I had no idea why he was saying that to Elena, but I didn't care. It was an asshole thing to say. "What's wrong with you?"

He arched a brow at me, but it had that hint of smirk that suggested he was amused by me.

"I swear, you goons are the most insecure men on the earth," I say.

Elena puts her hand over mine. "Maybe let's not upset him."

Donovan's expression shows intrigue. "Insecure? Do tell me more."

"Why else would you live your life picking on people smaller than you? You feel small, and threatening us makes you feel big. It's disgusting."

"What's disgusting is how Elena spoke to Niko. Do you have a death wish, Princess? You must. Why else would you call him inept?"

Shocked, my head snapped to Elena. "You did what?"

She shrugged. "He said he'd protect you and Kate. I thought he failed. My anger got the best of me."

Donovan sipped his wine. "Niko showed more restraint than I've ever seen." He studied her. "He must like you." The waggle of his brow suggested Niko must like her in bed.

"You're crass," I say with disgust. But what's strange was that I got the feeling Elena liked it too. Despite what my father thought, I'd never had sex. Not with my boyfriend who promised to take me away, nor with my husband, Giuseppe, who was too ill to have any interest. I envy Elena if it's true that she enjoys Niko's touch.

DONOVAN WINCES, bringing me back into the present. His pained expression wrenches at something deep inside me. I don't like this man. He's always around me. Smirking. Winking. Sometimes being nice. Why? I don't like it, and yet, each time I look at him, something inside me softens.

I'm able to get the tweezers around the bullet and pull it out. Then I secure gauze over the wound.

"Lucy..."

"Shh, save your strength." I clean up the supplies. I don't want to look at him like this...weak and vulnerable. It makes me feel protective of him, and I don't want that. He represents everything I hate in life. Life in the Mafia for women is filled with misogyny and violence. We aren't able to make any choices, any decisions on our own. We're pawns to be sold off or exchanged. We are prisoners within the Family. It's distressing to me that Niko has offered my sister complete freedom, including a new identity, and she wants to stay here with him. I hope that whatever discussion she's having with Niko, he continues to push her away. With Giuseppe dead, maybe I can go with her. Would Luca, Giuseppe's son and now the Don of the Conti Family, allow me to leave? Elena and I could be free to live our own lives.

I hover over Donovan, making sure he's breathing. I check the bandage to make sure it's secure.

His hand wraps around my wrist. "Knew you... liked me." His eyelids are at half-mast, as is his smirk.

I lean in close, close enough to feel his ragged breaths against my skin, close enough that our noses nearly brush. The proximity is an annoying electric charge.

"In your dreams, Toady." I straighten because I have this terrifying urge to kiss him. "You think this is because I like you?"

The amusement in his eyes holds steady. Damn him.

"Listen to me, Donovan Ricci. I only helped you because you're important to Niko, and he... he's important to Elena. That and I hate the idea of my father winning. That's the only reason."

His smile falters but doesn't disappear entirely. Instead, it morphs into something softer. I watch as his eyelids flutter, once, twice, and then close.

"Stay with me, Lucy," he whispers. "This toady needs you..." His words trail off, and the smile he attempts to hold slips away.

"Stop being charming," I mutter.

"I'm growing on you."

"In a bad way. Now rest, you big oaf."

His lips twitch up again and then he succumbs to sleep.

I move away and past the men standing at the door.

"He should be fine until the doctor gets here." I exit the room and run into Liam.

"Doc's on his way up. I'm going to let Niko know. How is he?" Liam asks.

"He's sleeping peacefully."

Liam arches a brow, and I remember that sometimes, peaceful sleep means death.

"He's fine for the moment."

Liam nods and goes upstairs.

I make my way to the living area where Niko has a nicely stocked bar. I'm dying for something strong, but I opt for wine. It's always best to keep some of your wits about you when around a bunch of Mafia soldiers.

I sit on the couch staring out into the dark Manhattan night, praying that Niko and Elena aren't planning a life together. That she'll take the papers Liam made for her and start a new life. I make a mental list of what I need to do to try and secure my freedom as well.

I hear movement out in the hall. Curious, I go to the entrance to the living area to see what's happening. Everyone, including Elena, is gathered in Niko's office. No one seems to notice I'm not there. I don't want to be included, and yet, I want to know what's going on.

I ease my way closer so I can hear but not be seen.

"Donovan?" Niko asks as he guides Elena with him to his desk. She stands with him looking happy and regal, and all my hopes for her die knowing that she chose to stay with him.

"He'll live," Liam says. "Unless Lucia kills him."

There's a snicker in the group. Even Elena smiles. What the hell? What did that mean?

"Orders are to lay low, recover, and regroup." Niko lists out who is staying and who is coming to the compound. "We want Giovanni thinking he's won."

Smart. My father will gloat and get lazy.

"And then we show him he hasn't," Lou says.

"That's right."

Niko pauses, holding Elena's gaze. She stands by his side, nodding and smiling at him.

"Before we face what's ahead, there's something I need to let you all know." A smile tugs at the corner of Niko's mouth. "Elena has agreed to be my wife."

Murmurs ripple through the room. I close my eyes. Of course, I knew this was happening. I could see it in her as she stood next to Niko. And of course, with twins on the way, she was safer under his protection. But still.

"Smart move," Lou says. "Once Giovanni is gone, you can take over—"

"This marriage isn't about that. It isn't business." Niko brings Elena's hand to his lips and kisses it. "This woman has stolen my heart."

I cock my head, studying him, wondering if that could possibly be true.

"You have a heart?" Liam jokes.

Niko laughs. "Taking Donovan's role?"

Liam shrugs. "Since he's not here, I figured someone should."

"Congratulations," Niko's men say, and they seem to mean it. Even Lou. That's a relief. If they accept Elena, it will be better for her.

I step away from the doorway, and in that moment, I feel completely alone. My husband, who had been my friend for the last few years, has died. My sister is engaged and part of a new Family. I'm in limbo.

I hope I can stay with Elena and help with the babies, but I wasn't part of Niko's grand announcement, and that tells me that I should plan to return to Italy.

3

DONOVAN

I'm not dead. Unless I'm in hell and the fire in my chest and jackhammering in my head are my punishment for a life of crime. I peel my eyelids open and immediately regret it as the sun sears my eyes like death rays. My hand moves to shield the glare, but it's heavy, as if weighted down by lead. I'm in the penthouse, but not my space. It's an unused servant's room.

"Toady."

Pleasure breaks through the pain at hearing her voice. Lucy. I manage to bring her face into view.

"Can't stay away," I try to say, although the sandpaper in my throat makes it hard.

"Idiot."

"Lucia, please." Liam's voice is calm but laced with a hint of irritation. My Lucy has that effect on everyone except maybe Elena and me. Well, she irritates me too, but in a good way. Turns out I'm a sadist.

"You do know you're not bulletproof right?" she hisses.

I feel like shit, and yet her words make me happy. "Careful. It almost sounds like you care."

She sniffs, her face distorting into disgust. "Yeah... no."

"Lucia, he needs rest." Liam's hands are firm on her shoulders as he guides her away.

She jerks away. "Don't touch me." Her glare lingers on me for a moment, and then she's gone.

"I think she likes me."

Liam rolls his eyes.

"How is he?" Niko asks, striding into the room.

"I've been better, but I've been worse," I manage. "Feels like I've been hit by a truck."

"More like a bullet." Niko steps closer, worry and gratitude clear in his eyes. "You saved my life."

I shrug, but the movement feels like a knife in my chest. "It's my job." I can remember blocking him from Giovanni's shot, but everything after that is a blur. "Tell me you killed Giovanni."

"I wish I could. The motherfucker slipped through our fingers." Niko clenches his fist. "Right now, we're cleaning up the mess and dealing with the Abate territory. We're giving Giovanni a false sense of security."

"No shit? You're letting him off?"

"No." Niko's voice turns lethal. "We're regrouping and letting him savor what he thinks is a win. In the background, we're preparing to wipe him off the face of the earth."

Good. I remember before being ambushed, Niko's distraction over Elena. I have a feeling he loves her, but I also have a foggy memory of him telling her he wanted her gone.

"Is Elena okay?"

The change in Niko is instant. From a lethal killer to a man filled with sunshine. "She's safe."

Liam snickers.

I look at him and then Niko. "What?"

"I'm marrying her," Niko says.

"Makes sense. Good way to get at Giovanni—"

"I'm in love with her. And..." Niko looks at Liam. "I haven't announced this, but since you're family, brothers to me, I'll tell you. She's pregnant with twins."

Liam's brows rise to his hairline. "No shit?"

"Romeo's?"

Niko's eyes narrow, and all of a sudden, I worry he's going to throttle me. "Mine!"

"Ah, okay... good. I'm happy for you." I look to Liam for help, but he just shakes his head.

"You should get some rest." Niko pats my shoulder, and I wince as a pain lances through my chest.

"Wait... how did we get out?"

"Backup arrived. We got you here, but... fucking hell, Donovan." Niko scrapes his hand over his face. "I thought you were dead."

"Lucia saved you," Liam says.

"Lucy." I smile at her name.

"She stopped the bleeding, pulled out the bullet. All before the doctor could make it here," Liam finishes.

Lucy? My heart stutters. I want to think she helped me because she feels the pull between us, but I'm no romantic. I know she hates me. Another foggy memory returns of her telling me she only helped me because of Niko and Elena.

"Rest up," Niko says. "We've got a mess to clean and Giovanni to hunt down. And... I want both you and Liam to stand up for me when I marry Elena, which I want to do ASAP. She needs the added protection now that she's carrying my children."

"I'm honored, Boss."

He smiled. "You're my brother, Donovan. You and Liam. Now, rest."

I nod in acknowledgment, but my mind reels with thoughts of getting back to work. I don't want to rest, but my body is screaming at me to stay put. I close my eyes and give in to the darkness.

The dream gods take mercy on me and bring Lucy to me. I think it's a memory when I reach out and take her wrist.

"Knew you... liked me."

She leans in close, close enough that I can feel her warm breath on my clammy skin, her electric energy zapping along my nerves. "In your dreams, Toady." She moves away, and I hate the loss of her nearness. "You think this is because I like you? Listen to me, Donovan Ricci. I only helped you because you're important to Niko, and he... he's important to Elena. That and I hate the idea of my father winning. That's the only reason."

I think she protests too much, but I'm too out of it to say more than to ask her to stay. "This toady needs you..."

"Stop being charming," she mutters.

Warmth fills my chest. "I'm growing on you."

In reality, she called me a big oaf, but in dreams, anything can happen. In mine, she lies next to me. I feel the warmth of her body nestled against mine, and it fills me with a surge of healing and strength far more powerful than medicine. I pull her close, letting my hand slide over her curves. I don't feel pain now. Just lightness. Contentment.

How many times have I had this dream? Nearly nightly since the moment I nabbed her from the airport.

"What do you need? What hurts?" she asks.

I take her hand and guide it to my dick. "This needs relief." This is why I love dreams. Barriers such as the fact that she hates me don't get in the way. Neither do clothes, as in an instant, we're naked and her hand is stroking my cock. It feels so fucking good, but I want more. In dreams, injuries and pain don't exist, so it's nothing to roll her under me and slip into her tight, wet pussy. I move in and out, and it feels fucking amazing. I groan and arch, pumping into her until I release my load.

"Donovan?"

My eyes snap open to find Lucy standing over me, worry etched in her expression.

"You're okay. You're safe. It's just a nightmare."

Holy fuck. Did I just sleep fuck? My hand goes to my dick. My sweatpants are wet, a sure sign that I had a wet dream. Knowing Lucy won't appreciate knowing that, I don't share that bit of news.

"Lucy?"

"Yes.

"I'm surprised you're still here."

She straightens. "It was hard not to come with the way you were thrashing and groaning."

I bite back the smile at the memory of my dream fucking her. "Thank you for being my nursemaid."

"Yeah, well, it appears you still have more lives."

"Wouldn't be the first time I've used one." I cock my head to the side. "Why are you still here? Unless, of course, you do like—"

"Maybe I like watching you squirm."

"Or maybe you care."

"Yeah… no. I like seeing you taken down a peg or two."

I remember how she once called me insecure for picking on people smaller than me. "You like that your father shot me?" I ask.

Her breath hitches. Pain and fear for me flash in her expression, but it's gone so fast I wouldn't have seen it had I not been staring into her beautiful face. "You live another day so you can take him down."

"Damn right." All of a sudden, I wonder what Giovanni did to her to make her hate him so much. It had to be more than handing her over to Giuseppe. Elena has no love for her father, but Lucy has a deep-seated hate. Given the chance, I'm certain she'd kill him herself. As much as I know Niko wants to be the one to end Giovanni's life, I can't deny I'd like to see Lucy put a bullet into Giovanni's head. For the first time in my life working for Niko, I consider disobeying him so that Lucy can get her vengeance.

"Of course, you could beat me to it," I say.

Her expression reminds me of the day I took her from the airport and told her I saw a fierce woman out to protect her sister. It was like I'd given her a gift by seeing more to her than just her value in Niko's plan for vengeance. It was that expression that gave me hope she didn't hate me as much as she tried to project. If I played my cards right, I'd wear her wall down and instead of wet dreams, I'd have this fierce, smart-mouthed, sexy woman for real.

4

LUCY

"You like that your father shot me?"

No, I don't. In fact, it's scary how much I hate that my father shot Donovan. Not that I'll let him know that. "You live another day so you can take him down."

"Damn right. Of course, you could beat me to it."

And with those words, I'm again struck by the way he seems to be able to see me... see into me. It's the first time I've felt that from anyone. Even Dylan, who I knew loved me, who promised me a new and better life, didn't see into my soul as Donovan does. Damn him. Donovan is a magnet, drawing me in with his strength and that infuriating charm. Yet, he's also the embodiment of everything I loathe. How can I be drawn to him when he represents the shackles that I've spent my life trying to break?

And yet, I would like to kill my father. It's a deep-seated desire that I rarely give thought to because I'm not like these people. I'm not a murderer. But given the opportunity...

I won't have the opportunity. First, I don't know where my father is. I know he's hiding. It's one of the many things I learned today as I lurked about the penthouse, eavesdropping. I've learned that

Tiberius Abate is dead, as is his son at Elena's hand. I'm so proud that she was able to take his life in preservation of her own.

With Tiberius and Romeo dead, the Abate business is up for grabs, and Niko plans to take it. Although I hate this world, in some ways, I'm glad to hear of Niko's plans. It will keep him busy, giving me an excuse to stay with Elena to help her during her pregnancy.

"You like that idea." Donovan's voice interrupts my thoughts.

"I just want him dead."

I need to check Donovan's bandages as the doctor instructed us to do, but I hate getting so close to him. I hate the dark eyes that hint of mischievousness. I hate the warmth of his skin. I hate the scent of him. Mostly, I hate how much every part of me responds when I'm close to him.

But checking his bandages means I don't have to talk about my innermost thoughts, so I sit on the edge of the bed, carefully lifting the taped gauze, fighting the urge to kiss his chest. *Seriously, Lucia?*

His hand covers mine, and I have to close my eyes in an attempt to ward off the warm flow of something I can't name.

"I wish I could kill him for you, but Niko has a special bullet for him."

I shrug and pull my hand away. "As long as he's gone and can't hurt Elena or her babies."

"God... babies. How long was I out of it?"

It's not my place to tell Elena and Niko's personal business. "You haven't missed much. Niko isn't going after Giovanni yet."

"Wants to regroup and catch him off guard."

So Niko told him. "Plus, he's got new priorities. Elena. The twins."

"Elena's doing okay?"

"Better than you," I say. "She's strong."

"Like her sister."

God, how does he do that? How does he say things that make my heart do cartwheels?

I fold my arms across my chest, a shield against his irritating charm.

"Even so, you don't have to carry it all alone."

"What? You're going to protect me? You can't even get out of bed. Seems to me you could use a lesson in self-preservation yourself." The words tumble out, tinged with anger I don't fully understand. I tell myself it's for this idiotic world we live in, but deep down, I think it's at him for nearly getting himself killed.

"Maybe." The corner of his mouth quirks up. "But who'd save reckless bastards like me if not for guardian angels masquerading as ice queens?"

The metaphor strikes a chord deep in my chest, and I push off from the bed to gain distance from the growing urge to move closer to him.

He chuckles like he knows what he's doing to me. I want to slap his amusement off his face. Or maybe kiss it off.

"Say, how come you don't have babies?" he asks.

I whirl on him, gaping. "None of your business."

"Surely, even an old man like Giuseppe could get it up."

I shake my head at his vulgarity, and at the same time, I'm glad for it. It helps push away the warm feelings. "As I said, it's none of your business." I grab the clean gauze to replace his bandage, pressing extra-hard and enjoying the wince of pain on Donovan's face.

"You don't like me."

"Finally, you get it," I say, putting away the medical supplies.

"I'd think you'd be grateful."

I make a face. "Why?"

"I did what you asked me to do. Remember? The other day at the compound when you first arrived? You made me promise that I'd protect your sister. I jumped in front of Niko and took that bullet because he's my Boss, but also because I knew Elena needed him. I fulfilled my promise."

He's right. I need to be grateful. Not that I care so much about Niko, because I'm still not sure about him. But Elena loves him, and when he looks at her, I believe I see love from him.

Before I can offer up my thanks, he asks, "You never asked me to protect you. Why?"

"Because I don't need or want your protection. And you're mistaken if you think taking bullets is brave. It isn't brave, it's foolish."

He shifts in the bed, grimacing slightly, but the smirk doesn't fade from his lips. "You're welcome, anyway."

"What do you want, a reward? Do you think I'll be so grateful that I'll fall into your arms because you've proven yourself so gallant?"

His smirk turns lecherous. "I'm grateful that the idea of you in my arms has crossed your mind."

I want to punch him in his wound.

"I know I've thought about it. Dreamed about it. Tell me, what have you fantasized about me, Lucy?"

"Nothing," I lie. Donovan with his big beefy, muscly body has haunted my dreams more than once. It makes me wish I'd packed my vibrator when I came to New York.

"Lucy." His voice is soft, coaxing, and I hate that my name sounds different when it passes his lips.

"Stop saying my name like that!"

"Like what?" His eyes never leave mine, searching, probing and I feel myself failing at protecting myself.

"Like it means something to you." God, I've revealed too much.

"Maybe it does. I have feelings, you know."

Yeah, right. "Your feelings aren't my problem, Donovan."

"I could be good for you."

I take a step back, putting more distance between us. "You aren't my salvation, either."

The smirk fades, replaced by something softer, something dangerously close to understanding. "I'm not trying to save you, Lucy. God knows, you don't need anyone to save you."

"Then what do you want from me? Why do you keep poking at me?" Dammit, I've said too much again.

He shrugs. "I don't know, actually. I only know I like being around you. What I don't get is that if you hate me so, why are you here? It's almost as if you're concerned about me."

"Your health isn't my concern."

"Of course." For the first time, the smirk is gone. His tone has an edge of bitterness. I should be glad that I'm getting through, and yet, I feel bad about my words.

"Why would my health be your concern, and yet, here you are."

I swallow and hope I look indifferent. "Consider it... professional interest. Your dying complicates things."

"Everything about you is complicated, Lucy."

It's stupid, but his words hurt. I start toward the door.

"Where are you going?" He almost sounds disappointed.

"Somewhere you're not."

"Always so caring, my ice queen." He's mocking me.

"No." I turn toward him. "I'm not one of your conquests, Donovan. I don't belong to you, to Niko, or to any of this."

"Lucy—"

"Let me make this clear. I'm here for Elena. That's my sole purpose. Not to be a pawn in some power struggle."

He tries to push himself up, his face contorting in pain. Concern flickers inside me for a moment, but I ignore it.

He gives up, lies back. "Always so fiery."

"Fire burns, Donovan. You should remember that."

"One day, you're going to let someone in. And when you do, all these walls you've built won't mean a damn thing." The certainty in his voice stirs something deep within me, and it terrifies me because a part of me hopes he's right.

But I push the feeling away. "That day isn't today." With one last look at his stubborn face, I turn and exit the room. With each step, I rebuild the walls, higher, stronger. I have to, because Donovan's world is filled with blood and tears.

It's a death sentence.

5

LUCIA

Two days later, I've been able to avoid Donovan, and because I'm not lurking about anymore, I'm able to avoid Niko and his men. My focus is on Elena, who isn't throwing up as much anymore, but she's still tired. Right now, she's resting while I'm in the kitchen, sitting alone with a glass of water, feeling like I'm in limbo. At any minute, Niko can tell me to leave, even if Elena wants me to stay. Or maybe Luca will order me back to Italy, a command that Niko would likely enforce as it turns out they're professional acquaintances.

My solitude is interrupted when Niko enters the kitchen carrying a glass of something potent. He has a large, foreboding presence that ensures no one forgets the power he wields.

"Lucia." His tone is casual, and yet, there's an undercurrent of command. "You and Elena will be staying here—"

"I thought we were going to the compound in Long Island. You said we'd be safer—"

"You'll be safer here."

I arch a brow. "So, before, you were lying. You just wanted Elena out of the way—"

"Careful—"

"No. Kill me if you must."

He jerks back. His expression suggests he thinks I've gone off my rocker.

"I've lived my entire life under the threat of pain or torture or death. After a while, it's too exhausting to be afraid."

I think there's a slight upward twitch of his lips. Great, he's humored by me as well. He sits down, and there's something about his coming to my level that hints of his approaching me not as a Don.

"I love your sister. Before… let's just say it was difficult to be around her thinking she wanted to leave. You and Elena are safe in both places, but I want her close. I want to avoid what happened the other day when she got it in her head to come to the city."

Okay, so I can't blame him for that since Elena's plan put us in danger.

"I've beefed up security here, and Donovan will be staying onsite with you both."

Crap. "Is that necessary?" I hope my voice is steady and doesn't reveal my annoyance at this plan.

"Absolutely." Niko takes a sip of his drink, eyes assessing. "Donovan is best positioned to ensure your safety, especially with the recent threats."

"Surely, he's too important to you in business, especially if you plan on taking over the Abate family."

"He's recovering—"

"All the more reason to have someone stronger to protect Elena."

He arches a brow. "What's your deal with Donovan?"

"I just don't want him here, Niko." The words slip out unintentionally.

"I can't imagine why. He's practically the only one of my men who tolerates you."

"I don't need a reason."

"Neither do I. Your feelings don't dictate security measures." His voice is firm, telling me there's no discussion. "Donovan stays."

"So what I want or Elena wants—"

"No. Your desires are secondary."

"Secondary." I wonder why Elena loves this man when it's clear that Niko doesn't give a crap about what she or I want.

"Let's get something straight." He leans forward, and the relaxed, friendlier version of Niko is gone, replaced by Don Leone. "You're only here because you're Elena's sister. She needs you. But make no mistake, Lucia. If it weren't for her, you'd be on the next flight back to Italy."

A shiver sneaks up my spine, but I hide it, not wanting him to see my fear. I nod my understanding.

"Good." Niko stands. "Have a good afternoon."

He turns to leave, but before he does, I say, "End it. End my father and his threat to Elena."

"Done."

I don't trust him with my sister's or my life, but in that moment, I feel quite certain he'll make sure my father never gets to Elena again.

I stare at the empty space where he stood moments before, the air still thick with his authority. My purpose here is crystal clear—as Elena's sister, nothing more. I should be used to being relegated to less-than. It's where I've been all my life.

The memory of my father surfaces. Him in his tailored darkness, his voice menacing, promising punishment for any misstep. The man who tortured and killed Dylan while I was forced to watch.

Niko mirrors him, another Don in a fine suit, wielding control as effortlessly as breathing. Why has Elena chosen this life? Me? I can't help but feel that I could have a different life now. Giuseppe and I had even discussed it, although he died before anything could be put into place.

"Mrs. Conti." Maria, one of the maids, enters the kitchen. "Is there anything you need?"

"No. Thank you."

She nods and turns back to her task, letting me sit as my brain ruminates over my situation. It's gone from Niko to my father to Elena, and now, Donovan. The pull I feel toward him—strong, confusing, infuriating—contrasts with my revulsion at the thought of falling for someone so entrenched in the life I despise. He's part of this world, a world where men like my father and Niko dictate the fate of those around them without a second thought. How can I desire someone so deeply rooted in the very thing I loathe? It's a dangerous game, this attraction. One I can't afford to play.

"Luce?"

Startled, I snap my gaze upward. Elena stands there, her face alight with the happiness of true love and impending motherhood. Her hand is on her belly, now a gentle swell.

"Everything okay?" she asks, her tone light as she sits in the chair Niko vacated moments ago.

"Of course." I don't want her to know my inner turmoil. I need to be strong. I'll do Niko's bidding, and perhaps Elena will change her mind and decide this life isn't for her, after all.

"Good." She takes my hand, squeezes it.

"Do you want lunch upstairs?" Maria asks Elena.

"No. I'd like it here with my sister." Her smile is bright toward me. "I'm so glad you're here. I missed you so much."

I force a smile in return. I can see she's happier than she's ever been.

"Are you okay, Lucy? You seem... distant." Concern laces her words. Even with time apart, she can still see the cracks in my strength.

"Fine. Just thinking about everything. The city isn't exactly the safest place right now, but Niko insists—"

"We have the best protection" Her optimism feels naïve.

"Sure. Of course."

She looks down, and I hate that her smile has faltered. "I want to keep you here with me. I don't know how I can do this... pregnancy and motherhood without you. But I know you have a life in Italy. I can see that you and Niko... and Donovan..." She looks up again. "If you want to go—"

I take both her hands. "I'm not going anywhere. You're my family, and where you are is where I want to be." I take a breath, hoping she doesn't get upset at the reminder I'm about to deliver. "But I'm only here because Niko is allowing it. Your choosing to stay means you choose to live by his rules."

Her eyes narrow. "You don't think Niko cares about my happiness? The only reason he brought you to me was for my happiness."

"That's not completely true." I remember the brutal interrogation Niko gave me when Donovan kidnapped me from the airport.

Elena tugs her hands back, and I hate her reaction. For a moment, I wonder if there were a choice between me or Niko, who would she choose? I don't want to test it.

"Look, I know I'm here now because he wants you to be happy. I'm just saying that if he decides it's time for me to go, I'll have to go."

She shakes her head. "He won't decide that. I understand the choice I've made and the sacrifices that come with it, but you're not one of them and he knows it."

Again, I see the strong woman I'd seen the other night. I hope she's right.

"Okay," I say.

"Good." Elena's smile returns, full and unguarded, and I envy her ability to find joy despite the shit show that our lives are swirling in. "I'm just so happy you're here with me."

"Me too." And I mean it. For her, for those unborn babies, I'll stand up against anyone, including Niko and Donovan, and especially my father.

Maria sets two plates on the table.

"Mmm, I'm hungry," Elena says. "I hope I can keep it down."

"I hope so too."

She tentatively takes a bite of fruit. I join her, enjoying the food but missing my cook in Italy.

She's quiet for a moment, and I get the feeling she wants to say or ask something. Finally, she says, "You haven't really talked about Giuseppe or..."

"Mourned? Cried?"

"I don't know. Everything is so focused on me or Niko's revenge that you haven't had time..."

"Honey, my feelings aren't important here. In Niko's house, you and revenge are all that are important."

She frowns. "Not to me. You're important. Are you okay?"

"I'm fine." Not that I'm not sad. Giuseppe was good to me when he could have been a beast. I'll miss our chats and his insights into running a Mafia organization. But he's gone now. The one salvation is that he died of a sickness, not by an enemy's bullet. Not many Dons die of old age.

"Luce..." She sighs heavily.

I force a smile. "I'm okay. Really."

She isn't convinced, but she says, "Okay, just remember I'm here if you need to talk."

After lunch, I leave the kitchen, escaping to my room for true solitude. The hallway is quiet, in contrast to the noise in my head. I'm almost to my room when Donovan steps into my path.

His presence is a jolt to my system. The color is back in his cheeks, the smirk at full wattage on his face. He's dressed in jeans and a T-shirt that molds to every line on his chest, including the bandage covering his wound. He exudes stability and strength.

Our gazes catch and hold. Heat floods my cheeks, a telltale sign of the effect he has on me, and I curse myself inwardly because there's no doubt that he'll notice. I school my features into irritation.

His gaze is unwavering, as if he's trying to read my mind. I'm a little afraid he can, or can at least see into my soul.

I give a slight acknowledging nod and then turn the door handle to my room. I enter and look out into the hallway where he's still standing, still watching. His eyes flicker like he's waiting for me to react. Of course, I don't.

He shakes his head, but he doesn't have his usual smirk, so it feels like he's disappointed in me. It annoys me that he makes me feel that way, so I curse him. I didn't set out to be an ice princess. I've developed my cold strength from necessity, for survival. I can't let Donovan's sexy smile and boyish charm cause me to forget who he is, what he is, and how easily he could kill me if Niko ordered it.

6

DONOVAN

The bullet hole, midway between my heart and shoulder, is healing. I'm a lucky bastard. If the bullet had entered any further left, Niko would be planning my funeral. I wonder if Lucia would have come and if she'd be sad? Probably not.

I'm not a hundred percent, but I'm well enough to get back to work. And by work, I don't mean babysitting two Mafia princesses as Niko is apparently wanting me to do. I hope that our meeting today at the office will result in my getting back to it. Maybe I won't be hunting Giovanni Fiori down, but I can make sure everyone else is doing their jobs—collecting loan and gambling debts, etc.

Lou is driving us from the penthouse to the pizza restaurant where Niko's office is located in the basement. The place has the best pizza anywhere in New York... hell, anywhere in the world except maybe Italy. It makes it easy to launder money there. Of course, the clubs are the best places for business because not only can we run our gambling businesses through it, but we can launder as well.

"Thought you'd be laid up for weeks," Lou says with a glance to me.

"Rest is for the dead. And I'm not done living. Not yet."

He laughs. "You're like a fucking cat. Just be careful, you may be on your ninth life."

"Bring it on."

He shakes his head. "I hear you're gonna be babysitting. At least that's safe."

I arch a brow. "Have you met Lucy?"

"She is a firecracker. And hot."

My fist balls, not liking that Lou has noticed Lucy. I like Lou. I brought him into the business, so he's like a brother. But I'll beat the shit out of him if he so much as looks at Lucy.

"But she's got a mouth on her. Niko should make her show more respect."

"Any man who can't take a little back talk from a woman shouldn't be in this business."

He glances at me again, his brow arched. "What? Do you like her or something?"

I shift in my seat, worried I've given too much away. "Lucy and Elena are leverage against Fiori, nothing more." The lie tastes bitter, but admitting my attraction to Lucy is like admitting a weakness, which isn't an option in this line of work.

"Still, didn't peg you for the protector type," Lou says, skepticism lacing his tone.

"Neither did I." I'm irked that Niko plans to make me one. Hopefully, he's changed his mind.

We park in the alley behind the restaurant and make our way inside and down the stairs to Niko's office. We reach the door guarded by men who nod and then step aside, granting us passage into Niko's inner sanctum.

Inside, Niko sits at his desk like the king he is while *capos* and soldiers cluster around.

"Let's get to business." Niko's voice cuts through the din of voices once he sees me enter. "The vultures are circling. Like Giovanni, they think they smell blood in the water and want to come after us."

"Let's feed them their own carcasses," Lou says, followed by murmurs of agreement from the other men.

"Patience. First, we take care of our business. Remind everyone that all is well and the consequences for thinking otherwise, especially if Fiori or any of Abate's men come sniffing."

"Marco, I want extra surveillance on all clubs. We've had two enemies waltz right in. And if it turns out someone in the Leone Family is connected to Abate or Giovanni, I want to know."

"Should we take care of it?" Marco asks, his tone eager with the idea of killing a traitor.

"Let me know first."

"Right, Boss." Marco nods.

"Lou, I want you with the street-level guys. Boost our presence and peace in the community, if you know what I mean. Remind them who holds the power."

"Will do, Boss." Lou leans closer to me and whispers, "I wonder if you'll have to knit for your duties."

I shoot him an irritated glare. "It's easy to torture and kill with knitting needles."

He smirks.

"Now, we also need to get into Abate's territory."

I straighten because that's right up my alley. I can take men and insure that Abate's business becomes Niko's.

"Pete, I want you and your men, along with Dex and his men, to get in there and persuade his soldiers and *capos* to join us—"

"Or die." Dex high-fives Pete.

"Yes, but find out who in the Family thinks they can take over. With Romeo gone, it's likely a *capo*, but maybe Carlo Marchetti, Tiberius's consiglieri, could be eying it."

"He has a legit law firm," Pete shares.

"So? I have legit businesses."

Pete shrugs.

"Everyone else, you know your roles. Visibility and strength, brute force if needed."

I know Niko is focused on protecting his business and taking over Abate's, but how long will he let Giovanni alone? The fucker set us up and nearly killed me.

I shift from the wall, the bullet hole beneath my shirt itching. I'd rather the soreness than itching. I ignore it to focus on the job at hand.

"What about Giovanni?" I ask. "When do we move on him?"

"Patience, Donovan." Niko leans back in his chair, steepling his fingers, his eyes on mine.

"He thinks he got one over on you, Boss," Lou says. "You gonna let him think that?"

"For now, yes. Don't worry, justice will come. But Giovanni must think he's won. That's when he'll slip. That's when we strike."

Niko pauses, watches the men who are all nodding. They're on board, except maybe Lou, who is scrutinizing Niko. Perhaps he thinks Niko is being weak. But I trust Niko. Even when I don't like his decisions or don't understand them, I trust him.

"Let him think he's holding all the cards," Niko says. "In the meantime, we fortify. We take what was Abate's and make it ours, and by the time Giovanni senses the noose, it'll already be too tight to slip."

"Damn right!" several men bellow.

"You know your jobs. Get to it." Niko stands. "Donovan, you stay with me."

The *capos* and soldiers disperse, leaving me alone with Niko. My spirits rise. He's going to give me my assignment and it's not going to be to babysit Elena and Lucy.

"Have a seat." It's not a request.

I sit down and try not to squirm as he studies me.

"How's the wound?"

Instinctively, I press my hand over it. "Fine. Doc says the problem was the blood loss, not the wound itself. I'm feeling good. I even worked out this morning." Of course, it hurt like hell, and I had to change my bandage as I'd reopened the wound. "I'm ready to get back to work."

"Your job for right now is to keep Elena and Lucia safe."

Fucking hell. I must be making a face as Niko's brow arches like he's ready for me to argue with him. I'm close enough to him that I can question him without worrying he'll shoot me. Usually.

"That's what I've been reduced to? Babysitting?" Frustration seeps into my words.

"You think protecting women is unimportant?"

"I think I can be a better use to you doing something else. You have plenty of others who can babysit."

"Mikey babysat, and look what happened to him."

My jaw tightens. Elena talked Mikey into driving her from the compound in Long Island to the city. Giovanni's men forced them off the road, put a bullet in Mikey's forehead, and kidnapped Elena and Lucy.

"He was young and inexperienced. You have plenty of other men who won't let the women talk them into doing something stupid."

Again, his dark eyes scrutinize me. I do my best to hold my own against it.

"What would you say is most important to me?" he asks.

His question is loaded. Until recently, I'd have said vengeance for the murders of his mother and brother. But we're talking about Elena and Lucy right now, so I have to consider his priorities have changed.

"Elena."

"Exactly." His voice softens in a way that not many others see. At this moment, he's a man, not a Don. "Elena and the twins are my world, Donovan, and I'm entrusting their safety to you, the one man I know I can trust."

I feel the weight of his gaze and the meaning to his words. This is an honor.

I nod. "Of course. I'm honored. What about Lucy?"

His lips twitch up slightly like he's amused. What the fuck for?

"She stays because Elena wants her here, so yes, you're watching out for her as well. It could be more difficult as she's obstinate, but at the same time, she understands her place and that if she steps out of line, I have no qualms about sending her back to Luca. I think she'll behave for Elena's sake."

"I understand." And I do. I'm nothing if not a good soldier. I know my place.

"Good." Niko leans forward, letting me know that his next words are deadly serious. "Because Donovan. You're the last line of defense. I expect you to hold, with your life if needed."

"That goes without saying, Boss."

His features soften as he sits back again. "I know. I trust you with everything. But don't think I'm just expecting you to fall in line. I have plans for you, my friend."

That could mean just about anything. A bonus. Taking over an area of the business.

"Right now, we're letting Giovanni think he's won. He might think you're dead, or at least out for the count."

I nod even though on the inside, I hate the idea of anyone, much less Giovanni Fiori, believing I've been bested. I wonder what he'd think if he knew his daughter had nursed me back to health. That I'd had a wet dream involving fucking her.

"When the time comes and Giovanni is dead, the Fiori operations will be yours."

My pulse doesn't just skip, it trips over itself in shock. It takes several seconds for his words to sink in. He's offering me a crown. My own empire.

"Mine?"

"You've got the instincts for it. The respect. The loyalty of our men. When you eliminate Giovanni, you're not just ending a threat—you're stepping into a role you were born to play."

"Boss." It has a nice ring, although one I never thought I'd hear referencing me.

He smiles and shakes his head. "Come on, Donovan. You know you're more like an underboss. We never made it official, but you are. You're my second in command and the best one to take over Fiori's business."

"What about Liam?"

He snorts. "Liam has a tough enough time straddling being an advisor and sometimes soldier with his work at the FBI. Besides, despite what he does for me, he doesn't want to be in this world. He'd have to go to Bratva anyway, if he did."

I nod, knowing Liam's history growing up in Bratva. "I'm honored again."

"The point is, when all is said and done, the Abate and Fiori families will be history. I need you, someone I trust, to take over Giovanni's business."

"Maybe I should take over the Abate business since Elena is a Fiori. The Fiori family might be easier to deal with if she's—"

"They won't care. Giovanni made sure women had no status, no respect."

I think about Lucia and what she might have gone through at Giovanni's hands. I knew she'd been sold off to Giuseppe Conti and that there were rumors it was because she'd dared to sleep with someone outside the Family. Giovanni killed this man, and for once, I couldn't blame him for that. I'd want to kill him too for touching her.

"Under our banner," Niko continues, "You have the vision, Donovan. You can expand, innovate… lead."

It's everything I've been groomed for, fought for, bled for. The prospect of running Giovanni Fiori's empire sends an electric surge of power and possibility through me. And yet...

The rush of excitement fades as another thought creeps in. A vision of Lucy's face, her eyes flashing with that fierce disdain she reserves for men like me. For all things Mafia. It's idiotic to even think about her. Lucy is unattainable, she's made that clear. Even so, I can't help but reach for her. Something about her draws me in.

But she's clear. Her hatred for this life, it's a barrier thicker than the doors of Fort Knox. Could she ever see past the blood on my hands, the legacy of violence? Would she even want to?

If she did, I'd have to step away from this life. I'd have to become something else, someone else. But who? Who would Donovan Ricci be without Niko and the Leone Family?

"Is something wrong?" Niko asks.

"Not at all. Just… letting it soak in." I'm being an idiot. *I want to fuck her, not marry her*, I tell myself. This pull I have toward her is lust, nothing more. What sort of moron lets his libido dictate his life? Not this one. Niko and the Family are the only world I've known, the only one I've mastered. So much so that Niko is offering to give me an empire.

This is who I am. If Lucy can't accept that, then that's the answer. Maybe I need to head down to the club in Jersey for the next virgin auction. Nothing like a tight pussy to make me forget Lucy. Yeah, that's it. It has been awhile since I've had a woman. That's probably why Lucy affects me. Fucking another woman will get her out of my system.

"I'm honored, Niko, really."

He stands and comes around his desk. I rise to greet him.

"You've earned it." He gives me a hug. He pulls back, but his eyes are intense as he says, "When the time comes, Donovan, you'll end Giovanni, not just for retribution, but to cement your place. You'll have the respect and fear of the other Families. You'll take your place—"

"What? You've had a special bullet just for him. You've spent years planning to kill him to avenge your mother and brother."

"Make no mistake, I want Giovanni dead. But it doesn't have to be my hand that stops his heart from beating. Like I said, my priorities have shifted, which doesn't mean that I won't seek justice for my mother and brother. It's only that you'll be my hand that takes care of it."

I nod. "Consider it done."

"Good. Giovanni's last breath will herald the rise of Donovan Ricci." He puts his hand on my shoulder. "But first, you keep Elena and Lucia safe, and heal. Your time isn't here yet, but almost."

When I leave Niko's office, I'm a mixture of excitement and fear that I'll fuck it all up. Mostly, I feel strong. Fierce. Invincible. I'm Donovan Fucking Ricci, and the world is mine. If Lucia Fiori doesn't want a part of me, then too bad for her.

7

LUCIA

Elena sits on the window seat, one hand rubbing her belly, the other making notes on her upcoming nuptials. I sit at the table offering my input on her plans. Not that I know much about weddings. Mine was in a church, but it was only me and Giuseppe, with Luca in attendance. I was wearing the cream-colored dress my father forced me to wear on the flight over to Italy following Dylan's murder.

"I wonder if Niko would like flowers."

"What do you want?"

"I want flowers. I mean, I know we're just having a small wedding, probably here, but still—"

"Why not a church?" Although now that she's showing, I wonder if the Catholic church would marry her. Then again, Niko likely has an in with a priest.

Elena shudders. "My last church wedding didn't go so well."

I arch a brow. "Isn't that when Niko kidnapped you?"

Her smile is sweet. "Yes, but there was shooting and blood. And I spent some time in the trunk of a car."

"I guess I can see not wanting to tempt fate again, but surely, Niko would do better with protection. If you want a fancy wedding—"

"I don't want a fancy wedding. This isn't about showing off. This is a love match. All that matters are Niko and me."

I resist rolling my eyes at the words *love match*. Not that I don't believe love is involved. I know Elena loves Niko.

"Has he told you that?" I ask.

"What?" She looks up from her list to me.

"That he loves you?"

Her brow furrows as if she's wondering why I'm asking the question. "Yes. Of course. You don't think he loves me?"

"I just want to be sure. I don't want you to get hurt." I'm not sure that Niko loves her in the same way she loves him. I'm not sure any man who makes his living running criminal syndicates and murdering people is capable of love. With that said, my sense from Niko is that he does care for Elena. I just hope it's enough.

"I won't get hurt." Her expression softens. "I wish you could feel the way I do. I know you said you cared for Giuseppe—"

"We were fond of each other, but it wasn't love." I rise from my chair and go to sit with her on the window seat.

"I'm glad you had that, but love…" Her face turns up, her expression serene. "It's so wonderful."

"Then we'll make sure you have a beautiful small ceremony." Right now, Elena is all I have in my life, and I want her to be happy and safe. Maybe I don't like her choice to stay and worry that her love is misguided, but there isn't anything I can do about it except support her. I reach across the space between us, covering her hand with mine. "Nothing is going to ruin your day. Not if I have anything to say about it."

A smile tugs at the corners of her lips. "I'm glad you're here with me, Luce. I don't know what I'd do without you."

"From what I've seen the last few days, I know you'd be fine without me. You're a lot stronger than I'd given you credit for."

She laughs. "I'm channeling my inner Luce. I remember how you'd always stand up to Mom and Dad. You were so brave."

Memories flood, and I close my eyes to stop them.

"Will you ever tell me what happened?" Her words are soft, tentative, as she has to know that the past is painful.

I open my eyes. "Maybe someday. But not now. Not when we have a wedding to plan and babies to prepare for." I hope my tone is cheerful and excited. I don't want to have darkness seep into any part of Elena's world any more than it already has.

She nods and then yawns.

"Go rest," I urge softly. "Dream of walking down the aisle to Niko without a care in the world."

"I'm so glad not to be throwing up all the time, but I could do without the fatigue."

I stand up. "You're growing two babies. I can imagine that's tiring work."

She rises and retreats to her bed. Once she's lying down, I leave her and head to my room. There is a lot to do, not just for the wedding but for the babies as well. I don't know what's on Elena's list, but I pull out paper and a pen from the desk in my room and begin my own.

Once I have a few things jotted comes the urge to go buy them now. I put the list in my purse and head out of my room. The penthouse is quiet. Really quiet. Like no one is here. If that's the case, I could just walk out.

A sudden, glorious feeling of autonomy fills me, imagining going out in the world on my own. As I near the door, Maria appears.

"Maria. I need to go out. Just for a little while."

Her gaze moves around the area, and I know she's looking for Niko or one of his men.

"It's okay. I promise," I tell her. "Or if you'd rather act like you never saw me, that's okay too." After all, I don't want to get her in trouble.

I exit and head to the elevator. With each step, a growing sense of freedom builds. I anticipate being in the city as just another person. Not Lucia Fiori Conti, Mafia widow or pawn depending on whom you ask. I'm just a regular woman.

The elevator dings, and a giddiness bubbles in my chest as I wait for the doors to open. I'm sure I'm smiling like a loon.

The doors slide open, and I step forward, only to be met by a wall of man. His hands grip my arms, probably because I'm about to walk into him, but maybe to manhandle me. Either way, it sends undesired tingles up my arms. I jerk out of his grasp and step into the elevator.

One dark brow arches. "Where are you going?"

"Out," I say it with authority. Like there's no question.

He stands in the open door of the elevator, preventing it from closing as he looks up and down the hall. "By yourself?"

"It's none of your business."

He rolls his eyes and steps into the elevator, pressing the button for the garage.

"I don't need a bodyguard. Elena's inside. Go babysit her." My shoulders square. Can't he see that I don't need him?

"Rules are rules." He steps away from the panel, closer to me. His scent surrounds me as the doors slide shut, sealing us together. His scent surrounds me, making my blood heat. It's out of anger, right?

"I'm not made of glass."

"Never said you were. But the streets aren't safe." His voice is low but insistent. It says there will be no discussion.

"Who is watching Elena? I'm sure Niko would rather have you…"

There's a flicker in his eyes that makes me think he recognizes what I'm saying is true. But when we get to the garage, he talks to one of the men on guard, who nods.

"Come on, Princess." He guides me to a vehicle with a waiting driver.

"I'm not a princess," I snap.

"Right. You're a Don's wife. Should I call you queen?"

I like the idea of being a queen, but queens are rulers, right? I have no authority. No freedoms.

"I'm perfectly capable of shopping on my own."

He stops by the car and leans in, nearly nose to nose. His heat and his scent assail me this time. "No."

It takes a minute for his word to get through the fog being near him often brings. "You're insufferable."

"That's why I get paid the big bucks."

Ugh! "Fine," I relent, moving to get into the SUV. "You can come."

"Thought you'd never ask." The words are light, like he's laughing at me as he scoots in beside me. I want to punch him, but I'm not convinced that he wouldn't strangle me.

I let the driver know where I want to go, and then I sit back, my gaze out the window, pretending Donovan isn't there. It's not easy to do. The man is the size of a linebacker. The intensity of him rolls off him, snap, crackling along my nerve endings.

When we get to Madison Avenue, the driver lets us out. I step onto the sidewalk, the city's pulse instantly wrapping around me. Donovan falls into stride beside me. Growing up, my protection detail always stayed several steps away from me. Close enough to intervene, but far enough that I could breathe.

"You're too close, Toady." I move laterally to create space.

He moves with me. "Too bad, Brat."

Brat? God. I like Princess better. I stop short and glare up at him. He stops and with his usual smirk waits for me to speak.

"Why is it bad… entitled, to wish to be able to live life without being bossed or bullied?"

His brow furrows like he doesn't understand what I'm asking.

"Why am I brat simply because I'd like to buy my sister a few things for her wedding and babies on my own?" I look at a woman passing me. "Look at her. She's alone. Is she a brat?"

He sucks in a breath like he's trying to stay calm and reasonable. I should appreciate the effort, but the idea that I'm getting on his nerves for something so basic as shopping on my own grates on me.

"No, but that's because she doesn't have a city full of wise guys who'd love to kidnap her or kill her."

"No one here wants me—"

Now he does roll his eyes. "Wake up, Lucy. Just a few days ago, your father had you kidnapped."

Oh, right. It isn't that I forgot. It's just that I'm sure Elena was the target. I was in the way. I knew for all intents and purposes, I was dead to my father the moment he sold me to Giuseppe.

"You're a brat for being selfish and ungrateful. You don't think I have better things to do than trail you around the city?"

I purse my lips at him and make my way to the bank.

"Are we robbing it?" he quips as he follows me in.

"Will it get you arrested and out of my life?"

He snorts. And damn it if my lips don't quirk up as well.

I make my way to the ATM, entering the card that Giuseppe gave me just before I left Italy. I press my PIN and the screen flashes my balance. Relief floods through me—enough to cover Elena's whims without tapping into Conti funds that might draw Luca's attention. I send a silent thank you to Giuseppe for thinking of giving me my own account.

I hear a whistle and turn to see Donovan looking over my shoulder.

"You're rich."

I smirk. "I'm a Don's wife, remember?"

He laughs. "Right. Not free, but with enough money to fund a small country. Poor little rich girl."

His words effectively wipe the smirk off my face. Damn him again.

I take out a significant amount of cash. If anyone is tracking the account, they'll see where I got the money but not where I spend it. I stash the cash in my purse and head toward the upscale baby boutique.

I'm immediately entranced by the tiny clothes and baby accessories.

"Those babies aren't here for a while."

I want to ignore him. "I've accepted that you're my bodyguard. Now act like one. Keep your distance and don't talk to me."

"Okay, Brat."

Ugh.

I move around the shop, pretending that the hulking presence following me around isn't associated with me.

"Need help choosing?"

I arch a brow. "You know about baby clothes? Tell me, Donovan, how many kids do you have?" For a moment, my stomach clenches as I wait to find out if he has a woman. Or many women. And a brood of kids.

He feigns thinking about it. "No kids. Not that I know of, anyway."

I roll my eyes. "Just what this city needs, a bunch of Ricci bastards."

His eyes darken. "Careful, Brat."

I snap my mouth shut, not so much because I'm afraid he'll retaliate but because my words were offensive. I have no problem speaking my mind and even being rude, but there is a limit and I was about to go over it.

Luckily, Donovan stops trying to chat. I turn back to the task at hand, gathering lovely little onesies and pajamas, a few blankets, and a couple of stuffed animals. Donovan trails behind.

But I find myself distracted by him even so. With each step, my awareness of him grows. Worse, there's a part of me that wants to know what it means. To give in to it.

I force my focus back to the baby items, to anything but the man who makes my body heat and my mind fill with fog.

I chance a glance at him and find him watching me. I can't read his face or his mind.

"Everything okay?" he asks.

I shrug and go back to shopping. I gather the last few items and take them to the counter. Then we exit the store.

"Where to next?" Donovan asks.

"I want to get Elena something blue for the wedding."

"How about a garter?"

I stop and look up at him. "What?"

"A garter."

"I was thinking of a handkerchief or maybe something with a sapphire."

He grins mischievously. "Garter is more fun. And sexy. Niko will like it, and I imagine Elena will too if the way she looks at him is any indication."

I gape. "What are you talking about?"

"Are you a prude? You do know that Niko can barely keep his hands off her and Elena likes it. A lot. That's how they're having twins. Surely, you know all this."

I want to slap him. "Of course, I know about all that." Just because I've never had sex with a man doesn't mean I don't understand where babies come from.

"I knew it. Giuseppe might have been old, but he could still get it up."

"What is it with you and sex?"

"Well, I like sex. Don't you?" His tone is teasing. His goal in this conversation is to goad me, and it's working.

"I think I'm ready to go home."

"Car is up here." We continue up the street, and I can feel him laughing at me.

"You know, your sister is lucky to have you," he says, breaking the silence.

"She's all I have."

"Niko and the Family are all I have."

It makes no sense, but at his words, I wonder about Donovan's story. Where are his parents? Does he have siblings?

My thoughts are interrupted when Donovan grabs me. I can't lift my hands to defend myself unless I drop my bags. He pulls me close and presses me against the side of the building. My breath hitches, caught in the suddenness of his proximity.

His head dips to the side of my neck. "Play along." His breath teases my skin, his lips graze along my jaw.

I'm stunned not just that this is happening, but that I'm not doing anything about it. His mouth moves to my cheek, soft and fleeting. My heart thunders in my chest.

The bags drop and my fingers fist in his crisp white shirt.

"That's right," he whispers.

Footsteps approach. His head turns slightly, and I follow the direction. I see two figures pass, their glances sharp and assessing.

Donovan's mouth travels to my jawline, a whisper of contact that sends delicious sensations over my skin and my eyes fluttering closed. I'm a bundle of raw nerves, every sense heightened, every neuron firing under his touch.

And then he's gone.

As quickly as it began, it ends. He pulls away, a gust of cold air rushing in to fill the void. I feel like I've been doused in cold water.

"Let's move." Urgency laces tone as he grabs my bags and guides me with a firm hand at my back toward the SUV.

Humiliation fills me. And because of it, anger wells. Not just at him for causing me this humiliation, but at myself for wanting more of his touch.

He ushers me into the car. It pulls away even before the door is shut.

I let out an exasperated breath.

"Are you okay?" He sounds genuinely concerned.

I look at him, and I don't see any hint that he was affected by our closeness. The humiliation grows.

"I'm fine." I bite out the words.

"Fine," I lie. I turn to look out the window, wishing I could be like him and think nothing of his touch. But the imprint of his lips still burns against my skin. It's like a brand that has marked me as his.

I don't speak to him the rest of the ride, or in the elevator up to the penthouse. I go straight to my room, trying to ignore the fact that he's on my tail.

Right outside my door, he says, "By the way, you won't be going out anymore. Whatever you need, ask Maria. She can get it for you."

"You're not the boss of me," I say, although I don't know why. Reality proves me wrong. I open the door and rush in, hoping to shut him out.

His hand shoots out, stopping the door from slamming in his face. "Don't test me on this. You know who those guys were, right? You understand what's going on. Your father, the Abate men, others who want to bring Niko down, they're all out there waiting for an opportunity, and like the spoiled brat you are, you nearly gave them one. You get that, right, or has life in Italy made you soft?"

I smirk. "If they came sniffing, it was because of you, Donovan. No one cares about me."

His brows narrow. "That's not true."

"It is. I'm nothing in this game anymore. I'm certainly nothing to Niko or you. You proved that."

He continues to look at me like I've grown an extra head. "How did I prove that? I had your back all afternoon. I've had it since we've met."

"Right. When you kidnapped me? Tied me up? That was having my back?"

He gives me a sheepish smile.

"One thing is for sure, you don't have to kiss me to protect me." I try again to shut the door, but he prevents it, stepping into my room.

"I didn't kiss you."

"Yes, you did!"

His brow furrows and the mortification grows deeper. God, did he forget? Am I that forgettable?

"You kissed my neck, Donovan, and my... my jaw—" My voice breaks, the humiliation of it all bringing tears to my eyes.

"It was fake, Lucy. I wanted to make sure they didn't see us. I had to do something."

"Fake." I close my eyes because I don't want him to see how much his words hurt. "You can go now. I'm in my room. And I'll stay here forever if it means I never have to see you again."

His head cocks to the side, and I don't like how his dark eyes are assessing, scrutinizing, figuring out my inner turmoil.

Then he smirks. "Are you pissed because I didn't give you a real kiss, Luce?" He stalks toward me. "You wanted more, is that the problem?"

"No." *Liar*, my body says. I step away from his advancing steps until my back hits the wall.

"That's it, isn't it?" He leans in like he did earlier today. His lips brush over my jaw, and I betray my resolve by sucking in a quick breath.

My hand presses against his chest to push him away, or maybe to hold him close. His nearness, the way my body aches from it, makes it hard to think.

His lips trail along my jaw to my chin. He lifts his head for a moment. "That was just for show." Then his mouth covers mine, firm, fierce, and my fingers grip his shirt as I feel my world spin away. This isn't my first kiss. Dylan and I had many kisses. But this one, I feel an inferno is building, sparks flying, all the proverbial clichés about kissing I've ever read in books. It's all that and more.

Need rolls through my body. All the reasons to push him away have vanished. All I want is this. His kiss.

Like he did before, he abruptly pulls back. I'm expecting his usual smirk, but instead I see desire.

He gives his head a quick shake and that irritating smirk is back. "In case you're not clear, that was a real kiss."

8

DONOVAN

I'm in serious trouble. I've just kissed Lucy and if I don't get out now, I could just possibly rip her clothes off and fuck her right here against this wall. That is if she doesn't slap me and scream, in which case, I'd be in serious shit with Niko for trying to fuck his fiancée's sister. Lucy belongs to the Contis, so perhaps Luca would try to kill me.

I pull away, but her fingers clutch my shirt, tugging me back. Like a fucking magnet, my lips are on hers again, drinking in her luscious lips. If I have to die, this will be a good parting gift.

My hands tangle in her hair as the kiss burns like wildfire, untamed, out of control. She responds with a moan that vibrates through me, igniting something primal. The taste of her is intoxicating, a mix of sweet and spicy.

My hands roam over her curves, inventorying them, searing them into my memory. I find her tit, round and soft with a nipple as hard as steel. I rub my palm over it, loving how she shudders and moans at my touch. My other hand slides lower, gripping her ass, squeezing the firm flesh. She gasps and arches, her body pressing against my achingly hard cock. Her fingers clench tighter on my shirt, nails grazing over my nipples, sending another jolt of need through me.

But then it hits, like a sucker punch to the gut—or the dick. I can't do this. She's not mine to have. Crossing the line and fucking Lucy could blow my life out of the water.

"Dammit." The curse is more for me than for her. I jerk back, and for a moment, she doesn't move. In her eyes, I see a storm of emotions that morph from desire, to confusion, to pain. Like a fucking coward, I can't stand there and watch it. So I turn and walk away.

Fucking hell.

I can't seem to get out of her room fast enough. I run my fingers through my hair as the taste of Lucy's luscious lips lingers on my mouth, the sound of her moans echoes in my brain, the feel of her soft body burns against my skin. As I make my way down the hall, the memory of it all chases me. The way our bodies crashed together, fierce and demanding, blowing up every rational thought with insatiable hunger.

I've kissed a few women in my time. I've been carried away by lust before. But that... with Lucy... it wasn't just a kiss. It was a detonation, rocking me to my core. Breaking away from Lucy was the hardest thing I think I've ever done. It took every ounce of willpower I possessed. Even now, as I head down the hall before I do something crazy, all I want to do is turn around and drown in Lucy. But I can't. I know Niko still has questions about her. She's Elena's sister. Lucy's married... or at least she was until recently. She's like a forbidden fruit, and holy hell, do I want to take a bite.

I continue downstairs, trying to get my mind sorted before running into Niko.

"Damn." I shake my head, trying to dispel the image of her pressed against me. Reminding myself that she isn't mine and can't be mine. Lucy is a complication in a world where complications can cost you everything. Niko trusts me to protect her, not to give in to the desire that could jeopardize it all.

Lucy's safety is my responsibility. I can't afford distractions—not even ones that promise a sensual paradise.

"Check-in," I bark to one of the men standing in the foyer.

He jumps to attention. "All secure."

"Garage? Perimeter?" I scan the area for anything out of place.

"All secure. I ... I can go down—"

"Call down. Have everyone report in. Anything suspicious, let me know."

"Got it."

I focus my time on doing what Niko asked me to do—keep the women safe. I oversee security rotations, double-check locks and surveillance feeds. The screens flicker with silent images of hallways and doors, nothing amiss. But I've been around long enough to know that the quiet can hide all sorts of monsters.

As dusk falls, Niko strides into the penthouse with Liam in tow. They head straight for the office, and I'm on their heels.

"Report to me," Niko commands before I even close the door behind us.

"Giovanni's got ears and eyes in the city. They're looking for her." Liam makes himself comfortable on Niko's couch.

"Elena?" Niko's scowl is fierce.

"Lucia."

A frown creases Niko's brow. "Not Elena?"

What the hell? Why would Giovanni care about Lucy after all this time? Yes, he'd kidnapped her after orchestrating the car accident, but the target had been Elena. Right?

"It appears that Giovanni has accepted that Elena belongs to Niko now," Liam explains.

"Doesn't make sense," Niko muses, sitting down behind his desk. "Elena's his blood, pregnant with Leone heirs. She's more valuable."

"Giovanni tends to sell his daughters. She's of no value if she's not a virgin," Liam suggests.

"Then why Lucy?" I ask. "She's married... or was. She's not a virgin."

"And the babies make Elena a bigger target. Giovanni knows he can get to me through them," Niko states. "Lucy isn't anything to Giovanni."

I bite the inside of my mouth to keep from blurting out that Lucy is important too. But along with the disrespect is the risk of showing my hand. Of them figuring out what she does to me.

"You'd think the guy would be grateful to me for his not having to pay that debt to Tiberius," Niko grumbles.

"Maybe not going after Elena is his form of gratitude," Liam offers. "Or he knows she'll be harder to get at. All he has to do is bide his time with Lucia. She'll probably go back to Italy, and he can get her then. Hell, maybe he's already talked to Luca."

"No."

Liam and Niko look at me. Niko with an arched brow. "No?"

Hell. "I mean, Luca is your ally."

Niko shrugs. "The question is, why Lucia? What makes her so valuable to Giovanni?"

My teeth grind at Niko's question. He doesn't see her as anything but a pawn in this ugly game we play.

"He had to have heard about Giuseppe and he knows she's back. Maybe he thinks he can sell her again," Liam suggests.

"Over my dead body," I murmur.

"Did you say something, Donovan?" Niko asks.

"I wish we'd killed him when we had the chance."

Niko nods. "His time is coming soon. Don't worry, Donovan. The countdown for Giovanni has started. Before long, you'll be in charge."

I imagine Lucy at my side looking over Giovanni's dead body and taking over his business. But no. She doesn't like this life. All I can do for her is to keep her safe.

"Do you think Lucia knows something?" Niko asks. "Something Giovanni wants to keep her from telling us?"

"That seems unlikely." Liam gets himself a drink from Niko's bar, apparently deciding we'll be here for a while.

"Why?"

Liam sips his drink and shrugs. "It's been years since he sent her off to Italy. She's been with you, Niko, for days. I don't doubt you put the screws to her. Did she say anything?"

"She wasn't tortured." Niko glares at Liam.

"She doesn't like her father." I decide I need a drink too and go to the bar. "If she knew something she thought could hurt him, or moreover, help Elena, she'd have said it."

"How do you know?" Liam asks.

I still as I'm about to pour, worried Liam can see through me. That he can see I'd rather be lost in Lucy's body than here with them.

"She said as much, remember, Niko?" I glance at Liam. "When we were putting the screws to her."

Liam purses his lips and rolls his eyes at me.

"Donovan's right. She asked me to kill her father."

I gape. "When?"

He shrugs. "Recently. It doesn't matter. What matters is why Giovanni is looking for her."

"Maybe it's as simple as he wants to kill her." This time, Liam sits in one of the leather chairs, taking another sip of his drink.

"Why?"

"It's Giovanni Fiori we're talking about here. She was his prize until she took up with some young man. Rumor is that Giovanni made her watch as he put a gun to the kid's head and blew it off."

I recoil at the idea.

"She disrespected him by being with another man. She ruined herself... in Giovanni's eyes. Honestly, I think she was lucky he didn't kill her then. Giuseppe must have paid a pretty penny to have her."

I'm trying not to gape as I hear all this.

"Maybe we should send her back," Niko says.

A maelstrom of thoughts whirls through my mind. Lucy, back in Italy? With Luca? My jaw clenches as I wrestle with the desire to keep her close and the need to ensure her safety because maybe she would be safer there.

"That only works if Giovanni believes that Luca sees her as being part of the Conti family. And it doesn't stop Giovanni from negotiating with Luca to get her back," Liam says.

I have this horrible thought of Niko negotiating with Giovanni as a way to protect Elena.

"Elena won't like anyone negotiating anything that results in Lucy going back to Giovanni," I say.

"True." Niko's word gives me some relief.

"We should keep her close," I say, hoping I sound like an advisor and not a man who has a hardon for Niko's soon-to-be sister-in-law.

Niko nods. "She could be the key to luring Giovanni to his death."

The idea of using Lucy as bait doesn't sit well, but I bite my tongue. Niko has decided to keep her close, and that's what I focus on.

"Besides, Luca has his hands full making sure no factions see Giuseppe's death as an opportunity," Liam reminds Niko.

"That won't take long. Everyone knows Luca's been in charge for years." Niko dismisses Liam's concern. "Besides, Giovanni may have his ear to the ground for Lucia, but he's hiding. There's no doubt about it. The Feds are circling, waiting for the fallout of the firefight the other night."

"Waiting is fucked," Niko says.

Liam laughs. "You were the one who said we should bide our time."

"I know. And it's still a good plan, but it's also fucking frustrating." Niko runs his hands through his hair. "What about Chief Emerson? Any word?"

Liam stiffens, just for a second, before he's back to his usual ice-cold composure. "Captain Emerson is still MIA. Presumed dead."

"Who?"

Liam shrugs. "Could be you, for all I know."

Niko shakes his head. "Not me. I'm thinking Giovanni. Elena was friends with Emerson's daughter, and that fucking bastard likes to make his daughters pay."

"What makes you ask?" Liam goes to the bar for another drink.

"Elena's friend is important to her. It would be nice for her to have her friend around."

I'm surprised by how much Niko is bending over backward for Elena. But then, that's love, right? He values his woman above all else. But it pisses me off that while he wants to bring Elena's friend back, he a moment ago wanted to send Lucy back to Italy, use her as bait to get Giovanni. Fucking hell.

"Is it possible to bring Kate back?" Niko asks.

"I can look into it." Liam, ever the stoic agent, nods once, sharply, but there's something to it that I can't place. Kate Emerson seems to be a topic Liam is uncomfortable with.

The meeting breaks, and I decide to take another pass through the penthouse to insure all is well. Needing a break from the penthouse, I head down to the garage. I check in with the men and decide to hang with them. I'm still doing my job protecting the women, I'm just doing it far enough away to avoid seeing Lucy.

At nearly ten, I head back up and do a final walk-through of the penthouse. It's like a fortress, but that doesn't mean there aren't potential weak spots.

Speaking of weak spots, I think as I pass by Lucia's room. I stop, thinking how easy it would be to knock on her door. To pick up where I left off hours ago. I can already taste her lips. Feel the softness of her body.

My dick is hard as a rock. Every muscle in my body is taut. It's scary how fucking much I want her. But at what risk? At what cost?

"Damn it," I whisper, clenching my fists. My job here is to protect, not to indulge in selfish desires.

I take a step back. The retreat feels like defeat. Since when do I give in to fear? I stare danger in the face every day. Yes, indulging in Lucy would be a gamble, but some gambles are worth the risk. She could just be the biggest gamble of all.

But not tonight. Tonight, I have a date with my hand in the shower.

9

LUCIA

God, that man! I hate him.

How could he do that to me? He's Mafia, that's how.

I faceplant on my bed, angry that I brought my humiliation on myself. Of course he'd kiss me like that as a punishment or simply to remind me that I had no power. My despair is made worse by how much I liked his kiss. How feminine and desired I felt. But it was all a lie. God, he's probably laughing at me right now, at how gullible I am.

Lying on my bed and wallowing in my humiliation only makes it worse, so I force myself up and go on with my day, doing my best to rid Donovan Ricci from my mind.

I sort out the items I bought and think about when the best time to show them to Elena will be. Then I clean up my room that doesn't need cleaning. I read a book without knowing what it's about. I can't get Donovan's kiss out of my head, but I'm determined to try.

That evening, I join Elena and Niko at dinner. Elena chatters away and Niko simply smiles.

Me? I'm still trying to forget Donovan's lips on mine, which is hard since I swear I can still taste him.

"Lucy, you're quieter than usual." Elena's brow furrows with concern across from me.

I look up, feeling a bit like a deer in the headlights. "Ah... uh... just thinking about Giuseppe."

Elena's eyes soften, turn sympathetic. "Are you okay? Do you want to talk about it?"

Guilt fills me that I'd use my dead husband to hide the truth about kissing Donovan. "No. Tell me how the wedding plans are coming along."

Elena's face brightens and beside her, Niko captures her hand in his, his thumb stroking her skin with tenderness. I study them for a moment, recognizing the genuine affection that exists despite the darkness and danger that consume much of Niko's world.

"I've got something special planned," Niko says, his eyes never leaving Elena.

"Oh? What?"

His brows rise with a hint of mischief. "It's a secret."

Elena laughs, and I'm so happy to hear it. I still don't know about Niko, but if he can make her smile and laugh, then I have to accept him.

After dinner, I head up to my room, inviting Elena to join me for a surprise I have for her. I reach for a soft cotton baby onesie and hold it out to Elena.

"Isn't it adorable?" I ask.

"Aww. It's so cute." She takes the onesie, her eyes, looking more and more motherly all the time, taking it in.

"Plus, I got all this." I show her the items I've laid out on my bed.

She hugs me. "Thank you. These are so cute. But Lucy, you shouldn't have gone out. It's not safe."

"Relax, Toady was with me," I say, a nickname for Donovan that drips with disdain yet betrays my constant awareness of him.

Elena's smirk cuts through the cool air between us. "You know, everyone thinks Donovan has a thing for you."

My heart clenches, but I brush off her words because it's not true. I'm a pawn. A toy. A thing he chose to put in its place.

"I can't imagine why."

"It's probably how he looks at you. Or maybe how he likes to tease you."

I gape. "You don't think that too, do you?"

She shrugs. "I don't know. I mean I don't know Donovan very well. He always seems like a jokester to me."

"He's a joke, all right," I mutter, folding up the clothes I bought for Elena's twins.

"You seem upset. Did he do something?"

Yeah. He kissed me and then humiliated me. "He's breathing, isn't he? That's all it takes."

Elena rolls her eyes. "If I didn't know better, I'd think you liked him."

"Your hormones are messing with your mind."

She laughs, and I hope she doesn't see through me.

LATER IN BED, I toss again, the sheets tangling around my legs. The room is dark, save for the sliver of moonlight that creeps across the room. I should be exhausted, but instead, I'm keyed up. Donovan's kiss lingers on my lips like an imprint. My fingers brush against my mouth, half expecting to feel the pressure of his all over again.

I roll onto my back and stare at the ceiling. This place, this opulent prison, suddenly feels too small. I can't escape him. He's everywhere. Maybe it's time to think about going back to Italy. I'm dead weight, really. I use up resources I'm sure Niko would rather have for Elena. It would be easier for Donovan to protect one woman rather than two. And Elena doesn't need me. I can see that she's a strong woman. She has Niko and her twins on the way.

So maybe it's time to return to Italy. With Giuseppe gone, what's left for me is only closure, not a future. But here…

Unable to sleep, I decide to call Luca. It's early in the morning in Italy, but I know he's up. I put on my robe and head downstairs. The house is quiet, and I almost feel like I'm sneaking around. I hope none of Niko's men think that.

I pause outside Niko's office, watching through the half-open door. He hunches over his desk, his focus on the papers scattered before him.

Taking a quiet breath, I tap softly on the open door. His head snaps up, eyes narrowing slightly as he sees me.

"Can't sleep either?"

"Something like that." I cross the threshold. "Do you have a phone I could use? I need to make a call about Giuseppe's funeral."

He leans back, studying me like he's assessing whether I'm telling the truth or not. It occurs to me that he's likely as suspicious of me as I am of him.

I hug myself, feeling the chill of the room, or perhaps it's the coldness of guilt seeping into my bones. My relationship with Giuseppe was never the stuff of fairy tales, but we had a mutual respect and affection. So why does the memory of Donovan's kiss feel like a betrayal?

He stands, stretches. "You can use this one." He motions to the phone on his desk. He steps around the desk and heads to the door.

"Thank you, Niko."

Alone now, I approach the desk. The phone sits there, but I hesitate. Most people take phones for granted, but in my world, the phone could be a lifesaver or a killer. It had been a phone call that had tipped my father off about Dylan.

My hand hovers before the phone. Giuseppe would have laughed at my hesitation. "My little shrew isn't afraid of anyone or anything," he used to joke. Being called a shrew is offensive, except Giuseppe said it with such affection.

I'd told him all about Elena's predicament, the danger she faced, and when she vanished, taken by a rival family, he encouraged me to come to Elena.

"Take care of her," he had said, his voice weak but resolute. Had he known then that he wasn't long for this world? Is that why he sent me? He didn't want me to be around when he passed? Or is that thought to relieve the guilt I have for not being with him in his last days?

I push all the thoughts aside, focusing on the task at hand—contacting Luca. I press the numbers and listen as the phone rings. But when the call connects, it's not Luca. It's his voicemail.

"Luca, it's Lucy. Just checking in," I begin, feeling unsure as to what to say. Luca was always kind to me, but that was probably because I was good to Giuseppe and Giuseppe cared for me. Would Luca's kindness continue now that Giuseppe is gone? "I wanted to discuss... Giuseppe's arrangements. I, ah..." I have no way for him to call me back except through Niko. "I'm with Elena at Don Niko Leone's." Hopefully, Luca will know how to reach Niko. I remember that Niko had once commented that he knew Luca.

I replace the receiver and stand alone in Niko's office. There's nothing to do now except go back upstairs and try to sleep. I decide a glass of wine might help with that, so I make a stop in the kitchen to pour a glass and then return to my room.

When I close my door and look at my bed, the sheets a mess from my restlessness, I decide a warm bath might help me settle down.

In the bathroom, I run the water in the large tub and uncap the lavender oil, putting a few drops in. I take my robe and nightgown off and submerge myself into the warm, fragrant water. I drink several sips of wine and then close my eyes, letting the warmth sink into my bones. I focus on the tranquil scent of lavender to clear my mind of worries and Donovan. Instead, he lingers like a ghost, haunting me.

Why? Of all the men I could find myself drawn to, why big, rude, Toady Donovan?

I think about Dylan and his tentative and sweet kisses. Sometimes, we touched each other through clothes, in a sweet innocence. But that had been it. And as lovely as it was, it wasn't anything like what I felt at Donovan's touch. Dylan was like slow, liquid wax, whereas Donovan was like a blowtorch, sending fire through my blood.

My heart races from the undeniable truth—Donovan didn't just kiss me. He ignited something fierce and raw, something I can't douse with reason or will away with stubborn denials. Which isn't to say

Queen of Misfortune 71

that I'll ever kiss him again, because I won't. Never again will I allow him to use my feelings to humiliate me.

The lavender's soothing scent weaves through the steam, but it does nothing to calm the storm Donovan has stirred inside me. I close my eyes, and there he is—Donovan, with his stormy gaze and the hint of danger in his touch. The firm fullness of his mouth. The sensations he sent roaring through me when he rubbed his hand over my nipple. The way his arousal pressed against my belly. The fantasy unfurls so clearly, it's like he's here. His hands roam with intent, touching me here, there, everywhere.

A sigh escapes me as I settle into the memory. But where Donovan abruptly walks out in reality, in my mind, he stays. He continues to kiss and touch me. And I touch back.

My hand slides down my chest, pinching my nipples as I imagine Donovan doing the same. Sweet sensation flows through me. I may be a virgin, but I know pleasure and I seek it now. Donovan's lips on mine. His hands fondling my breasts. Each kiss, each touch building up the tension as I slide my hand down to my clit and stroke it.

A gasp escapes, and for a moment I stop. I think about the wisdom of pleasuring myself in Niko's home. Are there cameras or microphones? I look around and decide I'm being paranoid.

The image of Donovan returns. His beguiling smirk. His hard hands.

I rub my clit, faster, harder. The tension coils, tightens to the brink of shattering, and then I tumble over into bliss.

In the aftermath, I lie still and the self-deprecation rolls in. What have I done? I'm such an idiot, indulging in fantasies about a man who doesn't see me as a person. A man who represents everything I despise. A man who could destroy me without even trying.

Now angry from the emotional chaos Donovan has sown within me, I rise from the bath. I consider a shower as if I could wash away the longing and the guilt. Realizing I can't, I dry off and put my nightgown back on.

I finish my wine and climb into bed, closing my eyes. Of course,

Donovan is there, but this time, I focus on all that I'd like to do to the man to torture him. To wipe that smug smirk off his face. When I fall asleep, he's begging me... no, not to live, but for me to make him come.

10

LUCIA

The next morning, I have breakfast with Elena in her room. The sun is out, filling the room with a warm glow.

It's still not as radiant as Elena, whose hand gently rubs the swell of her belly. "Thank God these little ones let me keep my food down."

My heart swells with joy for her, but there's a tightness that coils around my chest. It's envy. She seems to have everything a person could ever want. Love and happiness. With Giuseppe, I had comfort and contentment, and I felt lucky to have it considering the very real alternatives. But I can see that Elena has more than that, and I envy her that.

"The time will go by fast, I imagine. Are you and Niko ready?"

She laughs. "Probably not."

"Before, you said he didn't want—"

"That was when he thought I wanted to leave." She sighs as she looks at me, knowing my not-so-subtle questions are due to wanting to be sure she'll be okay. "Every night, he talks to them and tells them about all he's going to give them. He's going to spoil them."

"They're going to grow up like we did," I say carefully.

Her eyes narrow, and I see the woman who took charge the other day when Niko and Donovan had been ambushed. "No. They won't. I'm not Mom, and Niko isn't Dad."

I've offended her. "No, of course not. But you're in that world."

"They'll be loved and protected." She pushes her plate away, and guilt clutches my gut that I'm ruining the morning.

"I'm sorry, Elena. I just... I want you to be happy and safe. At one point, you had a plan to leave and—"

"And now I want to stay. You don't have to if you find my life so repulsive."

I sigh and sit back. "Do you want me to leave?" Where would I go? I liked it in Italy all right, but I don't just want to be comfortable and safe.

She stands and goes to the window. "I want you to accept my choice." She turns to me. "My choice, Luce. Niko and the babies are what I want."

I rise from my chair and join her. "Okay. That's all I need to know." I want to hug her, but she seems mad. I look down. "I left a message for Luca last night."

Her eyes widen. "You're leaving?"

I shrug. "I'm in the way. I take up resources that Niko can use to better protect you and hunt down Dad." I pause. "You don't need me."

"But I want you here."

The little crack in my heart starts to mend. "Really?"

"Yes. You're my big sister. I need your help and advice about... well... everything."

"I don't know how well I can advise. My life isn't like yours. I've never had a baby."

"Will you stay? If Luca lets you?"

I look down, hating the reminder that my life isn't my own. Hating that Elena had a choice to take control of her life, but I didn't.

I nod. "Of course. I don't want to miss these two little beings." I press a gentle hand to her belly.

Niko strides in, going straight to Elena for a kiss, and he rubs her belly. "How are you all this morning?"

"Good. Better now that Luce says she'll stay if Luca allows it."

Niko turns his attention to me. "Did you reach him last night?"

"I had to leave a message." I can't read his mind, but I wonder if he's peeved that he wasn't involved in the decision about my staying. After all, it's Niko's home, Niko's Family.

"As long as Elena's happy, you can stay with us as long as you like."

Elena gives him a kiss. "Then it's settled."

"Not quite," he says.

Elena frowns, and I tense. "Today, we're heading out to the compound. Maria will be in shortly to pack for you."

"Is there a reason? Did something happen?" I ask, worried that the security here has been breached. Has someone gotten through Donovan? Is he okay?

"It's a surprise." He winks at Elena. "Now, get ready. We leave in an hour. You too, of course, Luce." He leaves the room.

Elena's eyes sparkle with a new kind of excitement. She's practically giddy. "Do you think it's for the wedding?"

"You know him better than I do."

Maria walks in and scurries about to pack for Elena. I leave them, going to my own room to pack. I don't really have anything for a wedding, but I have a summer dress that might work. I also bought a little black dress, more out of habit than necessity. The rest of my clothes are jeans, shorts, and a variety of tops.

An hour later, the convoy of black SUVs slices through the city like a presidential motorcade. Niko is pulling out all the stops to ensure our safety on the way out to Long Island.

"Feels like we're moving an army," Elena murmurs beside me, her fingers dancing nervously over the swell of her belly.

I'm relieved. After all, the last time Elena and I were on the road, we had an accident and were kidnapped. "Better too many soldiers than too few."

The ride feels longer than the two-hour drive, but finally, we enter the gates of the fortified walled compound where Niko has a sizable mansion.

"Home, sweet fortress," Elena teases, her voice filled with relief as she undoes her seatbelt.

I exit the SUV, stepping out into the expanse of manicured lawns and stone pathways. My gaze lingers on the colorful blooms. It gives life to a stone gray home that feels like it came out of a Gothic novel. It's a metaphor for Elena's life, I decide. Niko, dark and foreboding like the house, and Elena, vibrant and radiant like the flowers.

Once inside, Niko takes Elena's hand, carrying her bag in the other as he leads her up the staircase. I can't hear what they're saying, but I strongly suspect it's the type of words involved in foreplay based on the smiles and giggles. I swallow down the lump of longing in my throat. How I ache for the happiness Elena has found.

"Mrs. Conti, I can show you to your room," the maid—Rosa, I think her name is—says.

"Thank you."

I'm put in the room I stayed in with Elena when I first arrived in New York. It seemed like a lifetime ago, and yet it wasn't that long at all.

"Would you like me to help you with your clothes?" Rosa asks.

"No, thank you. I've got it. You can check on Elena."

Rosa's lips purse. "I believe Don Leone has her taken care of."

I roll my eyes. "I imagine he does. But I'm fine. Really."

She nods and leaves the room. In the silent aloneness, I wish I'd asked her to stay. The feeling of emptiness seems to be growing and I don't like it.

I put my clothes away and then sit in the window seat looking out over the gardens. Maybe I'll take a walk and enjoy the warmth of the sun and take in the lovely setting. A walk could help clear my head.

I rise to leave when Donovan's hulking body fills my doorway. He watches me, eyes dark, the corner of his mouth curved into his usual smug smirk.

"Need something?" The words come out sharper than I intend. They give away the hurt I still feel at his actions.

"I have to go out later tonight. I thought you might like to come." His voice is casual. It's not a demand.

"With you?" Why would he think I'd want to go somewhere with him?

He shrugs. "I figured you'd want to stretch your legs a bit."

"Not with you."

I turn back to the window seat. Maybe he'll leave and after a few minutes, I can go for my walk without worrying about running into him.

"Are you mad about—"

"Out."

I don't look toward him, but I know he's here. It's like his energy is radiating through the room.

"Well, if you change your mind and want a small taste of freedom, meet me in the foyer at seven. Dress nice."

I glance at him, searching for a sign of mockery. There's something tantalizing about the offer, but it has nothing to do with Donovan. It must be the idea of a little freedom. Of being somewhere other than holed up in Niko's home.

I SPEND the rest of the afternoon going through a mental tug-of-war on whether I should go with Donovan or not. In the end, my sense of adventure wins out and I'm shimmying into my little black dress. I'd already done my hair and makeup, first like I was going out on the town, and then remembering this isn't a date since Donovan has business to deal with, I tone it down.

You know, everyone thinks Donovan has a thing for you. Elena's words come back to me. For a moment, I consider that but then dismiss it. Maybe I'm a conquest for him, but that would be it. Besides, I don't want to be in his world. I wonder if I can escape it, though. And if I did, would that mean I couldn't see Elena anymore?

I push all the troubled thoughts away and make my way downstairs at seven to meet Donovan. I wonder if he'll be surprised that I'm taking him up on his offer. Maybe he'll be annoyed. If that's the case, he shouldn't have invited me.

I descend the staircase and see Donovan standing at the bottom, his attention on his phone. I reach the last step, and still, he doesn't turn. My presence is inconsequential. It's a feeling that has me ready to go back upstairs and hide in my room forever.

"You look lovely, Mrs. Conti," Rosa says as she enters the foyer and heads upstairs.

"It's nice of you to notice. Thank you, Rosa."

Donovan finally turns, and his eyes travel the length of me, igniting a trail of heat despite the chill of my indignation.

He smirks. "That'll do."

I bristle at the casual approval. Like I'm chattel or something. "Are you sure? Do you need to check my teeth?" Inside, I'm feeling like an idiot for reveling in his perusal of my body. It's pathetic how starved I am to be seen as something of value. As more than a tool or a pawn.

Niko strides into the foyer. "A minute, Donovan."

Donovan obeys with a nod as he steps over to Niko. I watch from my peripheral vision, pretending to adjust the strap on my heel. The muscles in Donovan's jaw clench as he listens, his eyes flickering to mine for just a split second before returning to Niko. There's a promise in that look, or maybe a warning. I wonder what they're plotting. Exchanging secrets? Planning a murder? I wonder if this outing is a ruse for Donovan to pick my brain about my father or encourage me to leave Elena. I wouldn't put anything past those two.

The conversation ends with Niko giving Donovan a pat on the back. Niko exits toward his office, and Donovan steps back to me.

"Let's go."

His hand is low on my back as we walk out the front door. I try to be irritated by it, but the sizzle his touch sends up my spine is hard not to like.

The driver holds the door open, and I slide into the leather seat.

"Seat belt," Donovan murmurs as he settles next to me, close enough that I can catch the faint scent of his cologne—a mix of something dark, like the threat of a storm.

The car moves up the drive and out the gates. For long moments, we're silent, a surprise from Donovan who always has a quip or a joke.

"Why did Niko allow me to come with you?" My question breaks the quiet. "After all, you insisted that I'm not allowed out anymore."

Donovan's gaze remains fixed on the world outside the window. He's a statue, all chiseled features and controlled strength. But his pause tells me he's weighing his words, and it sends a chill down my spine.

"Things change," he says finally, turning to face me, his expression unreadable.

"For whom? Me? You know you don't own me, right? Niko doesn't either."

A muscle ticks in his jaw, the only betrayal of his irritation. "It's not like that, Luce."

"Then what's it like?"

He blows out a breath and shakes his head, like I'm an annoying little sister. "Security is easier out here. And it's tighter than ever. I thought you might like to get out. That's all." It almost sounds like he cares. But I won't make a mistake in believing that.

Finally, he turns to look at me. "Why did you come?"

He's turned the tables on me, and I'm unable to look at him for fear he might see the truth. I look out the window. "I wanted to get out. Where are we going, anyway?"

"Niko has a club out here. I've got to meet someone there."

All of a sudden, I question why I'm along on this outing. "Am I some sort of bait?" I recoil as a new thought comes. "Are you trading me or something? Luca won't—"

"Fucking hell, Lucy... no." He holds his hands up in surrender. "You have no involvement in my meeting. I really just thought you'd like to get out of the house and have some fun."

Am I being unreasonable? No. I know how men like Niko and Donovan think and work. Still, I doubt Niko would have Donovan do something to me because that would make Elena unhappy, and Niko wants her to be happy.

"You're paranoid."

I gape at him. "Can you blame me?"

His expression confuses me because it looks like hurt. "Nothing is going to happen to you. I promise."

I want to believe him but I know I can't. My fate really lies in Niko and Luca's hands. One word from Niko, and Donovan would have to follow orders even if it was to hand me to my father or send me to Italy or kill me.

We arrive at the club and Donovan escorts me up to the bar. The throb of the bass vibrates through my body. I can't remember the last time I'd been to a club. It fills me with excitement for at least the possibility of fun and forgetting how lonely my life has become.

He settles me on a stool and calls over the bartender. "Whatever she wants. On the house." Then he turns to me. "Behave yourself." His lips quirk up and he winks. He's back to being smug Donovan. But I get whatever I want on the house, so I turn to the bartender and order an Old-Fashioned with his most expensive whiskey.

I SIP my drink and look around the club. Across the room, Donovan has settled into a booth, leaning forward toward the man with him. I'm not sure whether he's trying to listen better or is threatening the man.

I decide that if I'm out in the real world, I'm not going to give attention to Donovan and whatever business he's up to. It's been so long since I've been out. My life in Italy was for the most part calm. It was clear from day one that my marriage was about caring for Giuseppe during his illness. I did the best I could knowing being his nurse was a better situation than ending up with someone abusive. There had been a lot of rumors about Giuseppe and his violent streak, but I never saw it. In fact, my impression was he never used it on those he cared for. Outside the Family, yes, but not inside. That was so different from my father who would kill anyone, including me and Elena, for power, money, or to save his own skin.

Life in Italy was slow and calm, but often boring. I had a few female friends, wives of Giuseppe's *capos*, but they were older than me. I tried to take up hobbies, but none stuck. I enjoyed walks around the compound, but I longed to see more of the country, of the world. I wanted to see or at least talk to Elena and know she was all right.

I look down into my nearly finished Old-Fashioned and realize that I've gotten some that I wished for. I'm away from my home. I'm with my sister, and she's happy. So, why do I feel so empty and lost?

Loneliness seeps in, cold and relentless. In the reflection of the mirror behind the bar, I catch glimpses of life playing out. A couple leans into each other, sharing secrets and smiles. Friends toast to whatever triumph brought them together this evening. And here I sit, alone, invisible, inconsequential. I take another sip, wishing the expensive whiskey would dull the pain of my epiphany.

I'm considering ordering another drink when someone sidles up next to me.

His shoulder brushes mine. "Can I buy you a drink?" A smile tugs at one corner of his mouth as if he knows exactly what runs through my mind.

"Depends on the drink." I feel like I'm playing with fire. It's dangerous, and yet I don't want to stop because at this moment, I feel alive.

"Whatever you want is yours."

"That could be dangerous."

He smirks. "Nothing is going to happen to you. I promise."

11

DONOVAN

I sit in the booth of Niko's club across from the informant when I'd much rather be taking in Lucy. Fucking hell, that dress she's wearing nearly gave me a stroke. It shows off every fuckable curve of hers.

The man across from me is twitchy. He keeps glancing toward the door like he expects a bullet with his name on it to come whistling out of the darkness.

"Spit it out. What do you have on Giovanni?"

The guy swallows hard, his Adam's apple bobbing. "He got clipped in the shootout with you and Don Leone. Been laying low... but he's been sending scouts. They're looking for someone."

"Who?" I push, already knowing the answer and ready to rip someone's arms off.

"The daughter."

My jaw clenches. "He has two. Which one?" On the off chance that Liam's intel was wrong about Lucy being the target.

"The one from Italy."

"Lucia?"

"I think that's her name." He nervously glances toward the door again.

"Focus, Joe. Anything else? Where is Giovanni hiding?" That was the point of this meeting in the first place.

He shrugs. "He moves around."

So he's not that hurt. He's not hiding to heal. He's hiding because he knows we're after him.

"Is he planning anything on Don Abate's territory?"

"That I don't know. He wants the girl."

Why is the question.

"Thanks for the info." I keep my voice level, though inside, I'm anything but calm. The man nods, downs his drink, and then rises, eager to escape. I nod his dismissal, and he disappears into the shadows.

I sit back and try to decipher the information he gave me. It seems like I wasted my time as I haven't learned anything new except that Giovanni had been hit during the encounter at the warehouse.

But the trip to the club isn't a total waste. It was worth it to see Lucy looking like a goddess. I look at her at the bar. She's sitting alone, her posture elegant, yet a wariness hangs on her lovely features.

Her gaze is fixed on the throng of bodies that move to the pulsating beat of music, but it's clear she sees none of them. The air around her is charged with a sadness that tugs at something deep within me.

Why the hell does Giovanni want her now? With Giuseppe dead, maybe he thinks she's vulnerable, an opportunity waiting to be exploited. Or maybe he's threatened by her. It wouldn't surprise me. Despite her icy exterior, there's a fire in Lucy that could put the fiercest *capo* to shame. She's got the makings of a Boss.

The thought of her as a Boss makes my lips twitch, as well as my dick. I like the fire in her, the fierceness even when it's directed at me. But as I watch her, the sorrow in her features dims my amusement. Giuseppe's death... could it be the cause of her sadness? Is she grieving him? Did she care for the old man? Giuseppe was good to her. Could he have been more than just a name on a marriage certificate? It seems so unlikely, considering how she ended up being his wife and the age difference. But what do I know of love and marriage? Zip. Nada. Zilch.

But that isn't my concern now. Giuseppe is gone. Giovanni is very much alive and has set his sights on Lucy.

She shifts slightly, her arms wrapping around herself, like she's fortifying herself against the world. Does she feel vulnerable here? Does she know what her father wants from her?

I watch as a man steps up to the bar next to her. He leans over Lucy with a familiarity he hasn't earned.

My jaw tightens. My hands curl into fists.

They talk, his smile clearly conveying that he wants to fuck her. She appears indifferent at first but then says something that appears to make the man think she's interested. His hand creeps up her thigh, and I see red. But I wait and watch because for all I know, she wants to fuck this man.

Time slows, stretches taut like a wire ready to snap as I watch. Lucy looks down at his hand on her thigh, then, with the grace and fury of an ice queen, she tosses her drink across the man's shocked face.

That's my girl. I'm at the bar so fast, my fingers closing around the man's collar, yanking him away from Lucy with a force that sends others at the bar scattering. There's a collective gasp around us, but no one intervenes. They know who I am. Who I work for.

The stench of his cheap cologne fills my nostrils as I drag him through the parting crowd. He thrashes, curses spilling from his lips. I wonder if he's a tourist as no one around her who knew me would dare such disrespect.

I tighten my grip. "Got a death wish, pal?" The words come out low and even, every syllable a promise of pain. The desire to kill this man is coursing through my veins. I hope he pushes me so I have a good excuse to carry out his death.

I get him out into the area behind the bar. It's dimly lit just for situations like this. I push him hard, and his body slams against the building.

"Didn't your mama ever teach you not to touch what isn't yours?"

"Fuck off—"

My fist lands a blow in the center of his face. "If you're smart, you'll learn manners and respect. Unless you want to die here."

"What is your prob—"

My fist meets his gut. "You're my problem."

"I just—"

"What you should be doing is apologizing to the woman you put your grubby hands on."

"She didn't say she was with—"

Another blow lands on his stomach. "Doesn't matter, asshole. You know what? I'm sick of this shit." I let my fury loose, blow after blow, each strike making the man howl or whimper. When I'm done, he's a crumpled heap, breathing ragged, eyes glazed with fear and pain.

"I'm not sure that was necessary."

I glance up at Lucy. She's watching the man, but her expression is unreadable. But at least she's not pissed at me.

"Are you all right?" I ask her.

Finally, her gaze turns to me. "Better than him."

One of my men appears. "Everything all right, Boss?"

"Yes. Maybe you can take care of this piece of trash. I'm going to take Mrs. Conti home."

"Mrs.?" the man whimpers from the pavement. "She never said—"

The words are interrupted when my man kicks him. "Shut up."

I escort Lucy to the car, and we drive right back to the compound in silence. I note that she's got her stoic ice princess persona on, but there's something underneath it that doesn't sit right.

When we reach the house, I guide her inside and through the familiar halls of Niko's opulent mansion. I take her through to the back of the house where I have my own private apartment. She steps inside without hesitation, and for a moment, relief washes over me that she isn't fighting me. It makes me wonder if the incident was more upsetting to her than I'd realized. Or maybe she doesn't know that this is my private room. How would she? I doubt she's seen much of the house.

"Make yourself comfortable." I guide her to the couch, but she doesn't sit.

She surveys the room with a guarded expression, taking in the living space that doubles as my sanctuary within the compound. Her gaze lingers on the large bed before drifting to the windows. I wonder if she's seeking an escape.

I head to the mini bar, pour two fingers of whiskey, and offer it to her. She accepts it with a nod, her fingers brushing mine, sending a jolt through me.

"What happened back there?" I ask.

She sips the whiskey, her throat working as she swallows. "Why do you care?"

Her question stings more than it should. I care. I shouldn't, but I do. It gnaws at me, this concern for a woman who's built walls so thick, I wonder if even she can see over them anymore.

"Because I do," I say, leaning against the bar, arms folded.

"Shouldn't you be off charming some other girl who actually wants your attention?"

I arch a brow. "You sound jealous."

She scoffs. "To be jealous, I'd have to care about you, and I don't."

"Ouch." I press my hand to my chest, in mock pain. "What's got your panties in a bunch, Princess?"

She sips her drink and then walks up to me, handing me the glass. "My panties are just fine."

She starts toward the door, but I can't let her go. My hand reaches out, taking her by the wrist and tugging her back.

"You haven't finished." I push the glass toward her, our fingers grazing again. This time, I'm ready for the electric shock of her touch, but it still rattles me.

She downs the drink and hands it back, but I don't take it. Instead, I reach for the bottle and pour more. Then I tug her to the couch.

"Donovan, I don't—"

"Too bad, Princess. You're going to sit here and tell me what the fuck is going through that pretty little head of yours."

"So now you think I'm dumb?"

I push her until she plops on the couch. Then I stare at her, wondering how she came up with the idea that I think she's dumb.

"No. Why would you say that?"

"Pretty little head... that indicates that you think I'm dumb."

I roll my eyes. "I don't think you're dumb. Irritating, yes, but—"

She starts to rise, but I step up in front of her, glaring at her with an expression that should tell her I'm not having it.

"You're like a petulant teenager," I say.

"And you're an overbearing—"

"Toady, yes, I know."

She purses her lips. "I was going to say oaf, but Toady works too."

I cross my arms. "What's your problem?"

"You." She turns her head away.

Deciding she's not going to run, I sit on the couch next to her. "Is it Giuseppe?"

She frowns at me. "It's not your business?"

I remember how I kissed her the other night and then how she tossed the drink on the man tonight. I felt like she'd been into the kiss with me. She hadn't slapped me or reacted like she had with that dickwad tonight. But maybe I'm wrong. Maybe she is putting on a strong front but deep down, she worries I'll touch her again.

"Are you afraid of me? Because you don't have to be. What happened the other night—that won't happen again."

Pain crosses her beautiful face, but it's fast, barely perceptible before she's got her cool, indifferent mask on again.

"Oh, you made that clear." She looks away.

I'm confused because it almost sounds like she's upset that I won't kiss her again. "What do you mean?"

When she looks back, there's no missing the anger or the pain underneath it. "You're the worst, Donovan, do you know that? Why do you hate me? Why do you torment me? Is this some plan you've concocted with Niko to make me leave?"

I stare at her in total incomprehension. "There's no effort to make you leave, and I'm not tormenting you. If anything, it's the other way around."

"Can I go now?" She starts to rise, but I stop her. At first, I prevent her from standing, but the effort brings me close to her. So close that I can see the depth of her dark eyes so filled with sadness. So close that I can inhale the scent of her... sweet and spicy. So close that I could taste her sublime lips if I just dipped a bit closer. The need for her is a rush of adrenaline. It drives me forward until my mouth consumes hers.

12

LUCIA

What is happening? Why is Donovan kissing me again? Is this more punishment? More trying to keep me in my place? Better yet, why aren't I stopping him?

Like before, his tongue slides along the seam of my mouth, coaxing my lips to part, which they do. His tongue dances with mine, and it's shocking how something like French kissing can feel so divine. It's just a kiss, but my entire body has lit up. Neurons are firing. My blood is pumping.

And then his hands begin to roam, and my body turns into liquid fire. Hot. Pliant. I should be stopping this, but I'm too weak to fight against the need Donovan brings out in me. The need to be seen. The need to be touched. How strange that he's the one who can make me feel that, is the one I want to make me feel that.

He pushes me back on the couch as his lips trail down my neck. "You're so fucking sexy. I nearly came in my pants when I saw you on the stairs."

"You did not," I say on a gasp as he tugs the bodice of my dress down and my breast pops out.

"I did."

I can't refute him because his lips wrap around my nipple and suck hard, stealing my breath. I arch into him, closing my eyes as sensations I've never felt radiate through me.

He moans against me as his large hand kneads my other breast. "Are you wet for me, Lucy?" His other hand slides under my dress. A part of me feels like I should stop this. Another part of me is shouting, *Hallelujah, finally*! His fingers press against the panel of my panties. I hiss out a breath as a new type of sensation floods through me.

"Mmm, my little ice princess is hot and wet." He moves down my body, and I'm wondering what he's doing. He pushes the skirt of my dress up and presses his nose to my panties and inhales. "Just like you, sweet and spicy."

His fingers grip the waistband of my panties and tug them down. Again, a feeling that I shouldn't be allowing this tries to rise, but I'm too captivated by Donovan and what he's doing. That is until he leans in as if he plans to use his mouth on me.

"Wha–What are you doing?"

He kisses my inner thigh, sucking slightly. "I'm going to eat you up, Princess. Make you lose control for once."

I don't really understand what that means. I move to put my hands over my private part, but he grips me by the wrists.

"One taste, Lucy. I might die if I can't taste you." Then his tongue slides through my folds.

"Oh, my God." I arch again as the sweetest, most torturous sensations flood through me.

"That's right, open for me." He releases my hands and pushes my thighs open wider. I feel exposed and vulnerable, but only for a split second. Only until his tongue is on me again, licking, lapping, flicking.

My body jerks and undulates of its own accord. Tension builds in my center, cranking up tighter and tighter until I can barely breathe.

Donovan releases my wrists. His hands slide under me, lifting like he's serving my intimate bits up for his meal. He moans, and the vibration of it reverberates through me. My fingers grip the couch as pressure builds. I might be a virgin, but I know where this is going. I've pleasured myself before. But oh, my God, I've never felt like this before. My body is taut in anticipation. My center is on fire.

"Come for me, Lucy," Donovan murmurs against me as he moves one hand to my belly. "I want to drink you up." His tongue slides inside me, and he uses his thumb on my hardened nub.

I cry out as my world pulls in and then snaps, explodes in a kaleidoscope of sensation. It floods my entire body down to my toes.

"Mmm... fucking fantastic," he murmurs again as he continues to lick me until I can't hardly take it anymore.

Finally, he stops. His body moves up mine until he's over me. His erection behind his slacks is massive as it presses against my belly. He kisses me, and at first, I don't want it. His mouth has been down there... it seems icky. But then it isn't. More than the taste is the sense of intimacy. No man has been this close to me, has touched the parts of me that Donovan has.

"Is that what you needed? A release?"

His words stop the warm fuzzies floating inside me. I look up to his signature smirk, and it hits me that this is nothing for him. He's done this to countless women. It's only sex.

"It feels like that's what you need." I push at him. "But not from me."

He's a huge man, but he moves off me. "God, now what?"

I hate that tone in his voice. It suggests that I'm being unreasonable. Or an ice princess. Just as his comment about my needing a release did.

My movements are jerky as I straighten my dress and slip on my panties. "You're a ____"

"A Toady, yes, I got it."

"A jerk, Donovan Ricci." I hate that my voice is quavering. Like I'm on the verge of crying. How does this man make me want so badly one minute and then make me feel like nothing the next?

His eyes narrow as he watches me. "Did I hurt you?"

All the time, I want to say, but I don't.

His features soften and he steps toward me. "Lucy." His hand reaches out to cup my face, but I'm already feeling crazy and humiliated.

I move back. "Please stay away from me." I rush from the room, fleeing upstairs to my bedroom. Like a spoiled princess, I suppose. I flop on my bed and lose it. I'm not sure why, exactly. All I know is that I feel such emptiness and loneliness. And for a moment, when Donovan touches me, that seems to be gone. It's like he sees me. But when it's done, I feel worse than before because I know it's not about me. I could be any woman. Sex isn't love. It isn't respect. It won't fix what's broken inside me.

THE NEXT DAY, I do my best to push everything away. It's not easy. How do I forget that my father sold me to my husband who just died? Or that my father caused a car accident to kidnap me and my sister? Or that my sister could have total and complete freedom from this world but chose to stay? Or that I've let a man who doesn't respect me touch me intimately simply because I'm feeling lost and alone? A hot shower doesn't wash all that away.

Luckily, distraction can help keep it at bay. When I go down for breakfast, the house is awash with activity preparing for a wedding. Elena is radiant as she jumps up from the dining room table to hug me.

"It's today. Niko has arranged everything."

"How exciting. How can I help?" Focusing on others always works to keep my pity parties at bay.

"You'll be my matron of honor, right?"

"Right." God, who is standing up for Niko? Probably Donovan. Ugh. "Who is the best man?"

"Liam. It was going to be Donovan too, but he's taking care of all the security today."

Thank God.

Elena frowns. "Are you all right? You look... I don't know, sad?"

I plaster on a smile. "What's there to be sad about? My sister is getting married and it's for the right reasons. She's in love."

Her smile is radiant. "I can't believe it. I'm so lucky Niko found me."

"Kidnapped you, you mean."

She gives me a sly grin. "It's a good thing I sold him my virginity."

I still can't believe she did that. In her desperation to escape my father, she'd done something so over the top crazy. And yet, because of it, she is here, happier than I've ever seen her. Maybe I need to do something crazy. The image of Donovan between my legs flashes in my mind. I give my head a shake. That wasn't crazy. It was stupid.

I spend the rest of the morning helping Elena get ready for her wedding. She stands in front of the mirror and studies herself, her hand on her belly.

"Mom was so mad that my dress didn't fit right when I was supposed to marry Romeo," she says.

"You were pregnant then?"

"Yes, but I'd been losing weight. She told me to just lie down and do whatever Romeo wanted. That it would be easier." She turns to me. "She never knew relations between a man and woman could be loving and pleasurable for both."

I scoffed. "She married Dad. He doesn't know how to love, and I'm sure didn't care about her pleasure. Hell, she's not much different from him."

Her eyes soften. "She was like us... a woman without agency, turned hard by a lifetime—"

"Don't, Elena." I can't hear her try to justify our mother.

"What?"

"She is as bad as him. Trust me on this." I'd spent so much time caring for and protecting Elena, and part of that was keeping truths from her. Truths about our mother.

"But she didn't have a choice—"

"She had plenty of choices." My voice is teetering on rage, so I pull it back. "This is your wedding day. Focus on that."

She studies me for a moment but then nods and turns back to the mirror. "Was your wedding nice?"

I was terrified when I arrived at my wedding. Even seeing

Giuseppe old and infirm didn't alleviate my fear that he'd hurt me. We were married several months, with me tending him every day, before I understood he wouldn't hurt me. After that, we forged a sweet friendship.

"It was lovely," I lie. "Now, you need something borrowed, so here is a necklace that Giuseppe gave me."

Elena's eyes tear up. "Pearls. Oh, and a sapphire. It's beautiful."

"It's borrowed, blue, and something old. I'm not sure that's how the tradition is supposed to work… but we're under the gun. We just need something new."

Elena laughs. "You take such good care of me."

The moment is bittersweet as I know she won't need me after today. She probably hasn't needed me since the moment she tried to escape our father. She's become a strong, independent woman.

There's a knock on the door and Rosa enters. Her eyes tear up when she sees Elena. "Oh, you're so beautiful. Don Leone is going to be in shock."

"Thank you, Rosa."

"He asked me to give this to you." Rosa hands Elena a small box.

Elena glances at me. "Maybe this is the something new." She opens the box and inside are two dazzling sapphire earrings.

"He said it was new and blue," Rosa says. "I see you have blue already."

Elena looks in the mirror as she puts on the earrings. "It goes perfectly." She turns around. "Well?"

"Rosa is right, Niko is going to be shocked."

While not traditional, Elena opts to not have anyone walk her down the aisle. After all, she's giving herself to Niko. Outside, in the lovely garden filled with colorful blooms, she joins her life to Niko's. I swear I see tears in the man's eyes when she first comes into his view. It actually helps me feel more comfortable about the two of them. I know Niko is a killer, a ruthless, determined Mafia businessman. But I have no doubt that he loves my sister. There is no one better to give her what she wants and keep her safe than him.

The best part of the wedding and small reception for me is that I don't see Donovan. I wonder if he's even at the compound. So, all in all, it's a lovely day. That is, until Niko informs me that I'll be returning to Manhattan later that night with Liam.

"Why?" I'm part angry but also part afraid. Now that he's married, is he going to get rid of me? Not to kill me, but to ship me back to Luca? Or just to separate me from Elena?

"I'm on my honeymoon."

"Oh... right." Due to the tensions between my father and Niko, the decision is to postpone a real honeymoon until my father is dead. Instead, they'll have their honeymoon here at the compound. "I can stay away—"

"You're going to Manhattan. Rosa has packed your things."

"Does Elena know?"

"Do you really think she wants her sister on her honeymoon?"

He has a point.

"You'll be safe with Liam. Donovan will keep you safe while there."

"Don't you need him here with you?"

He arches a brow like he finds my question odd. "We're plenty protected here. Besides, he has work to deal with in the city."

Ugh.

It's after nine when Liam loads me into his car and we head back to the city. I'm not sure what to make of him. He's very serious, even more so than Niko. I've learned that he was once Bratva but is now in the FBI. Was that by design, or had he wanted out of the criminal life? If that was the case, why is he essentially Niko's *consigliere*? These are all questions I don't dare ask him. Instead, we talk about Niko and Elena and our favorite Italian wines. He asks my opinion of the best pizza in New York. Of course, I say Niko's place. Is it the best? Maybe not, but it's pretty good.

When we arrive at the penthouse, he escorts me up. Maria is there to take my bag to my room. Donovan is there too, and my first sight of him after last night makes my insides roll over. He barely glances at me as he tells Liam they need to talk.

I go to my room and settle in. It's late, after midnight, but I can't sleep, so I head downstairs to get a glass of wine. Once I have my glass, I make my way toward the stairs.

"Settled in?"

I stop but don't turn at Donovan's voice. "Yes."

"Good."

I turn. "You missed the wedding."

He's leaning against the doorframe of Niko's office, his arms crossed. "No, I didn't. I was there. I left after."

"Oh."

"Luca Conti wants a meeting with Niko."

My stomach tightens. "About me?"

"I don't know. He'll be here in two weeks."

I feel like he's telling me that in two weeks, I'll be gone. Gone from Elena. Gone from him.

For a moment, we stand, gazes caught. I have this feeling like I should apologize for the night before. Before I can figure out what to say, he straightens.

"Have a good night, Mrs. Conti." He enters the office and shuts the door.

It takes me a minute to register that he didn't call me Lucy. Something only he does. Mrs. Conti is so formal. He's now all business. No humor. No warmth. Not with me, anyway. For some reason, that makes me feel even more alone than I'd ever felt.

13

DONOVAN

Two weeks. Fourteen days of dodging Lucy. Do you know how fucking it hard it is to protect a woman who can't stand the sight of you? I've gone over that night I ate her sweet pussy. She was into it, that I know. But as soon as it was over, she was angry. Why? What the hell happened on the way down from that massive orgasm I gave her?

Please stay away from me.

It hadn't been a demand. It was a plea, and it broke me in two. The only thing that makes sense to me is that the intimacy was too much for her. She doesn't like touchy feely things. The only person she's close to is Elena, and I suspect Elena doesn't know half the things knocking around in Lucy's psyche.

I need to stop ruminating on this. I've got to get my head in the game because the shit is heating up with Giovanni. And then there's Luca Conti, whom Niko and Liam met with earlier today. All I can think about is Luca taking Lucy back to Italy. It kills me, and yet, it would likely be for the best for both of us.

I'm heading from my apartment in the penthouse to Niko's office. He and Elena returned here last week, although the way he interrupts the day to go fuck his wife makes me think they should have stayed gone two weeks.

"It's the hormones. They make her need me," Niko had said, waggling his brows suggestively.

"Fucker. Why rub it in that you're getting laid everyday—"

"More like two or three times," Liam had quipped.

"Ah, Donovan, don't tell me your charm has worn off. Or maybe you've just fucked every woman in New York and have lost interest," Niko had retorted.

I haven't fucked Lucy, at least not in real life. In my dreams and fantasies, she has a starring role.

I push that discussion out of my mind so I can focus on the meeting we have today. I round a corner and nearly run into Lucy. For a second, I drink her in. We've been in the same location for weeks, but I feel like I haven't seen her.

Her brows draw into a frown and I remember my place.

"Mrs. Conti." I step to the side to let her pass. She seems even more pissed now that I've pulled back and only act professionally around her. The woman is driving me mad. "Is there anything you need?"

"From you? Never." Her reply is brisk, dismissive. It hurts like hell, which is a new thing for me. Why can this woman stab me in the heart so easily? Why do I allow it? I must be a fucking sadist.

"Okay." I nod, stepping back, respecting the chasm she's drawn between us. I watch her walk away. Her back is straight, chin lifted, like nothing can get to her. It's armor, that much is clear, but armor against what? Protecting her feels as natural as breathing, but she doesn't want my protection. She's got barbed wire around herself, and I'm tired of getting scrapes and scratches each time I go near her.

I breathe again once she's gone, flexing my hands.

"Boss needs you," someone calls from down the hall, and I square my shoulders, schooling my features into the impassive mask of Niko's right-hand man. All this is good preparation for when I take over Giovanni's business. Being able to kill the feelings, dull the pain, to focus on the job are all skills I feel I've honed, but Lucy is making me rethink that.

I enter Niko's office. Liam is there, but it's only us. No other *capos* or soldiers. Not even Lou, who I feel is on the brink of a promotion. He's really proven himself since the ambush by Giovanni.

Niko stands at the window, his hands in his pockets, his gaze out the window. He's partly surveying his kingdom but also deep in thought.

Liam is hunched over the desk, eyes scanning sheets of paper that can only spell trouble.

"Situation's escalated," Liam says without looking up, his voice low. Despite growing up in the Bratva, his Russian accent is mostly gone except when he's tense, like now.

"Give him the details." Niko's voice is tense.

"The FBI has been monitoring an organized crime site on the dark web. Lucia's name has come up."

My heart stops in my chest.

Liam moves to a tablet, his fingers typing across the keyboard. A website pops up, and he hands me the device. On it I see Lucy's face. It must be five or more years old. She doesn't necessarily look younger. She looks less hardened. Less guarded. More innocent.

"Christ," I mutter, bile rising in my throat.

"It's a dark web auction site." Liam takes the tablet back. "Starting bid… half a million dollars."

"Half a—" I can't finish. That's my Lucy they've put a price tag on. A goddamn commodity for sick bastards with too much money.

"Does it have a time frame?" Niko's question slices through my spiraling thoughts.

"No, but bids are coming in. It won't be long before Giovanni thinks there's enough to take the bid and close it down."

Rage is seething, dripping from my pores. "He can't do that if he doesn't have her."

"Find the host server, track the source." Niko ignores my comment.

"Already on it."

"The fucking gall." I run my hands through my hair.

"Apparently, Giovanni thinks Lucia's widowhood makes her his again."

"Like fucking property. That man would sell his wife…" Liam doesn't finish the sentence as something on the screen catches his eye.

"This reeks of desperation," Niko states. "I think our time of waiting is over."

"No shit," I blurt out. "He can't sell Lucy. Not again."

Niko arches a brow at my outburst. Liam looks up from his tablet. I've probably tipped my hand.

"It would crush Elena," I add, hoping it hides my personal attachment to Lucy.

"That's why we won't let it happen. We'll turn Giovanni's desperation against him," Niko says.

"He's worse than we'd imagined," Liam says as he goes back to the tablet.

"What do you mean?" I ask.

"To his family," Liam says.

I look at Niko, wondering if he'll enlighten me. "Elena is lucky I stole her when I did. But Lucia…"

"Lucia what?"

"His daughters were never family to him. Hell, I don't think he sees them as people."

I'm about to pull my fucking hair out. "What does that mean?"

"Giovanni wanted to get into trafficking… women."

Bile threatens to come up. "Lucy?"

"When it appeared that she wasn't as pure as snow, he sold her to Conti," Niko explained. "Ruined his plans to make her his first sale as a sex slave."

"Holy fucking hell." I swallow hard. "Does she know this?"

Both men blink at me like it's an odd question. It tells me they don't fully see her as human, either. Not that she's just a commodity, as Giovanni saw her, but her feelings aren't something they're considering.

"I don't know," Niko says. "Elena hasn't said anything, but I'm certain there's plenty Lucia didn't tell her."

"She probably does," I say. Her hardened, guarded personality starts to make more sense.

"Has she said something?" Niko asks, his brows narrowing as if he thinks I know something I haven't told him.

"No. It's more about how she acts. She doesn't trust anyone. She'll die for Elena, but that's about it for people in her life."

"Giuseppe was good to her, at least that's what Elena said."

"Giuseppe is dead," I point out.

Niko nods and turns his attention back to Liam.

"What do you need me to do?" I'm ready to arm up and walk into whatever shithole Giovanni is hiding in and take him out. She doesn't want me. Doesn't need me. But heaven help the person who tries to hurt her.

"We could put her in Witness Protection if she's willing to testify against Giovanni," Liam offers.

Niko shakes his head. "Even if she'll do that... I want her in Elena's life, if possible."

"You're getting soft," Liam murmurs, but Niko ignores him.

"We could bid on her," Niko offers. "Smoke him out with a bid to stall or dupe him. It could draw Giovanni into the open."

"Risky," Liam says.

I agree. If we failed, Lucy would... well, I can't think about what would happen to her. My mind races, analyzing angles, anticipating moves.

"Luca Conti says he'll take her back to Italy." Liam watches me closely, and I know he's curious about my reaction. I suspect he's on to me. "She'd be safer there."

He's probably right, except I don't think anyone can protect Lucy as well as I can. No one is more motivated to keep her safe than me, that I know.

"Do you trust him?" Liam asks. "I know you've done business with him, but clearly, so has Fiori. For all we know, he's a part of this auction plan."

"She's Luca's Family." Niko goes to his bar and pours two fingers of whisky.

"So's Giovanni," I snap. "What's the point?"

Niko arches a brow at me over the rim of his drink. "Giovanni sold her to the Contis—"

"To Giuseppe," I argue. "Not Luca."

"They married. That makes her part of the Conti Family."

"Do we know that's how Luca sees it? Or that he doesn't see Lucia like Giovanni does?" Liam glances at me, and I suspect he knows my turmoil, and in an unusual act of empathy, he's siding with me.

"No. We could ask her. She has talked about going back to Italy," Niko states.

"She's still here, though, isn't she? Elena is pregnant. Surely, Lucy would rather be here with her than in Italy."

"Then what do you suggest?" Niko watches me, calculating.

"She stays here, with us. Anything else is non-negotiable."

"Even if it means war?" Niko asks.

"We're already in a war."

Niko sucks in a breath and downs his drink. "Before we do anything, we need more intel. We can't afford to fly blind."

"Understood." It's important that I don't forget my place, which I've come precariously close to doing.

"There's something that has been bothering me," Niko continues. "How did Giovanni get one on us?"

The three of us look at each other as we ponder the question.

"You think it's someone in the Family?" I ask.

He nods.

"Then we do an internal sweep." He's right. Something was off about that night.

"Discreetly. Once we're certain of our own, we'll deal with Conti and anyone else who thinks they can lay claim to what's ours."

Has he just said Lucy was his? Under his protection? That could go a long way to protecting her.

"Why wait longer?" I ask. "If Giovanni was injured, as our intel told us, let's not wait until he's better. "Let's go after him."

"It's not like we haven't been looking for him." Niko's lips twitch upward like he's amused by me.

"No, but what better way to find him than to walk in and take what's his?"

"Niko already did that with Elena." Liam sits back and watches with an almost bored expression.

"I'm talking about his business. He can't be in all places at once, especially if he's healing. His New York business is the biggest, so he's not going to be too far from that. Let's go after his Jersey business, making him come out if he wants to keep it."

"What if he doesn't come out?"

"Then the Jersey business is yours. Or let me do it."

Liam snickers. "Sounds like Donovan wants to go rogue and start his own Family."

But Niko's narrow eyes tell me he's on board with my plan. "Do what you need to do."

14

LUCIA

Today is an exciting day. Elena and I, along with Maria, are making a doctor's visit to check on the babies. As we reach the landing in the penthouse, I see an army of Niko's men at the ready.

"Something must be happening," Elena murmurs next to me.

I nod in agreement as I scan the men, looking for Donovan. Not because I want to see him or because I'm worried about him. It's because I hope I don't see him. Something deep inside me says, *Liar*.

Niko enters the fray, his expression full of genuine love as he reaches out his hand to help Elena down the last few steps.

"How are you feeling, *cara mia*?"

"Excited."

"I'm sorry I can't go with you. I want to, you know that, right? But right now, things are tense. As it is, I wouldn't let you go if there were any way possible to have the tests you need done here."

She gives him a sweet smile. "I know. I understand. But you have to get this sorted, Niko, because you have to be there when the babies are born."

"I will move heaven and earth to make that happen."

I wonder how many men will be killed to make it happen, but I don't say that. Why be snarky at such a sweet moment?

Niko looks at me. "You're going as well?"

I nod.

His jaw tightens. "I'm not sure that's a good idea."

My anger rises. Elena's expression falters. "I need someone there with me."

"*Cara mia*, it's dangerous." Niko runs his fingers through his hair.

I glance at all the men. "What's going on? What are all your men here for?"

"They're for Elena."

Elana gapes. "What? I don't need an army—"

"You'll have an army." His tone indicates there's no getting around it.

"Then it should be safe for me to go with her, right?"

His jaw ticks again.

"I need her, Niko." Elena's voice has its own force to it. I'm proud of her. "We need to go now or we'll be late." She eyes all the men. "It will take two rides in the elevator to get us all down."

"And four cars," I add.

"There's nothing more important than your safety." Niko nods to his men, who move toward the elevator. "Take care of them."

Soon, Elena and I are making our way down to the garage. The number of men looking out for her seems over the top. I wonder how many are there because of me. Not to protect me, but because I add additional danger to Elena. If that's the case, perhaps I should stay behind. But wouldn't Niko say something if there were anything going on in regard to me?

My stomach churns. I hate this. But there's a small relief that Donovan isn't here. He's too dangerous in a way that has nothing to do with bullets or blood.

At the clinic, Elena, Marie, and I make our way to the exam room. It's clear that Niko has called ahead to arrange that Elena isn't left out in the open and that the section of the clinic is mostly empty. Fortunately, we're able to convince the three men still around us to wait outside.

"I doubt Don Leone wants his men to see something so intimate about his wife."

They blanch and nod, taking up station outside the door.

The sterile scent of antiseptic fills the air as the doctor enters the room after a nurse has taken vitals and information from Elena.

"All right, let's take a look at your little ones," she says as she spreads gel over Elena's swollen belly. I stand beside her, holding her hand. I'm probably not as excited as her, but it's close. I can't believe I'm about to see my nieces or nephews growing in my little sister's belly.

"Ah, there they are. Here we have Baby A" —the doctor points at the screen— "and right next door, Baby B." Her voice is calm, which tells me that everything must be all right with what she's seeing, because what I'm seeing is a whole lot of gray blobs.

Elena's breath catches. "Oh... look at them, Luce. Isn't it amazing?"

I squeeze her hand. "It is."

"Both heartbeats are strong," the doctor continues, pointing to an area showing a fast fluttering on the screen. "And they're measuring right on track."

Tears brim in Elena's eyes. She turns her head, looking at me with a radiance that fills me with emotion. I don't know that I've ever seen anyone so purely, joyfully happy.

"Would you like some pictures?" the doctor asks.

"Please," Elena whispers, still caught up in the emotion.

The doctor finishes her exam. "Everything looks great. You should be aware that twins increase the risk of complications. They also tend to arrive earlier than single births, so we want to keep a close watch. I'd like to have you back here next month."

"All right." Elena slides off the table clutching the photos of the twins. As we leave, her hand finds mine, squeezing tightly.

"Thank you for being here."

"Are you kidding? I wouldn't miss this for anything. As long as you want and need me, I'm by your side."

Elena loops her arm through mine as we navigate the sterile corridor toward the elevator. There are the three men who are outside the door, and three more are near the elevator. Where the others are, who knows?

We're several feet from the elevator when it dings and the door opens. A man in an expensive dark suit steps out. Niko's men stop and wait for the man to move away or around us. Instead, the man moves toward us. The guards react instantly, forming a blockade, their hands reaching for concealed weapons as protocol dictates. But as he nears, recognition shoots through me.

"Luca?"

"*Lucia, ho bisogno di parlare con te.*"

"Get away—"

"No, it's okay. This is Luca Conti... Don Luca Conti," I say, remembering his position now that Giuseppe is gone. "He says he needs to talk to me."

"Orders are to get you home," one of the men says in a flat, no questions asked tone.

"By insulting another Don? My husband's son?" The Mafia can be weird around family. In some cases, sentiment and family loyalty mean nothing. Like with my parents. But other Families, the center of the universe is the family, which is the sense I get from Niko.

"I just need a minute with him," I say.

"Luce, no." Elena's fingers tighten on my arm, her eyes wide, darting between me and the figure the guards shield us from.

"Let me speak to him." There's a command in my tone. "Take Elena home."

"Luce. No," Elena says again, but this time with more force.

"Elena, Luca is family to me." I turn my attention back to Niko's men. "Take her home. I can get back. Luca will make sure I'm safe." I turn to him, and he nods.

The men intend to argue, but Elena says, "Take me home. Niko will be expecting me." She glances at me with an expression that says she hopes I know what I'm going. The men follow her orders and escort her to the elevator.

Luca steps away into an empty waiting area, standing tall and imposing, and his dark eyes lock onto mine as I join him.

"What are you doing here?" And then I remember hearing that he'd come to town. Niko had a meeting with him.

Luca runs a hand over his face. "It's your father. He's trying to sell you again."

The words slam into me. For a moment, my world tilts. "No. He can't..."

Luca's jaw tightens, anger flashing in his eyes. "I'm afraid he is. He's been in contact, offering your hand in marriage."

I gape in incomprehension. "To you?"

He nods.

I like Luca, but I was married to his father. And even if it was only on paper, not a traditional marriage, it seems creepy to then marry my stepson.

"After everything... he would do this to me again?" Well, of course he would. My father would sell angels in heaven if he could.

Luca grips my shoulders. "Listen to me. I refused him outright. The idea of it is ludicrous. Not that you're not a good woman, Lucia, but—"

"No, I get it. I was married to your father."

"Right. So I told him no."

Relief and gratitude wash through me. But on its heels creeps a familiar sense of despair. If not Luca, then whom? How long before my father auctions me off once more? And can he do that? Aren't I a Conti? Wouldn't Luca have a say? What sort of deal had my father made to Giuseppe that I'm not fully under Conti protection now?

As if reading my thoughts, Luca says gravely, "He's started posting your... details on the dark web. In an auction."

A shudder racks my body. Again, I'm reduced to nothing human. Only attributes and selling points.

"I can protect you, Lucia, but you'd need to return to Italy with me."

I close my eyes as the weight of the world descends around me. But even as despair threatens to swallow me, a spark of defiance flickers to life. I am not that frightened girl my father made watch him murder her eighteen-year-old boyfriend and then shipped off to Italy to marry an elderly man. I'll be damned if I let my father control me again.

I will my tears not to fall as I take in a strengthening breath. "I can't leave New York. Not while Elena needs me."

Luca's brow furrows. "It's too dangerous for you here. Your father has reach, allies—"

"I don't care," I say fiercely. "I won't abandon my sister." Even as I say it, I have to wonder if I'm a danger to her. I think back to how Niko didn't want me to come today. Does he know what my father is up to? He must. Even so, I have no doubt that Niko can protect my sister. And I have to believe he'll carry out his promise to me to end my father.

"Does Niko know?"

"Yes. Of course. That's why I'm here. You'll be safe in Italy."

My mind is a whirl of confusion.

"I want nothing more than to honor my father's wishes to protect you." His voice softens. "But I cannot do that from Italy. Everything is set. You have a home, a life in Italy. My father left you an estate and enough money to live your days in peace with security."

I know about the money, but the estate is news to me. It suggests that Giuseppe knew he wouldn't be around much longer. He gave me my freedom, but also a place to be if I needed it. He treated me like a real wife.

"My father loved you, Lucia. You were always by his side, caring for him. He once told me you were too young to be bound to such an old man, but he was happy that he had you."

I feel guilty for not accepting Giuseppe and Luca's extreme kindness. "I'm grateful to you and Giuseppe. Really, Luca. But I can't bow to my father."

He inhales a breath, and I can see his expression turning from empathetic to serious. "I will not sugarcoat this. Returning with me is your best chance at safety. I can't stay here and I can't protect you here if I'm in Italy."

Of course, he's right. As long as I remain in my father's crosshairs, nowhere in New York is safe. And while I hate the idea that I need protection, I know I'm no match for my father. Niko protects me now only because of Elena. But if—or more likely, when—things heat up between Niko and my father, Niko will see me as a liability.

But abandoning Elena now, when she needs me most? The thought makes my chest ache. She's all I really have. Am I selfish, or am I looking out for her?

"I just can't go."

Luca watches me for a long moment, then nods. "I thought you might say as much." Luca pulls me into a fierce embrace. "I—"

Suddenly, he jerked away from me violently. "Keep your fucking hands off her."

Donovan's eyes hold a murderous glare, first at Luca and then at me. He grips my arm and tugs me toward the elevator. "We're leaving. Now!"

15

LUCIA

"Let go!" I try to escape Donovan's grip, but he holds tighter, his fingers biting into my arm.

"Don't test me, Lucy. You'll lose." His voice is dark, and I should be afraid, but I'm not. Is it because I'm tired of being afraid? Resolved that my life will never be free? That my end could very likely be tragic?

"Donovan!" Luca follows us. The fact that he knows who Donovan is tells me Luca and Niko have spent more time together or know each other better than I realized. "She is mine."

"Like hell," Donovan bellows, punching the elevator button. "She's mine."

What? I again try to pull away. "I'm nobody's." That I know for sure. Luca is offering me a safe haven, but I'm not his. Niko, too, offers some protection now, but I'm not a part of his Family.

Donovan looks down on me, his expression fierce. "Think again." Then he turns to Luca. "She's under Niko's protection, Luca. I don't know what the fuck you're up to."

Luca glances at me. "You have a place in Italy. Just say the word."

And what? Luca will kill Donovan and take me to Italy? Will Donovan end up killing Luca? Good God, this is crazy.

"It's okay, Luca. I appreciate your talking to me. But I need to be with Elena."

Luca nods and steps back. His gaze moves to Donovan. "If anything happens to her, it's on you, Donovan, and Don Leone. We won't forget that."

The elevator opens and Donovan pulls me in. "Ciao, Luca."

When the doors close, Donovan puts his face in mine. "Did I not make myself clear before? You don't go anywhere without guards."

"There were guards."

I feel the tension, the rage in him. It radiates around him. "Don't fuck with me now, Luce. I'm in no mood."

"How did you even know?"

"Your little tête-à-tête with Luca didn't go unnoticed. Why were you talking to him?"

The doors open, and he pulls me into the garage, loading me in his SUV. The driver squeals out practically before Donovan has the door shut behind him in the back seat where he keeps me trapped.

Suddenly, I'm wondering if Donovan is suspicious of me and my conversation with Luca. Perhaps I should be more afraid. Just because he kissed me... and gave me an orgasm... it doesn't indicate that I mean anything to him.

Maybe I'm brave. Maybe I'm an idiot. But I want to stand up to him. "None of your business."

"Think again, Princess. What did Luca want?"

I glare at him. "Luca is family. He's about all I have left."

"What about Elena?"

I turn to look out the window, watching the city blur past. "Elena belongs to Niko now." Perhaps it's time to face the truth. Elena doesn't need me. Not really. "Niko can get rid of me at any time." I have to consider that's why Luca found me. Because Niko wanted him to take me away. But if that's the case, why is Donovan dragging me back?

Donovan shakes his head and turns his attention out the window for the rest of the drive, the elevator ride up to the penthouse, and the walk to my room.

I try to shut the door in his face, but he pushes his way in. "Lucy—"

"Enough, Donovan! You've shadowed me since we left the clinic, spewed your accusations. You've done your duty. You've played the watchdog. Now leave me alone."

"Played?" He stops just short of touching me, his expression unreadable. "You think this is play?"

"No. None of this is very fun. I'm so tired of it all." I close my eyes, feeling so weary.

"Isn't it curious how you sidestep the question." A statement, not a query. "What did Luca want?"

Why doesn't he let this go? "I don't owe you explanations." I stride across the plush carpet, sinking into the armchair with feigned nonchalance. "Luca's visit was familial. That's all."

His gaze is piercing as he moves closer, invading my space. "So, your loyalty lies with the Contis now?"

"Where else would they lie?" My heartbeat quickens, wondering if something went wrong between Luca and Niko. Why does he care so much about my conversation with Luca?

"Are you going back to Italy?"

"Again, none of your business." I rise from the chair, not wanting to be penned in. But I don't know where to go, so I sit on the edge of the bed.

"It is my business, Princess. Everything about you is my business."

I look up at him, not understanding. "Because of my ties to my father and Elena."

"What you do impacts others. When will you get that through your... thick head?"

I look down. Maybe he's right. Niko is all about killing my father and protecting Elena these days, and so that would be the priority of his men, including Donovan.

"No. I'm not planning on returning to Italy. Elena needs me. I want to help her and the babies."

Donovan sucks in a breath and seems to release some of his tension. "Will Luca agree to that? To your staying?"

"It's not up to Luca."

He studies me, dark eyes searching. "You sure about that? Because Luca... he knows things. About your father."

"Luca thinks my father is a maniac. He wants nothing to do with him. Can't say I blame him."

"Did Luca tell you all that?" Donovan squats down in front of me. It feels like a sympathetic gesture, but I can't be sure.

"Yes." Wondering how much Donovan and Niko know, I add, "Luca said my father offered to sell me to him, and he refused. But he says I'm up for sale at some black-market auction instead." I watch Donovan closely. Does he know? Will he admit it if he does?

The subtle shift in Donovan's expression is a punch to the gut—a barely there clenching of his jaw, the way his eyes look away for a moment. It's enough for me to know he was aware of the auction, and the betrayal stings like a slap.

"That information would've been useful to me," I spit out, the words laced with venom. "But no, I had to hear it from Luca, of all people. He's always been good to me. Because of him and Giuseppe, I forgot how the real Mafia world works."

"It was Niko's—"

"Right, because you're a toady. A lackey."

His jaw clenches, but he doesn't respond.

I laugh derisively. "I was almost convinced that Niko and his Family were different too, but they're not. You're all the same. My father never told me what was going on until he was doing it either."

"I'm nothing like your father."

"Aren't you?"

He stares at me, taut with tension that doesn't seem angry as much as frustrated. I know comparing him to my father is cruel. There are some differences. And yet, in other ways, there aren't. Like how I'm not informed about things that could impact my life. How I can't be in charge of my own life.

I brace for the storm, the thunder of Donovan's wrath at my words, but instead, he sighs and sits next to me. When I meet his gaze, there's no raging storm. What I see is pain.

"Then why stay, Lucy?" His voice is low, softer than I've ever heard it, and it disarms me more than any shout could. "With Luca, you'd be safer."

The words hang between us, not an accusation but a genuine question. And something inside me crumbles. All those years building walls, and they start to fall. I don't want to tell him anything, and yet, it tumbles out.

"I've been a pawn in someone else's game since the day I was born. I was groomed to be my father's greatest asset in creating alliances for his personal gain."

"Your father is a fucking waste of breath." The vehemence in Donovan's voice soothes me.

"He wasn't alone. You may already know this, but at one time, I was going to be the first woman in an exclusive high-market trafficking business. Guess whose idea that was? My mother's."

Donovan's eyes close and his teeth gnash together. "She'll rot in hell with your father."

My lips twitch up slightly. Except for Elena, and Luca a little bit, no one has ever been pissed off on my behalf.

"Everything I am, everything I've ever been—it's all been bartered and sold." My voice is barely above a whisper now, the fight drained from me. "I was fortunate to end up with Giuseppe. He gave me respect. Made me feel valued. But that's all gone. I'm no one again. I have nothing. No one."

A warm hand finds mine, not grabbing, not claiming, just there. Offering. "That's not true."

"Isn't it? Elena is my sister, my blood, but Niko can force me out at any time. I imagine he wants to." I look at Donovan. "Do you know his plans for me?"

"He doesn't have plans to make you leave."

I look down. "I must have some value to get at my father."

Donovan shakes his head. "You have value to Elena. That's why you're here."

I nod. I accept it, even. If only I could be somewhere because I have value to someone who wants me for me.

"Lucy..." His voice is laced with something I can't place, something that sounds dangerously like care. Like he knows what I'm thinking. It's foreign, unexpected, and likely, I'm wrong, but for a moment, I let myself lean into his warmth. But only for a moment because vulnerability is a luxury I can't afford. I need to rebuild my walls, fast. I pull my hand back, folding into myself once more.

"Lucy, stop." Donovan's voice is a low rumble of frustration.

I ignore the warning signs he's giving to stop me from withdrawing from him. I focus inward.

But then, his fingers brush against my cheek, and my resolve falters. I glance up, and there's something in Donovan's eyes that looks like pain, like longing. It's unnerving how much he sees, how much he wants to see.

"Please, don't pull away." His plea wraps around me, a tether pulling me to him. "You are somebody. You're not alone." And then, as if he wants to prove it, he closes the gap, and his lips find mine in a kiss. The minute his mouth is on mine, a whoosh of emotion washes through me. It's not lust, per se. Its comfort. It's gratitude at being seen.

But it's wrong. I should push him away, reinforce the barriers that keep me safe. Instead, I melt into him, let go of the fight because deep down, I want this. I want to be seen, to be known, to be cherished.

His kiss deepens, and there's no space for thoughts, no room for doubts. There's only Donovan and the slow burn spreading through my veins, lighting me up from the inside out.

Donovan's hands roam over me, finding the zipper of my dress and tugging it down. My heart pounds in a frenetic beat as the bodice of my dress falls away. My bra follows. My instinct is to cover myself because I've never been like this with a man.

His gaze holds mine, and I see heat, raw desire, and it fuels a feeling of power within me. Then his eyes cast downward to my breasts, and I see something else in him. Something like reverence.

His touch is fire as he traces the line of my collarbone and down to my breasts. My breath catches, and I'm falling into the sensation, as I did the last time he touched me.

The warning bell clangs again, but then he says, "Beautiful." The word is like a caress. His lips suck my breast, and it sends an inferno that ignites my blood, turns my bones to liquid.

I reach for him, fingers tangling in the soft hair at the nape of his neck, pulling him closer.

He lifts his head, and his dark eyes are filled with longing. "Don't turn me away, Lucy."

I'm caught by him. I can't say no even if I want to. "I won't."

His fingers caress my face. "Good. Because I can't walk away another time." Our lips meet again, and this time, it's a dance of tongues. It's hot and sweet and more than I realized a kiss could be.

Soon, my clothes are gone and I'm lying on the bed. I feel like I should be embarrassed, maybe even ashamed. But the way he looks at me, like I'm a most precious treasure, keeps me entranced by him and what he's doing.

Donovan's hands and mouth roam over my naked body with the same reverence I saw earlier. I want to see him too, so badly that I push any remnant of doubt aside and tug at his clothes until he's fully undressed. He's all smooth skin over sculpted muscle. Except for the thin bandage still on his chest where he'd been shot.

The urge to touch him everywhere all at once has me hesitating, not sure where to start. Especially when I see his erection. Good Lord, how does something like that fit in a woman? Surely, it's too long. Too wide.

From somewhere, he pulls out a condom, and I'm glad at least one of us is thinking straight. He slides it on, and then he kisses and touches me again. His hips settle over mine, pushing my thighs apart. His erection nudges my center, and all of a sudden, I'm thinking, *Am I going to do this?*

Again, it seems like I shouldn't. I don't love being a pawn, but I know my virginity is one of my greatest assets. I could sell it like Elena did. But as Donovan kisses me and touches me, all I can think about is wanting this from him. As much as I have disdain for him, something pulls me to him.

And so, I open for him. He thrusts in, and I cry out at the stab of pain.

He stills, followed by a sharp intake of his breath and a flicker of something like surprise in his eyes. "Lucy... God..." It's a half-question, half-apology. I'm not sure why, but I suspect it's that I'm a virgin. Or I was until a moment ago.

I'm afraid that he's going to stop, that there's something wrong with what we're doing. But now that I've crossed this threshold, I can't bear the thought of not seeing it through. So, I grab hold of him. "Please, don't stop."

"I won't hurt you. Or... I'll try not to." The tenderness in his voice fills my chest with warmth. When he moves again, it's slow, smooth. He watches me like I'm his guide.

"Are you all right?" he asks.

I nod even though there is some discomfort. But soon, I feel different. The buildup of tension like he'd created the last time he touched me grows. I feel him inside me, the hardness, the ridges as he glides in and out methodically. I surrender to it, open to it.

"Stay with me." His voice is rough, like it's taking effort for him to speak.

I nod again because I can't speak. My breath is coming in pants. My hands grip at him, needing more, more, more.

"Ah... fuck... Lucy... I can't hold back."

"I don't want you to. I want to feel it all." It's an epiphany. I want to feel. Not trapped. Not like nothing. But life. I want to feel life.

He levers up on his hands, his body huge as it hovers over me. "Tell me if it's too much, baby... ah, fuck..." On the next thrust, he growls and withdraws again. He moves faster. Harder. My breath catches each time, but not from pain. No. This is glorious, the torture mixed with the pleasure. I don't want it to end.

"Come, Lucy... come with me." His hand reaches between us. His fingers brush over my hard nub. My world blasts apart into a million shining stars.

I cry out and hold on to him as if he's the only thing keeping me from falling apart.

"Yes... doesn't that feel good?" He drives in again, his head thrown back, and I know he's let go as well. For several moments, he continues to move in and out, slowing down until finally, he collapses over me. Quickly, he moves aside but gathers me close. He kisses my forehead, a gesture so intimate and foreign that it brings tears to my eyes. Who'd have thought this big, burly man would have so much tenderness in him?

I don't know what it means, or even if it means anything. Perhaps he does this with all the women he's with. But I let that go for now. Instead, I close my eyes, leaning into the comfort offered in his arms to fully experience this moment.

I can build my wall again later.

16

DONOVAN

When I dragged Lucy away from Luca and out of the hospital, I had no intention or even an idea that I would end up in bed with her. I was too pissed for that. My head nearly exploded when Lou called and told me that they were ordered by Elena to take her home, leaving Lucy behind with Luca. What the fuck was she thinking? The Conti family has good relationships with Niko, but the Conti family had also done business with the Fioris. For all I knew, Luca might've won the auction. Or worse, Luca and Lucy were a couple. After all, I caught them in an embrace, which was the second time today my head nearly exploded.

Once I got her back to the penthouse, in a stunning turn of events, my ice princess melted, sharing details of her life that made her difficult ways make sense. The emotions that ran through me, the need to kill everyone who hurt her, the need to protect her, the need to soothe and let her know that someone cared overwhelmed me until before I knew it, we were naked and I was thrusting inside her. Fucking hell, she was tight. Too tight. She was a virgin, and I had barreled through like a fucking rutting animal.

Now, as she lies quietly in my arms, I'm trying to make sense of that. Lucy's been married for years. Is it possible she never had sex with her husband? Giuseppe was old and known to be ailing, so perhaps it's possible. But what about the story that she had a boyfriend she'd slept with? That was the reason Giovanni killed him, wasn't it?

I lie still with questions running through my head. Questions about her virginity. Questions about whether the top of my head is still there because I don't think I've ever come so hard, so fiercely as I did with her. Surely, this time, my head did explode.

My dick is deflating, and I need to deal with the condom, but I don't want to move. I'm pretty sure once I do, Lucy's walls will go back up and she'll push me away again. Unfortunately, I'm about to make a mess. So, with one hand, I slide the condom off, pinching the ends to prevent any leakage.

"I need to deal with this." With more reluctance than anyone can imagine, I disentangle myself from her.

She looks up at me, and I can't decipher her expression.

Not giving her time to tell me to leave, I say, "I'll be right back." I disappear into her bathroom, tying off the condom and tossing it in the trash. I rest my hands on the vanity as I look at myself in the mirror. There's no doubt I'm going to hell when I die. A person doesn't live the life I do and not get punished for it. But I wonder if I'm going to end up there sooner once Nikko finds out what I've done. I truly believe that Lucy's virginity is hers to keep or give away, and clearly, albeit surprisingly, considering what she thinks of me, she'd given it to me. But in my world, virginity is like a commodity. A virginal woman is worth more than her weight in gold. Then again, no one believes she's a virgin, so maybe I'll be spared.

I turn on the cold water and grab a hand cloth, dousing it. When I leave the bathroom, I hold my breath wondering if Lucy is still there. I enter the room, and she's sitting up in bed, under the sheets which are pulled up to her neck. My heart cracks open with emotions I've never felt before. She looks confused and vulnerable, and all I want to do is wrap her up and protect her from a world that has been so cruel to her.

I stride over to the bed, her eyes watching my every move. I'm naked, and I can see the flicker of fire in her eyes when she takes notice of that.

I join her on the bed, gently tugging the sheets down. "This will help the stinging and bleeding." I set the cloth on her thigh and gently move it toward her pussy, not sure if I'm still allowed to touch her so intimately.

She puts her hand over the cloth, and I pull my hand back, maneuvering myself so I can look at her. I feel like I need to say something, but I'm not quite sure what.

She stares at me and then arches a brow, telling me my feisty Lucy is on her way back. "You're not going to say something like I should've told you that I never did this before, right?"

I shrug. "Your sexual experience is yours, but had I known, I might have been gentler."

"Might?"

I give her a sheepish smile. "I would've tried, anyway. I wanted you so fucking badly for so long. But once I did know, I did try to take things down a notch or two."

Her eyes widen, and she blinks like the proverbial deer. It's like what I said surprised her, and that fact surprises me. Is it that I admitted to wanting her? That shouldn't be a surprise. It's not like I haven't kissed her or touched her before. Or is it that I toned it down? Perhaps she doesn't expect anything from men except brute force. Considering her history, it's not a wrong assumption on her part.

We stare at each other for a moment and curiosity gets the best of me. "I meant what I said that your sexual history is yours, but considering you were married and what your father did before he married you off—"

"My father sold me."

The anger I have for Giovanni begins to simmer again. "I have a fantasy of getting your father alone in a room. I'd like to include your mother now too. And I'd torture them with excruciating, agonizing pain day after day, year after year into eternity."

"Get in line."

I let out a laugh. Although the topic isn't funny, there's something about Lucy's comment that breaks through the tension. "I think I'd like seeing you exact your revenge on your parents."

"You don't think I could do it?"

I laugh again. "I have no doubt you could do it, my little warrior princess. Hell, you could probably run your father's business. But it doesn't take away from the deep-seated rage I feel and the revenge I want to enact on your behalf." I raise a hand to stop her from speaking. "I know I'm being a misogynist toady, but that's how I feel." I watch her for a moment, wanting her to see the truth of what I'm saying in my eyes. "You have value beyond your virginity or your sexuality, and I know it's crazy to say now, considering what we just did, but you do."

She smiles, but it doesn't quite reach her eyes. It's almost as if she doesn't believe me. I have an urge to take her into my arms and show her that I mean what I'm saying, but it would be too soon. She needs time to rest and recover.

She hands the washcloth back to me and then scoots down into the bed, pulling the blankets up around her. "No one bothered to ask me."

I stop my exit from the bed and turn back to her. "What?"

"About my virginity. No one ever asked me. People just assume. That's one of the problems with all of you."

I grind my teeth, hating that she's lumping me into the group of people she hates. Even though I'm a part of it. I made the assumption that she was accusing everyone of making.

"No one asks because I don't think they really want to know. Or maybe they don't really care."

A mixture of irritation and guilt tightens my belly. I don't know what to say, so I get up, go to the bathroom, rinse the washcloth off, then hang it to dry. I return to the bedroom, and I desperately want to get in bed with her again. But she's rolled away from me. I'm a man who normally takes what I want, but that's the problem. That's where her resentment and bitterness stem from. If I'm going to earn her respect, I have to start by respecting her.

I get dressed and for a moment, I watch her. Her steady breathing tells me she's nearly asleep. I'm torn between wanting to stay and knowing I have a job to get back to. It's not going to be long before people are wondering where I am and come looking for me.

With great reluctance, I leave her room, knowing that by the time she wakes and I see her again, my ice princess will be back.

17

DONOVAN

It's been five days, and my prediction has been right. Lucy is keeping a wide berth. In all honesty, it's not as hard since now that I'm mostly healed, I'm spending more time out in the field.

I tell myself that being apart from her is a good thing. What's the point in being with her, fucking her, when nothing will come of it? Nothing could come of it. Sure, I'd like to do the whole marriage and family thing someday, but it won't be with Lucy. She's made it clear that she has no interest in the life I lead. It makes me wonder why she let me fuck her. She gave her virginity to me. Whatever the reason, I know it's not because she feels something for me. No, she has disdain for me and my world.

I think back to her comments about feeling like she was nothing and that no one cares for her. It's not true. I don't know what I'm feeling, but it's not nothing. But it's also not something I can spend too much time analyzing or wanting more of. Not with her, anyway. *So, her staying away from me is for the best*, I tell myself. Even as I think that, I'm scanning the area for her as I make my way to Niko's office. God, I'm becoming such a sap.

I enter Niko's office and stop short when I see that Luca Conti is there. This is a surprise visit unless Niko had arranged it. If he had set it up, why wasn't I notified?

Niko waves me in. "Donovan, come and shut the door."

Like a good soldier, I do as I'm asked and approach Niko's desk, studying him and Luca.

Niko turns to Luca. "Tell them what you told me."

Luca's eyes narrow and he studies me. I don't blame them. Just a few days ago, I'd nearly ripped his arms off after finding him hugging Lucy. What the fuck was that about? It makes it all the weirder that she let me fuck her.

"I'm not sure how this information is relevant to Donovan."

My hands bunch into fists even though I'm not sure why, except that now I can't get the image of his hugging Lucy out of my head.

"Aside from my wife, there's no one else here who is more invested in Lucia's well-being than Donovan."

I cast a glance toward Niko, wondering what he means by that. Is my infatuation with Lucy that obvious? I push all that out of my head because something's up and I need to know what it is.

I turn my attention back to Luca. "I apologize for the other day at the clinic. Don Leone charged me with Lucy's protection." I don't mean it, of course. With the image of Lucy in his arms seared in my head, I still want to rip his arms out.

Luca's eyes remain narrow on me, but he gives a subtle nod. "I have come to the conclusion that Giovanni Fiori is a madman."

I snorted. "That's not news."

"Although we took transitional actions in preparing for my father's death, his ultimate demise caused me to have to deal with issues back at home. This is why initially, I suggested that Lucia stay here with you. I understand her sister is pregnant, and I believe she very much wants to be a part of that."

I cross my arms over my chest thinking *so far, this sounds okay.*

"But when I got wind of Don Fiori kidnapping his daughters, including Lucia, and then the auction, I knew that she wasn't safe here."

My frown narrows into a scowl because suddenly, this sounds bad. Like he plans to take Lucy with him.

"I told Giovanni that Lucia is not his to sell, but as you know, she's in a bit of a limbo in terms of protection. My father cared for her very deeply and made provisions for her in Italy—"

"But as you said, she wants to be here with Elena and the babies," I say, not caring whether I'm overstepping Niko.

"That is what she told me as well when I saw her at the clinic." Luca arches a brow at me. I made my apology already, so I ignore it.

"My father made me vow to him that I would look after her, but I can't do that with her here and me in Italy. I think we can all agree that she would be safer from her father there than here."

My jaw tightens, but I hold back a burst of anger and irritation. I have to play it cool.

"If that's the case, why didn't you just tell Giovanni that she's part of the Conti Family? You made a vow, but it doesn't sound like she's part of the Family," Niko says, and I realize he's right.

Luca shrugs. "As you know, these things can be complicated. Don Fiori seems to believe my father didn't meet up to his part of the deal."

"What fucking deal? Giovanni sold her. Presumably, your father paid." I'm pissed, but this time, it's for Lucy and all she's had to endure. It explains so much of why she is the way she is.

Luca nods. "As I said, it's complicated. But that doesn't mean that she's not without help from the Conti Family." Luca turns his gaze to Niko. "And with Giovanni's sights set on her, she brings more danger into the Leone Family, does she not? Your pretty, pregnant wife is more at risk."

I want to run my fist through Luca's motherfucking face for reminding Niko of the danger. I look at Niko, hoping against hope that he isn't preparing to hand Lucy over to protect Elena.

"I have things I need to think about before I can make a decision. I think we all want what's best for Lucia."

What the fuck does that mean? Is he seriously considering this?

Luca watches Niko for a moment and then extends his hand toward Niko, who stands to shake it.

"I hope to have your response soon. I need to return to Italy, and I would like to bring Lucia with me."

I seethe with quiet anger as I do my best to give a polite nod to Luca as he leaves Niko's office.

Once he's out of the office and heading down the hallway, I turn to Niko. "Elena won't stand for this." Niko doesn't care about my thoughts on this as much as he wants to keep Elena happy.

Niko arches a brow as he sits back down on his chair. "Elena? What about you, Donovan?"

I sniff and do my best to act nonchalant. "You're the one bending over backward to keep his wife happy."

He nods as he steeples his fingers and continues to stare at me in a way that makes me think he can see into my soul. I don't like it when he does that.

"I'm also a man willing to do anything to keep his wife and his unborn children safe. Luca is right. Lucia is a liability to all of us."

Mother Fucker.

"But I'm not so certain that Giovanni's tentacles can't reach over to Italy. The truth is that she will never be safe as long as Giovanni lives or—"

"Then let's go kill that motherfucker. How long have you been dreaming of this, Niko? God, you could've done it when you kidnapped Elena from her wedding to Romeo." This whole situation is pissing me off. And while it's dangerous for me to blame Niko, I can't help it. Giovanni would've been gone already had Niko killed him as we'd planned at Elena and Romeo's wedding.

Niko sits back in that calm way that tells me I should be careful. Niko is one of those people who has a deadly calm before the storm. "Do you know why Giovanni doesn't care about Elena anymore?"

I shrug and sit down, hoping that will help relieve the tension flowing through my veins. "Because she's not a virgin?" But then I remember everyone believes Lucia isn't a virgin either, so that doesn't explain why he wants her back.

Niko leans forward again, resting his forearms on his desk. "Giovanni doesn't come after Elena anymore because he knows he can't. She is mine. She's mine in name. She's carrying my children. He'll need help to take me down, and no other Don will dare come after what's clearly mine."

I nod because in this weird criminal world we live in, there are certain rules. Then again, Giovanni Fiori often breaks them. Like now. "Lucia is a Conti. That should give her protection no matter where she is."

"In theory, yes. But Giuseppe is dead. She has the Conti name by marriage, but everyone knows that she was sold to him. She came here before he died, which could make some question their relationship. Luca has a vow to his father, but that means nothing to Giovanni Fiori."

I stare at him, wondering what he's getting at.

"The point is, Lucia has very little protection. She isn't in my Family or the Conti Family, technically. The default is that she's a Fiori, which is how I suspect Giovanni is thinking this through."

"So, what's the answer?" I feel like I'm missing something that Niko is trying to tell me. Or maybe I don't want to consider that he's saying Lucy needs to go back to Italy and marry Luca. "She becomes a Conti again by marrying Luca? Her stepson?"

Niko's lips tug up in a smirk as he sits back again. I'm wondering what the hell he's finding so amusing.

"Marriage can solve all sorts of problems for Lucia."

SEVERAL HOURS LATER, I stand outside the kitchen holding a large, flat box, hesitating and feeling a little nauseous. Inside the kitchen, I hear Elena and Lucy chatting away and sometimes even laughing. It's Lucy's laugh and desiring to hear it more often that propels me into the kitchen.

Both ladies looked up, startled and then concerned.

"Lucy, you need to come with me."

Elena stands, her hand going over her heart. "Is something wrong? Where's Nico?"

"Nico's fine. He's in his office."

Elena looks at Lucy. "I need to go see him."

Lucy nods. "Of course."

I let Elena go past me as she hurries out of the kitchen.

"Come on." I nod toward the door.

She purses her lips at me and jabs her fist on her hip. "What's going on?"

"I'm not kidding around here, Lucy. You need to come with me. If I have to pick you up and toss you over my shoulder, I will."

She looks at me with disdain I haven't seen in a while. I can't deny that it hurts a little bit. I'd like to think we had a moment those few days ago when we'd heated up the sheets.

"What is this about?"

"I'll tell you in a minute." There's no way I'm having this conversation in an open part of the house.

Tired of waiting for her to comply, I wrap my hand around her arm and tug her with me as I make my way out of the kitchen and to the stairs.

"You don't need to grab me."

"The fact that you don't listen tells me that I do." I lead her upstairs and into her room, only releasing her when we're both inside and I can shut the door.

"What is wrong with you?" She whirls on me, anger flaring in her eyes.

This is going to go so horribly badly, but I've faced worse things than Lucy Fiore Conti.

"Luca was here earlier today. He wants to take you back to Italy with him."

She rolls her eyes. "We've had this discussion before. I told him I didn't want to go." She cocks her head to the side and studies me. "Careful, Donovan. I might think you're jealous."

She doesn't know the half of it. "As you're aware, your father is trying to auction you." Immediately, I regret reminding her because her expression turns stricken.

I take a step toward her, wanting to comfort her, but she steps back and holds her hands up. "What is this all about, Donovan?"

"Luca made a vow to his father to take care of you. Going with him makes it harder for your father." The words taste like ash in my mouth.

"I'm well aware of the situation." Her brows furrow as if a lightbulb has gone off in her head. "Has Nico made arrangements with Luca? I suppose I can't blame him if I'm a danger to Elena."

My jaw is so tight I'm not sure how it doesn't crack. "As Nico's wife, Elena has the protection of the Leone Family. She's basically a queen. Your father is a certifiable psychopath, but he's not dumb enough to go after her, at least not right now and not without help that no other family will give him. You have people who want to protect you, but technically, your father sees you as a Fiori. Giuseppe is dead, and Luca refused to marry you. That leaves you twisting in the wind, Princess."

She sighs and crosses her arms. "So, what have you all decided to do with me? Hand me over to my father? Ship me off with Luca? Sell me to someone else?"

She's doing her best to be strong, but I see the pain and the fear hiding in the depths of her defiant eyes. I wish I could make everything okay for her, but I know I can't. This is the best I can do.

I toss the box I've been carrying onto her bed. "Get dressed and be downstairs in an hour. We're getting married."

18

LUCIA

"What did you just say?" My mouth is agape as I try to understand the words that just left his mouth. I had to have heard them wrong.

"I was speaking English. Do you need me to say it in Italian? *Ci sposeremo*," Donovan says in Italian that's pretty good for a man with an Irish name.

But I'm still in shock at his words, wondering what's come over him. Does he think he owns me now?

"Just because I gave you my virginity, doesn't mean you have to marry me."

Admittedly, I'm still a little unsettled by having had sex with him. Not that I didn't enjoy it. And I can't even bring myself to regret it. But it unsettles me how easily I had fallen into him. I feel like I'm slowly losing myself to him. Wanting to count on him. Wanting his strength. But I don't want this life. And marriage? That's ridiculous.

"I don't want to get married."

He jabs his hands on his hips and glares at me. "You've made that perfectly clear, Princess. This has nothing to do with the fact that I fucked you."

The harshness of his tone, the vulgarity of his words, makes me flinch. "Then what are you doing?"

"You're the one who said you wanted to be with your sister and help her with the twins. Getting married is how you do it. Or am I so repulsive that you'd rather go back to Italy with Luca? Maybe you want to pick up with him where you left off the other day in the hospital."

I stare at Donovan, not knowing who he is. It's like he's speaking another language. "Now what are you talking about?"

"I saw you two hugging. Is he going to be angry when he finds out that you gave your virginity to me instead of him?"

I've been slow on the upkeep of this discussion, but finally, I understand, and my anger breaks through. "I really want to slap you right now. You're being ridiculous."

His nostrils flare, and that along with his size and the narrowing of his eyes makes me think of a bull ready to charge. "If you want to stay here to be with Elena and those twins, you meet me downstairs in an hour or other arrangements will be made for you to return to Italy with Luca."

My anger is replaced with desperation. "What? No. Why?"

He moves toward me, standing so close I can feel the tension radiating off him. "Because your father is a menace to society and no one around you is safe as long as he has set his sights on getting you back. The only way to protect the Leone Family, to protect that sister you say you love so much, is for you to marry me because only then are you given the full protection of the Leone Family. Didn't you ever wonder why your father stopped going after Elena?"

I step back, trying to organize my thoughts. "Because she's married to Nico. She has no value to him anymore."

"That's right, Princess. And the best way to ruin your value to your father is to marry a toady like me. So, get dressed and meet me downstairs in an hour or pack up and get ready to return to Italy. It's your choice."

It doesn't feel like much of a choice.

Donovan strides out of my room, and before my door shuts, it opens again and Elena comes rushing in. She's dressed in a satiny pale blue dress one might wear out to a nice dinner.

"Tell me you're going to do it. Tell me you're going to marry Donovan and stay." She grips my forearms.

My past is rushing through my brain, all the moments of my life that are just like the one now. Moments when what I want doesn't matter. I look at Elena, and the envy I feel nearly brings me to my knees. Why is she so lucky to find a man who loves her and whom she loves? Is that too much for me to ask to have in my life?

I tug away from her. "Donovan doesn't want to do this. He shouldn't have to marry me simply because his Boss tells him to."

I sink on the edge of the bed as I realize that's what hurts the most. Donovan is only doing this to protect the Family. It isn't because he feels anything for me. It's why I've been avoiding him after our sexual encounter. It's easier to ignore these crazy feelings I have when I'm around him if I don't see him.

She pushes the box Donovan left on the bed back and sits next to me. "If you do this, you can stay, and you will be safe. Besides, Donovan might be a jokester and rough around the edges, but he's a good person. Like Giuseppe was."

I look at her, and as much as I love her, I don't understand why she doesn't see the pain this causes me. "What about love, Elena?"

She looks down, and I think she finally understands how difficult this is for me. "I'm being selfish, and I'm sorry. But I need you here with me. To help me with these babies." She shrugs. "It doesn't have to be forever. Once Dad is dead, you and Donovan won't have to be married anymore." She takes my hand and clutches it. "Or maybe by then, you'll be in love."

My mouth gapes again. "What?"

Her eyes soften and at the same time convey a message of *don't be so dense*. "It's no secret that Donovan has a thing for you. And as much as you try to hide it, I suspect you have a thing for him too."

God, is it that apparent?

"I know I've been much luckier in life than you have, Luce. And I know this is a big sacrifice. I probably shouldn't be asking it. I imagine you would have a lovely life in Italy. But I'm selfishly going to ask again that you stay with me and the twins. Let me help you get dressed so you can get married. And then everything will be back to how it was before. This is a marriage on paper. That's it."

"How are we supposed to fall in love if we avoid each other and have a marriage that's just on paper?" I quip to highlight the contradiction of her words.

She leans over so we're shoulder to shoulder. "I'm sure if you bat your eyes at Donovan, he'll come running like a little puppy. But don't tell him I said that. He has a reputation to uphold as Nico's fiercest enforcer."

I don't make a decision as much as I give in and take the path of least resistance, which is to open the box and get ready to meet Donovan downstairs in an hour.

Elena helps me, pulling out the dress and holding it up so I can see it. "My gosh, Luce, it's gorgeous. Look at all that silk."

I arch a brow. "Look at all that lace."

She laughs. "Do you suppose he knows how much you hate lace?"

I slip on the dress and look in the mirror. Elena has an expression on her face that would be normal for a woman helping her sister get ready for a wedding. Me? I feel like I'm on the verge of a breakdown. Donovan doesn't want me. As much as I act like he's a brute, I know deep down, he's a gentle giant with those he cares for. I can totally see him finding a woman he can love and dote on and who'd not only be a good Mafia wife, but also love and dote on him back. That's not me. Even if I could act like a good Mafia wife, I know I can't love him like he deserves. I'm too broken inside. My walls are too thick. My distrust is too high.

"Here, put this on for the trip to the church." She hands me a shawl.

"Church?"

"It needs to look real." She gives me a sympathetic smile and pulls out a few items from the pocket of the dress she's wearing. "Something borrowed." She hands me a pearl necklace and earrings. "Giuseppe's are nice, but perhaps they shouldn't be worn marrying another man. And here…" She blushes as she hands me a light blue garter. "Something blue."

I must be dreaming. A nightmare. This can't be happening.

I'm in a haze as she leads me to the bathroom and does my makeup and hair. She's chatting away like this is my special day. She can't possibly be so oblivious to my shellshock, so perhaps she's making the best of a less than great situation.

"You look beautiful, Luce. You always were the most beautiful woman I've ever seen."

I turn to her, tears in my eyes. "Beauty isn't a good thing in our world."

She grabs a tissue and dabs my eyes. "Dad is the worst in the world. Donovan will make you laugh. That's worth something, isn't it?"

I nod because there's nothing I can say or do. I suppose I should be glad that I know what's coming. I didn't have that when my father loaded me on a plane bound for Italy to marry Giuseppe.

She smiles, and I see sympathy in it. Even so, she says, "It's time to go."

I follow her out and down to a waiting car in the garage. En route to my wedding, I finally give in. This idea of having any sort of agency over myself is a waste of time. Freedom. Personal power. I'll never have them. I close my eyes, letting go of hopes and dreams, and instead, I build up the wall I'll need to survive.

19

DONOVAN

As I pace in the vestibule of the Catholic church, I'm kicking myself for being such an asshole to Lucy. I can face down my enemies in a gunfight, but it's a hell of a thing to face down a woman who disdains you and then to ask her to marry you. My pride had me being a jerk about it.

"You should be up front," Niko says, joining me.

"I need to talk to her first."

Niko arches a brow. "It's a little late for cold feet."

Niko's men stand by every ornate door and stained-glass window inside and out. They're watching for Giovanni's men on the off chance they get wind of this wedding and decide to do something about it. To my mind, that's why we shouldn't be here. But when I finally got Niko's hint in his office earlier and we made the plan to for me to marry Lucy to protect her, Niko said that if we were going to really piss Giovanni off and force him out of hiding or into making a mistake, we needed to leave the sanctuary of the penthouse. Of course, Niko has an army of men that any of Giovanni's men would see. There's no way they'd be as bold as Niko had been to crash a wedding to kidnap the bride.

"It's not that," I say in reference to Niko's cold feet comment.

He studies me. "You know this isn't an order by me, right? If you don't want to marry her—"

"I want to marry her... ah... I mean..." Fucking hell, what do I mean? I run my fingers through my hair. "This is for the Family."

Niko's lips quirk up into a smirk, but he puts his hand on my shoulder. "You're a brother to me, you know? In the past, that Irish blood of yours would have kept you out of the Family. It definitely would keep you from being a Boss. But you're my family, Donovan. *Mio Fratello.*" He pulls me into an embrace.

The heavy doors at the entrance groan open, and Elena steps through, her eyes lighting up at the sight of Niko. I wonder what it would be like to have someone, Lucy, look at me like that. Niko whisks her away from the door and into the safety of the sanctuary.

Lucy steps in, and my heart stops. She moves with an elegance that belies the steel in her soul. She's regal. Like a queen. It reminds me that I'm not deserving of her. But it doesn't stop me from taking in her breathtaking beauty. The dress does exactly what I thought it would. It hugs her perfect form, but not in a dirty, sexy way. In a goddess form sort of way. Her long, dark hair is pulled away from the front, cascading in long waves down her back. It's then I have to admit to myself that Lucy Fiori Conti, soon to be Ricci, has become my singular obsession.

I swallow hard, forcing my feet to move, to close the space that suddenly feels like a chasm. I yearn to claim her... no earn her, even knowing it's a wish that will never be fulfilled.

She stops short as I reach for her elbow. She pulls away. "You don't need to manhandle me."

I close my eyes, praying for strength. "We need to talk."

"Cold feet? It's the lace, isn't it?"

I don't know what to think. She seems to be babbling.

"Please," I say, gesturing toward a room off the vestibule.

She enters and looks up at me with wariness.

"About earlier," I begin, discovering my ineptitude for apologies. "I may have been... overzealous."

The silence stretches out, and when I turn, I find her gaze fixed on a stained-glass window depicting some saintly figure.

What is going on with her?

"I shouldn't have been so—"

"Toady-like?"

I sigh and shove my hands in my pockets.

"Yes. You do see, though, that if you want to stay with Elena and the babies, this is the only way."

"The only way Niko will allow it?"

I nod. "And Luca."

"Luca isn't the boss of me. Neither is Niko."

"No, but Niko is the Boss of the Leone Family, including Elena. You know that, Lucy. You know that what he wants takes precedence. The only reason he hasn't shipped you off yet is Elena, but with your father's actions, you're—"

"I know. You don't have to tell me again that I'm a danger to everyone." She shakes her head and looks away.

"Look, I don't know what you're thinking about all this, but I don't expect this to be a real marriage. All I ask is that you let me protect you."

"I get it. I have to stay in the gilded cage. I'm not new to this."

I step closer, yet the distance between us still feels insurmountable.

She folds her arms across her chest and looks up at me defiantly. "I agreed to this, so let's get on with it."

"What I wanted to tell you," I start, feeling like a teenage boy stumbling over my words. It's not a feeling I like, and the urge to be an asshole again threatens me. I mean, I get it that she doesn't like me, but I'm not an ogre. "Once Giovanni is no longer a threat... we can annul this marriage. You'll be free to do whatever you want, although anything with Elena will still have conditions set by Niko."

There's a flicker of something in her eyes, and I almost think it's pain, but more likely, it's annoyance. For a moment, she doesn't say anything. I stand there, my hands clasped behind my back, the word 'annulled' echoing in the space between us. The taste is bitter in my mouth, and it's another fucking sign of how much this woman has gotten into my soul.

"Only until Giovanni's threat is no more," I hear myself repeat to let her know this marriage is temporary, just a means to an end.

My gaze lingers on her, tracing the contours of her face, the determined set of her jaw, the way her hair cascades like dark silk. There's a beauty to her resilience, a magnetism to her strength that pulls at me, undeniable, unrelenting. It's fucking torture.

The door to the room opens, and Niko steps in. "It's time. We need to get this done and get out."

"We're coming," I say even though I wonder if Lucy is about to change her mind. I turn back to her, and it hits me how vacant her expression appears. She's a shell of the woman I'd come to admire and desire, and it guts me that I'm the cause of it.

I take her hand, wanting to believe she's allowing it because she wants my touch, but I know that's a lie. She's going through the motions.

"I know you didn't get to choose the first time you got married, and I'm so, so sorry you didn't get a choice this time either." Then I leave her there, under guard, as I go to prepare to marry a woman who doesn't love or respect me.

20

LUCIA

I thought I'd locked my heart up tight before I entered the church, but to hear Donovan tell me that this marriage didn't mean anything and it would be annulled as soon as my father was dead hurt. It's not like I didn't know that a divorce or annulment was a probability. I know exactly why this wedding is taking place. But hearing it from Donovan's mouth tapped into all the trauma I've been carrying since I was a child. It is a reminder that ultimately, I am nothing, I am no one.

Now I stand in the vestibule, waiting to walk down the aisle. Because men are everywhere, I can't make an escape. Would I run if I had the opportunity? Would I risk being caught by my father?

My life wouldn't be much different. I'd still be at the whims of the men who have control over my life. A pawn in their stupid games. At the same time, I have to admit, I'm much less likely to experience violence against me if I stick with Donovan. Plus, I can be with Lena. All I have to do is follow through on this wedding. So no, I wouldn't run away.

The doors of the sanctuary open and Niko appears. "I thought I would walk you up the aisle. If you'd like."

I can't imagine why he'd want to do that except perhaps Elena asked him to. Or maybe it's symbolic. Niko is handing me over to Donovan for safekeeping.

Whatever the reason, I don't have the energy to argue so I simply nod. He holds out his arm, and I loop mine through it. The doors open and from somewhere, a wedding march plays. I find it odd how they're pulling out all the stops for this. With Niko's clout, he could have hired a justice of the peace to come to the penthouse. But of course, this wedding isn't about me and Donovan. It's about sticking a middle finger to my father.

As I start up the aisle, my gaze first goes to Elena who's standing as my attendant. She is smiling, and I give her a wan smile back.

"Listen." Niko leans a little closer to me and murmurs, "I know that in your case, this is less than ideal, but Donovan really wants to do right by you. Maybe you can cut him a little bit of slack going forward."

I shake my head and let out a derisive laugh under my breath. I turn my head to look at him. "Is that in order, Don Leone?"

His brow furrows in confusion.

"You're the one who calls the shots. And in this marriage, Donovan will call the shots. I know how this works, so don't pretend that what I say or do really matters."

Niko looks surprised, and then his jaw tightens and he turns to look ahead. "But you had a choice, Lucia. You had the choice to leave. All I ask is that you flick that chip off your shoulder and act like you're a member of this Family."

Incensed that he acts like I'm the problem in all this, I look ahead to the altar where Donovan stands. His hands are clasped in front of him and he shifts from side to side as his dark eyes watch me approach. The intensity of his gaze hits me in the middle of the chest, causing my breath to hitch. I remind myself that he's a big goon, but it's hard when I take in the cut of his suit. Good golly, he's handsome. I hadn't looked at him when we were in the office off the vestibule, so I hadn't seen how shockingly stunning he is.

As we reach Donovan, he gives me a smile and holds his left arm out. I disentangle myself from Niko and step up next to Donovan, but I avoid putting my arm through his. It's petty, I know, but whenever I'm this close to Donovan, my brain short-circuits. It goes to places it shouldn't go, like thoughts of happiness. I remind myself of what he told me just moments before, that this wedding doesn't mean anything and when my father is dead, it will be annulled.

The priest begins the ceremony and I focus on him. He's a wiry, older gentleman whose gaze keeps darting over to Niko, making me wonder if Niko had threatened him to perform the ceremony. If a marriage is performed in a Catholic church by a priest under duress, is it legit? Under those circumstances, a marriage is null and void, and we wouldn't need to bother with an annulment. It's definitely something I could look up on the Internet. Assuming I'm allowed to have a phone or unsupervised access to a computer.

All of a sudden, I'm facing Donovan and he's saying words to me. "I take you, Lucia Conti."

I realize he's left out my maiden name. For some reason, I'm glad.

"...take you to be my wife. I promise to protect you and care for you in sickness and health all the days of my life." He slips a gorgeous diamond ring on my finger. The motions are real, but the vows have been changed. There's no talk of love or ever after. But there wouldn't be, would there?

I follow, repeating the words the priest has me say, and next thing I know, the priest announces, "Mr. and Mrs. Donovan Ricci. You may kiss your bride."

Donovan's eyes are soft as his hand cups my cheek. It's a tender gesture that I'm not expecting. The ache of yearning it causes is also unexpected. He leans in, his lips gently brushing against mine. Something inside me leads me to tilt my head, to lean into the moment. A small groan escapes him as he takes the kiss only slightly deeper, his lips firmer.

"Now might be a good time to go start that honeymoon," Niko says. There's a tension in his voice that tells me he's on alert. Perhaps my father is outside, ready to exact his revenge and take me as his prize.

Donovan pulls away and gives me his signature smirk. "Welcome to the Family, Mrs. Toady."

Moments later, Donovan has me packed into the back of an SUV. He sits next to me as the driver maneuvers through the streets at a clip that seems too fast for traffic in New York City, even at midnight.

"Where are we going?" I ask.

Donovan's hand covers mine and gives it a gentle squeeze. "Our honeymoon."

I jerk my gaze to his, wondering what that means. Hadn't he told me earlier that he wouldn't expect anything from me as his wife? Maybe we have to consummate the marriage to make it official. My girly parts light up in anticipation, betraying all my efforts to keep a distance between me and Donovan

His smirk graces his face again. "Don't worry, I give you my word that I won't force anything on you."

All those girly parts settle down. If they had expressions, they would look disappointed.

"Rest. We have a drive."

Sleeping feels like a better option than talking to my new husband, so I close my eyes. When I wake, it's two hours later and we're at a fancy hotel in Atlantic City. Donovan ushers me into the lobby of the hotel, and while nobody else can probably notice, I see many of Niko's men are already here. More than seems necessary for protection. This isn't a regular honeymoon.

Donovan goes to the check-in. "Honeymoon suite for Mr. and Mrs. Donovan Ricci."

I look up at him in surprise that he used his real name. Then I put two and two together. We're in my father's territory, and Donovan has just revealed that he's here. But I don't ask Donovan about it until we're inside the suite.

We're barely through the door when I say, "This whole thing is just some sort of bait to lure my father out?" I hate that the thought of this marriage being bait hurts me. It doesn't make any sense. I don't want Donovan. I don't want this life. So, why does everything

Donovan does to assure me that it's not expected of me make my heart crack a little bit more each time?

"No."

"But you used your real name."

Donovan's smirk turns menacing. "I want your father to know that I'm not afraid of him. If he wants to come at me, let him." He steps closer to me, rubbing his hands up and down my arms. "But I promise you, Lucy, he won't get anywhere near you. I don't just give you my word, I vow my life."

He said something similar during the marriage ceremony, but this time, there's something in his eyes and tone that seems different. Like he means it. Not that he didn't mean it before, but before, it was offering protection as part of his duty. Now, it's almost as if there's emotion behind it.

"Maria packed your bags, and they should already be in the bedroom. Go ahead and get ready for bed. I have some work I still need to do."

Once again, disappointment floods me. Perhaps it's time to face it. There's something about Donovan that I can't resist, no matter how hard I try.

I am exhausted, so I make my way to the bedroom, and I find all my clothes already put away in the dresser. I pull out a nightgown that isn't mine, and I wonder if Donovan put together a trousseau for me. I'm too tired to rummage around for the usual shorts and T-shirt I sleep in, so I toss it on the bed and start to take my dress off. The problem is that I can't reach the zipper.

Moments later, I feel knuckles brush the back of my neck, and it sends a shudder through my body.

"Let me help you." Donovan's voice is low and husky.

A finger trails down my back as he lowers the zipper. I close my eyes as an ache pools between my thighs. I'm about to turn around and throw myself into his arms when he steps back.

When I finally turn, he pulls out a small gun and sets it on the nightstand. "Do you know how to use one of these?"

I nod. "Luca taught me." He did it mostly because I was bored, and Giuseppe encouraged him to teach me.

For a moment, the scowl flashes on Donovan's face at the mention of Luca, but it's gone so quickly I wonder if maybe I imagined it.

"I don't think you'll need to use it. We've got this place locked down tighter than Fort Knox. But I'll feel better knowing that you have it. You go ahead and get some sleep. I'll be back in a few hours."

"Are you just having a meeting or are you going to do something dangerous?" I ask.

He smiles, but it's not a smirk. "Careful, Princess, I might think you're worried about this old Toady."

I drop my head down, looking at my fidgeting fingers. "You're my protector. The only one I trust to do that in the Leone Family."

The crook of Donovan's finger settles under my chin and lifts until I have no choice but to look up at him. His eyes are filled with something that I can't decipher. His gaze drifts down to my lips, and for a moment, I think he's going to kiss me.

"I won't let you down." He steps away and heads to the door. He stops and looks back at me. "It won't be long now, Lucy, and you'll be free."

He disappears through the door, and I'm left experiencing a torment of emotions as I take my dress off and slip into the satin nightgown. I climb into bed and try to will my brain to stop thinking, but it plays Donovan's words in an endless loop. *It won't be long now, Lucy, and you'll be free.*

But what if I don't want to be free?

21

DONOVAN

I like my job and I'm fucking good at it. But for the first time in my life, I don't want to go. I want to stay here and make Lucy feel like the queen she is. I want her to feel safe and cherished. But I can't do that with her father walking this earth, so I leave her in the bedroom while I head out to do business.

I remind myself that a vow of protection is what binds us, not love, not desire—though God knows, every fiber of my being screams for her. But Lucy wants freedom, not another cage, even if it's gilded with good intentions.

Once Giovanni is out of the picture, she'll have what she deserves—a life free from the shadows that have dogged her since birth.

"Nice wedding," Lou calls out as I slide into the passenger seat of the nondescript sedan waiting for me outside. "Shame you don't have time to consummate it." His tone is light, but the underlying sneer rubs me raw. Then he waggles his brows, and I imagine he's had lewd thoughts of Lucy. Lou is my friend, but that doesn't stop me from wanting to punch the smirk off his face.

But I can't afford to lose focus—not when Lucy's safety is at stake. "We've got work to do."

"Meeting with the Russians has my skin crawling." Lou's fingers drum a nervous rhythm on the steering wheel as we merge onto the road.

"They're not any different from any other Family."

"Yeah, well some Families try to kill us."

He's not wrong. I think back to when Niko and I were ambushed by Giovanni. How I ended up shot. How Lucy tended to me. I rub my hand over my chest, but it's not my healed wound that's aching. It's my fucking heart.

"Finding and killing Giovanni is what matters."

"Right." Lou nods, a soldier falling back in line.

The bright lights of Atlantic City dissolve into the rearview mirror as we drive to the outskirts where the meeting with the Bratva is set.

The twenty-four, seven diner's neon sign glows, the only light in the area. Lou parks in the nearly empty parking lot, and I step out of the car, my senses sharp as I survey the scene.

Niko appears from the shadows. "Everything good at the hotel?" His question is casual, but the weight behind it isn't lost on me. He probably thinks I had to tie her up to keep her in place. I wonder if Niko will ever come to truly accept Lucy, and vice-versa. I shake my head of that thought. There is no reason for that. Soon, she'll be free of us. We'll only see her in relation to her visit with Elena.

"She's sleeping."

We push through the door, the bell's chime announcing us to the aroma of strong overly-brewed coffee. Liam is seated in a booth with several other made men. He's not one of them, having chosen a career in the FBI, and yet, it's clear that his acquaintance with them is deeper. Likely, his dad, a member of the Bratva until his death, knew these men.

Fingers drumming against my thigh, I scan their stances, the set of their jaws. While I don't believe trouble is at hand, Lou is right to be on edge.

"Any news?" My question slices through the low murmur of conversation as we approach the table. Niko and I slide in while Lou grabs a chair and sits near us.

Liam glances up, offering a brief nod. "I've just been discussing that with Igor. Igor, this is Donovan Ricci and Lou Esposito. I think you know Niko. Donovan, Lou, this is Igor Peprov."

I nod my hello. Niko reaches across the table and shakes Igor's hand like they're old friends.

"It's been a while, Leone," Igor says in a thick Russian accent.

"Thanks for meeting with us," Niko responds.

Igor turns his gaze toward me. "Congratulations on your wedding, Donovan. A bold move." His eyes are assessing, calculating, like he's sizing me up.

I shrug. "You think so?"

Igor's lips twitch into what could be a smile or a sneer. "Some might say too bold. It's upsetting the delicate balance."

"You look agile enough."

He lets out a laugh. "Me? What do I care about the Italian squabbles?"

"What have you heard?" Niko leans forward, ready for business.

Igor shrugs. "News of the wedding and the woman being off the market have made the rounds."

My teeth clench at his reference of Lucy being off the market, like she's a piece of meat.

"After what you did to Tiberius Abate, people around here are antsy. Word is the woman is Fiori's daughter. You plan to use her to take over his territory here?"

My hands are fisted. Lucy won't be used for anything as far as I'm concerned.

"The plan is to erase Giovanni from the face of the earth." Niko says it calmly. Like it's the most normal thing to murder. I suppose in our world, it is. A beauty like Lucy shouldn't be around such darkness.

"Then why the girl? The wedding?" Igor asks. Something in his tone is off. I feel like he's disrespecting her.

"Her name is Lucia, and before me, she was Don Conti's wife."

Igor arches a brow. "Such passion. Do you love your new wife?"

Niko's hand settles on my thigh, a warning to keep myself in line. "What about Giovanni's men?"

"As I said, they're nervous about your intentions."

Niko chuckles. "If Giovanni's men are shaking in their boots over a woman, they're a bunch of pussies."

"Speaking of Giovanni" —Niko shifts in his seat— "any word on where he's skulking these days?"

"Nothing solid." Igor spreads his hands wide. "We've heard he's given up on getting the other daughter."

To that, Niko tenses. See? It doesn't feel good to have Igor-motherfucker talk about your woman.

"He's still focused on the other one."

My jaw tics. "Lucy," I correct again, this time aloud, feeling the weight of my ring pressing into my skin. "My wife."

"Your wife, right." The smirk on Igor's face grates on me. "The word is that the marriage is to bring her into the Leone Family and make her off-limits to Giovanni."

"She is off-limits," I growl.

Igor holds his hands up in surrender. "I'm just the messenger. However, you have to consider that Giovanni may not fear you, Comrade Donovan, as much as he does Niko. If that's the case, your bride might not remain yours for long."

"Careful," I warn, my jaw clenching until it aches.

"Would be a shame to lose her just when you married her. Did you at least have time to consummate the marriage?" Igor's taunt is a red-hot poker prodding at my self-control.

Again, Niko's hand settles on my thigh and I do my damnedest to rein in my desire to wipe the dirty linoleum with Igor's face.

Igor sneers. "I'm just the messenger, Donovan." He turns to Niko. "All I'm saying is you've upset the apple cart, so to speak."

"Any word on where Giovanni is?" Niko asks.

"No. Rumor is that he was wounded. But his whereabouts? No one has seen the guy since your run-in with him. Underground? Out of the country? Who knows?"

Fucking hell. I glance at Niko, wondering what he's thinking.

"The wife, on the other hand, she likes Atlantic City."

"Really?" Niko sounds surprised. "Even with the upset apple cart?"

Igor shrugs. "She thinks she's low-key and unrecognized, but she's not good at it."

"I wonder what she's up to?" Niko ponders.

"She needs to die too," I murmur.

Niko glances over at me, his brows furrowed in question.

"Probably a good idea. It's possible she's acting on Giovanni's behalf, rallying troops for a stand against the Leone Family," Igor says.

"Is she running the business?" Liam asks.

"That I can't say. I can tell you that Giovanni has two warehouses that have been busy."

"Any specifics?" Niko asks.

"Arms shipments, possibly more. High stakes… and possibly women."

I remember what Lucy told me about her mother's idea to make her the first woman sold in a trafficking scheme.

"The women… I bet that's Giovanni's wife," I say.

"Women." Igor sneers. "They blame men for their woes, but they're worse toward each other."

Niko is thinking and then he leans over to me. "Those warehouses, you take them out. Pull them out from under Giovanni's nose and take them over."

I nod, eager to exact revenge for Lucy.

"Then Giovanni," he continues, eyes searching mine, "you find him, you end it."

"Consider it done."

"Giovanni's Jersey territory will be yours." His nod is almost imperceptible, but I know what it means. He's anointing me. A Boss. It's an honor, and yet, it's bittersweet because in taking it, I effectively cut off any chance with Lucy.

"Ah, so the Fiori family has reason to fear. Good, I never liked that motherfucker," Igor says. "So, young Donovan, how do you plan to achieve such a righteous goal?"

I lean forward, forearms resting on the sticky surface of the diner's table. "I have plans. It could prove beneficial to the Bratva."

"Oh?" Igor arches a brow and glances at his men. "I don't know you. How can I trust you?"

"What do you need from me to prove myself to you?" For Lucy's revenge, I'll do whatever needs to be done, including asking for Bratva help and enduring whatever initiation I need to undergo to make it happen.

Igor's eyes narrow slightly, and then his lips part into a sneer and I know it's going to be a long night.

22

LUCIA

I'm a tangle of limbs, the sheets twisted around me. The clock's red digits burn into the darkness, marking each hour Donovan remains absent. He said a few hours. It's been an eternity.

A soft click pierces the silence, and my heart hammers against my chest. It's instinct, the way my hand darts over to the bedside table and closes around the gun he left for protection. My grip is steady, but the rest of me trembles, betraying my fear.

"Still up, *Tesoro*?" The voice is laced with amusement, cutting through the tension. Donovan.

Then it reaches my brain. *Tesoro*. The Italian word for treasure. I want to melt into it, but I resist.

He stands at the foot of the bed, his arms up in surrender. "Are you up because you're worried about me or waiting to shoot me?"

I realize I'm still holding up the gun. "I haven't decided yet." I set the gun on the bedside table.

He steps forward, the smirk clear even in the half-light. "And after I rushed back to our marital bed."

He's close enough now that I can see his face. He has a black eye.

"What happened?"

He shrugs as he pulls off his tie and tosses it aside. "Just a little initiation. I'm going to shower." He heads to the bathroom.

Not liking his answer, I leap from bed and follow him in. "What do you mean? Niko did this?"

Donovan turns on the water in the shower. "No. Bratva."

What the hell? I reach for his hand, and my breath catches at the sight of his knuckles – raw, split open. It's a reminder of the violence that takes up too much space in his life.

"What happened?"

"Occupational hazard," he quips.

"You were shot not that long ago, and now you're getting into a fight?" I'm sure I sound like a shrew, but seriously, how do men like Donovan stay alive when they're so reckless with their lives?

He stares down at me, amusement still dancing in his eyes. "I just needed to prove my worth."

I arch a brow. "Were you successful?"

He grins. "You should see the other guys."

My mouth drops open. "There was more than one?"

"Five." He holds up his other hand and beams like a schoolboy who's just won a trophy. "Three require medical assistance."

I purse my lips at him, angry that he's such an idiot and ridiculously happy that he's okay. "You're going to get yourself killed someday."

Donovan takes my chin and looks into my eyes. His expression softens, and he opens his mouth to say something but stops and steps away. He starts to undress, wincing as he removes his shirt.

"Donovan." My words are a whisper as I take in the cuts and bruises. My chest tightens as I watch Donovan, the way his body subtly recoils with each move from the pain he's trying so hard to mask.

He's about to shove his pants down when I realize he's nearly naked. I'd like to stay. I'd like to kiss his wounds and help him wash away the violence. But that's not what this marriage is. I turn to leave.

"You don't have to go." His voice is softer. He nods toward the shower. "You could join me, if you wanted."

"You're hurt."

He chuckles. "I promised I wouldn't expect anything from you, Lucy." His eyes glint with mischief, the smug smirk returning. "But I could ask, right? Joining me in the shower would certainly soothe the pain I'm feeling."

My heartbeat quickens—his playful tone, the promise of sensual delights, it tempts me closer to the edge of reason.

"It would be a nice, wifely thing to do," he teases.

It would be, except I'm a wife only on paper. "This marriage doesn't mean anything." My words bely the truth. I can feel the wall around my heart strain, threatening to crumble.

For a fleeting moment, his expression shifts. The humor fades, leaving behind something raw and achingly sincere. "I meant the vows I made to you."

His words linger between us as I try to understand them.

"The vow was to protect me, not... This—us—it was never about love or commitment. You said that yourself."

"Lucy..." He pauses, and he seems to weigh his words, or maybe it's whether to say anything at all. "What we're in... it's real to me."

I scoff, an automatic attempt to protect myself.

He steps closer, and the yearning to be in his arms is almost more than I can bear. His gaze holds mine, unwavering, intense. "You have my name, Lucy. My ring encircles your finger. That means something."

My breath catches as his hands reach out, not with the force of command but with the gentleness of an offering. Fingers graze my jaw, then trail down my neck. The world narrows down to the electricity of his touch sparking against my skin.

"That makes you mine." His fingers brush aside the strap of my nightgown. "Mine to protect. Mine to cherish." He pushes aside the other strap. The only things keeping my nightgown up are my breasts. The fabric rubs uncomfortably over my nipples.

But I can't give in to this. "This marriage was by Niko's order."

He shakes his head. "No, *Tesoro*. It was my idea."

Surprise jolts through me. "But you... don't want this." My heart races, a frantic rhythm, and I'm precariously close to losing myself in him, to believing words I know will only leave me heartbroken when the marriage is annulled and I'm set free.

His gaze holds mine. "I wanted you." He pushes my nightgown down, and it pools around my bare feet. "Ever since I picked you up at the airport—"

"You kidnapped me."

He chuckles. "Potayto, potahto. The point is, I've only ever wanted you." The words are a whisper, but they land with force, shattering my protective wall. In that moment, I teeter on the edge, caught between the pull of a life I want to escape and the allure of feeling seen, feeling cherished.

My life, my future, is wrapped up in this moment and what I choose to do. Stay or go?

The moment seems to hang in eternity. Finally, Donovan steps back. He reaches down and lifts my nightgown up. "Already, I've broken my vow."

I clutch the fabric around my breasts.

He kisses my forehead. "I'm going to shower."

I nod, feeling like I'm in a netherworld. Not quite part of this world. It's only when he steps in the shower and I feel the cool air from his absence that I come back into my body. I think of my sister and how she boldly grabbed hold of love. Could I do that too?

I let my nightgown drop again and step out of it. I take my panties off, and inhaling a breath, I step into the shower.

Donovan's back is to me, and it's covered in bruises. I brush my hand down it.

He turns, surprise lighting his dark eyes.

"A good wife would nurse her husband," I say in answer to his expression.

He smiles. "You're a good nurse." He takes my hand, lifting it to his lips. It's a sweet gesture from a man the size of Everest and who makes a living killing people.

I take the soap and lather it, then gently rub it over his shoulders and chest. Between us, his erection grows. When I see it, I look up at him.

He gives me a sheepish smile. "My dick just wants to make sure you don't forget to wash him."

Before I have a chance to touch him, Donovan takes the soap from me and pulls me into a mind-blowing, toe-curling kiss. If his arm weren't banded around me, I'd sink into a puddle of mush.

"Let me make you feel good," he whispers against my lips. "Like a good husband would."

It's hard to say no to Donovan's touch, so I don't. His hands roam my body, and each spot he touches lights up with a million electric sparks. He kneads my breasts and then bends over, sucking a nipple into his mouth.

"Oh!" I gasp, and my hands hold his head, not wanting him to stop. Each tug of my nipple sends a shockwave down to my center.

"Lucy." His voice is rough as he straightens. He turns me so my back is to him. His arms come around me, fondling my breasts again, pinching my nipples as his lips brush along my neck. I feel like my body is humming, like every nerve ending is firing, pulsing.

"I'm not worthy of what you've given me," he murmurs as one of his hands slides down my belly to the nest of curls between my legs.

I might have responded, but coherent thought is absent. All I experience is sensation as his fingers slip between my folds.

My hips rock, and I whimper. "Donovan."

"Yes, my treasure?"

My hands press against the tile wall as I reach for the stars, the pressure, the tension building tighter and tighter.

"Do you need more?" he asks.

"Yes... Oh, God."

He releases me around the waist and guides his erection between my legs. He doesn't enter me, much to my disappointment. I try to tilt my pelvis, wanting to feel him inside me.

"I don't have a condom," he whispers. "Let me take care of you." He slides along my folds as his fingers rub over my hard nub.

"You like my dick?" His breath is warm in my ear.

"Yes."

"Tell me." His movements slow down. Like he's holding my orgasm hostage until I say the words.

"I like your..."

"Dick. Or cock. Your choice."

I whimper as the ache intensifies.

"Say it, *Tesoro*."

I've always been a bold woman, much to my parents' annoyance. But I'd never engaged in sexy talk. I feel embarrassed to even try.

"Do you want to come?"

"Yes."

"Then tell me." There's humor in his voice, and I hate that he's teasing me. But my need to come is bigger than my need to be defiant.

"I like your... cock."

He groans, and I swear I can feel it thicken between my legs. "I love your pussy, Lucy." His fingers move faster over my clit, and he rocks his dick between my legs, sliding along my folds. The tension grows until the pleasure hits. Like a tsunami, it floods my system.

I cry out and my body shudders.

"So fucking beautiful," he whispers in my ear. "And mine." He turns me around, mouth consuming mine in a kiss that steals my breath away. "I want to fuck you so badly."

I look up at him, wanting that too. While I might have been late to the pleasures of sex, I'm not naive. I know without a condom, we risk a pregnancy. Oddly, I don't find the idea of that as problematic as I should. At the same time, I know that it would complicate everything. Despite what he said, we were still only married to protect me. I don't want to shackle him with more responsibility than he asked for.

"I could... you know..."

He arches a brow, his smirk returning. "What?"

I roll my eyes at his insistence that I be specific. "Use my mouth. I mean... you have to teach me—"

He lets out a feral groan. "You're going to be the death of me, woman." His hand cups my cheek. "Thank you for offering, but you don't have to."

I look down at his erection… his dick, and the desire to learn how to pleasure him blooms hot and wild. "I want to." I sink down to my knees.

His fingers lift my chin to look up at him. "Lucy—"

"Will you teach me?"

"Fucking hell… just seeing you on your knees in front of me is enough to make me come."

I flick my tongue out and lick the tip. It's soft, like velvet, and tastes like water and salt.

He groans. "Lucy… God… Put the tip in your mouth and suck. Like a lollipop."

I do as he says.

"Fuck, fuck, fuck…" His hips rock. "Baby… it won't take long."

A powerful feeling overcomes me. It's like feminine power. I hold this man's pleasure in my hands. He's surrendered it to me. Feeling bolder, I wrap my hand around his dick and stroke as I suck, taking more of him in my mouth.

"*Yesss*… oh, fuck… Lucy…" I glance up, and his head has dropped back. The cords in his neck are taut, straining.

Then he looks down at me. The desire, the need in his eyes encourages me on. "Feel that?" he manages to say through gritted teeth. "My dick has never been so hard. Fuck…" His head rocks back again, and his hips rock at a faster, shorter pace.

A moment later, he pulls away, and I look up at him, wondering if I did something wrong.

"Hold up your tits, baby."

I do as he asks. He strokes himself until he growls and his cum shoots out, covering my breasts. It shocks me at first, but then I'm fascinated by the thick, creamy liquid. I rub my fingers over it. I bring a finger to my mouth to taste it.

"Holy hell…" He keeps stroking, and more cum sprays over me.

Finally, he reaches down, taking my arm and hauling me up. He presses me against the tiled wall. "Is the top of my head still there?"

I look, not understanding what he's saying.

"Because you just blew my mind."

I feel the praise through my entire body. I realize at that moment that my walls have been completely demolished. There's no doubt about it. When this is done, I'll be heartbroken. But I also know that I can't do anything but take what I can from Donovan while I can. I'm going to experience the thrills and joys he brings and savor them. I'm going to sear the memories into my brain so that when it's over and our lives go back in their own directions, I'll be able to conjure them up when I need to be reminded of what it feels like to be in love.

23

DONOVAN

On my eighteenth birthday, Niko and Liam paid a woman to give me a blowjob. I wasn't a virgin. I'd fucked before. But I'd never had a woman suck me off. When it was done, I couldn't imagine ever feeling as good or coming as hard ever again in my life.

I'd had some interesting sexual encounters since then, but seeing Lucy on her knees with those plump lips of hers wrapped around my cock, fucking hell, I've never been so hard in my life.

We finish the shower, and once we dry off, I pick her up and carry her into the bedroom. I lay her on the bed and then hunt down my clothes for my wallet. Please, God, let me have a condom—maybe two—stashed away.

"Are you all right?" she asks when I return.

I hold up the condom. "Now I am. As soon as my cock recovers, I want to get inside you."

The blush that comes to her cheeks is adorable.

"In the meantime..." I climb into bed next to her and pull her close. Lucy's head rests on my chest, her breaths even and slow against my skin. I trace circles on her bare shoulder, feeling the warmth from her body seep into mine. This is fucking awesome. And unexpected.

I replay the moment in the bathroom when words spilled out of me.

I meant the vows I made to you.

I've only ever wanted you.

I expected snark, but her eyes widened and then softened. And then she was in the shower, letting me touch her. On her knees, giving me the blowjob of a lifetime.

I'm thrilled at the change in her, and yet, I'm cautious about what it means. She wants freedom. Once her father is gone, she can have that. I want it for her, a future where she can breathe without looking over her shoulder, laugh without it being laced with bitterness. She deserves to live, really live, not just survive.

What she doesn't want is this life I lead. Fucking hell, she doesn't even know that I'm the one who will take over her father's business when he's dead. It's a conversation we need to have, yet the words stick in my throat. I don't want to shatter this fragile peace that has settled over us, not when for once, she looks at me and I see something other than disdain in her eyes.

Maybe I can't tell her everything yet, but there are a few things she needs to know. "I have to stay in New Jersey for a bit. You'll return to Manhattan with Niko and Elena."

Her body stiffens against mine, and she turns to face me, eyes narrowing into a glare that could rival any made man's.

"I don't respond well to orders, Donovan." The defensiveness in her voice reminds me that she's had too many people trying to control her moves.

I lift my hands, palms out, a gesture of peace. "Hey, you said you wanted to be back with Elena. She'll be in New York. That was the deal, right?"

She flinches, and I feel like I've said the wrong thing. "The deal. Right." She sags back, pulling away, and I'm desperate to close the distance she's putting between us.

"You go back, stay safe with Elena. That's what matters."

She nods slowly, and I can tell I haven't fixed whatever I've fucked up. I feel like a big pussy bending over backward to make her feel safe and in control. A part of me wants to give up and act like she expects me to, tell her how things are and how they're going to be.

Instead, I ask, "Is there a problem?"

"No. You said this was a deal and I guess it is. If you want me to go—"

"Want you to go? I never said that."

Her dark eyes jerk up to look at me. "You just said—"

"I said it was the plan."

She looks down, and the vulnerability in her expression rips through my chest. "Do you want me to go?"

"Hell no. I just..." Is that what this is all about? She thinks I'm trying to get rid of her? "I thought you wanted to be with Elena. Besides, I'll be busy."

She adjusts her body, sitting up. She's magnificent and regal as she stares down at me. "What business do you have in New Jersey?"

I look her in the eyes, tired of pussyfooting around. "I'm going to kill your parents. And then I'm going to run their business."

She doesn't react until I tell her I'll be in charge. Her brows narrow. "Niko is giving it to you?"

I nod.

"You'll be a Boss."

I nod again, wondering what the fuck is going on through her mind and wishing I didn't care so much.

She looks down for a moment. "I can help you with my parents."

My brain comes to a screeching halt. "What?"

This time, she's looking me in the eyes. "I can help you take out my parents." The determination in her voice surprises me.

Her resolve rattles something loose in me—a mixture of admiration and terror. She's remarkable, braver than most men I know. But the idea of her in harm's way...

"Lucy, it's dangerous," I start, but she cuts me off with a look that could stop a bullet.

"More dangerous than everything I've already survived?" Her chin lifts, challenging me.

"Point taken. But the other point is that you've survived. Your father nearly killed me. I suspect he'll have no qualms about killing you."

Her eyes flash with fire. I hold my hand up before she can lambast me for being a sexist jerk. "Like it or not, Lucy, this is the world you're in... at the moment." I rake a hand through my hair, recognizing that I'm giving her more reasons to want to leave, more reasons to hold me in disdain.

"Regardless of what you think, Donovan, I'm already in danger. Sending me away won't change that. How can you protect me from here if I'm in New York?"

She has a point.

"What about being with Elena? You wanted to be with her."

She shifts, and for a moment I'm distracted by her gorgeous tits. "Elena has Niko now."

A swell of something warm and potent blooms in my chest. "And you have me."

Her smirk is a challenge, laced with a hint of vulnerability. "Sounds more like you've got me."

"Lucy..." The sappiness in my chest is back. It's a mixture of hope that she thinks more of me than as a toady and a desire to offer her the world. I can face down Giovanni's bullet, but hell if I have the courage to tell Lucy all the feelings threatening to bring me to my knees. Fucking hell. Is this how Niko felt with Elena?

"Donovan." She responds, watching me.

I sigh. "So, how do you suggest we deal with your parents?"

Her smile is radiant, with a hint of victory. "Do you realize they're your in-laws?"

I laugh. "Heaven help me. So, what are your plans?"

"I deal with my mom and you can deal with my dad."

I study her, partly in awe and then in fear because I see in her eyes that she plans to kill her mother. At the very least, she thinks she has it in her.

"Your mother?" I can't keep the surprise from seeping into my voice.

"I know how to push her buttons, make her reveal her plans. She can tell us where my father is."

"Lucy, she's dangerous." I need her to understand the gravity of it all.

"Exactly why I should be the one to face her." Her gaze locks onto mine, fierce and unwavering. "I've been surviving her games my whole life. Do you think women don't feel the need for justice? Revenge?"

"I'm learning to never underestimate a woman."

She gives me that triumphant smile again. It's sexy as fuck, and speaking of fuck... I laugh and tug her to me. "You've got the makings of a Boss."

A scoff escapes her. "Sure, if only I weren't a woman."

"Don't sell yourself short. There've been a few successful women bosses. And you've got what they had. You're fierce, brave... and have tits like a fucking goddess."

She arches a brow. "You know about the tits of other Mafia women?"

"No. Yours distracted me." I lean forward and lightly bite a nipple, tugging it.

She lets out a hiss, and I feel it harden between my teeth. I roll her under me and crush my lips to hers. Immediately, she goes pliant, and I'm filled with power that this strong, defiant woman would surrender to me. In that moment, the world outside this embrace ceases to exist. There's only Lucy. And as I hold her, I lose myself in the taste and feel of her. If she asked, I'd go to the ends of the earth for her. It's a terrifying realization that this woman could bring me to my knees. She could ruin me.

She arches into me. "Will you go inside me again?"

I'm struck by how hard and worldly she is most of the time, but still so shy and innocent when it comes to the pleasures of the flesh.

I lift my head and look down on her. "Are you asking me to fuck you?"

Her cheeks flush, and if I weren't already in love, I'd tumble over right now. "Yes."

"Then ask me."

"I thought I did."

I take her lip between my teeth and suck. "Ask me to fuck you."

She looks adorably shy. "Donovan?"

"Yes, *Tesoro*."

"Will you..." She looks away.

"Fuck."

"Fuck me?"

"Your wish is my command." I take my time exploring her body and what makes her sigh, what makes her moan until she's writhing.

"Donovan... please."

I grab the condom, ripping it open and sheathing my cock. I reach for her, tugging her over top of me. "You're in control, Lucy."

Her expression is confused, uncertain.

"Just straddle me and take as much as you want, at whatever pace you need." I can't believe I've just done that. My dick twitches in revolt. He needs a hard, fast fuck.

She maneuvers her body over my cock, rubbing her pussy over it. We both moan. I grip her hips to steady her as she slowly takes me in. It's fucking torture how long it takes her. A centimeter here, millimeter there. But then finally, I'm seeped so deep inside her I think I might be a part of her.

"What do I do?" Her hands rest on my chest.

I take one and kiss her palm. "Whatever makes you feel good."

She rocks, and we both hiss as pleasure spikes. She does it again, and again, and soon, she's adding upward and downward motion, and it feels fucking fantastic.

"Oh, God..." She's now riding me, lost in sensation. To watch it is like witnessing art in motion.

My dick is screaming for release, but I keep my focus on her. Only her.

"Donovan."

"Yes, baby," I say through clenched teeth.

"I feel... Oh, God..."

"Come, baby. Let go and come on my cock."

A low, guttural sound emits from her, growing until she's crying out and her pussy is so tight around my cock that I see stars.

"*Fuck!*" I buck underneath her as a tsunami of intense pleasure rocks through my body. I feel it all the way to the cellular level.

She collapses on me, and I bind my arm around her in a symbolic gesture of possession. Perhaps she won't be with me in the future, but right now, she's mine.

Exhaustion overtakes us, and we sleep. When I wake, she's curled up beside me, and I'm overtaken by a wave of emotion filled with aching longing. It's clear that I'm going to be fucked up by this whole experience when it's all said and done. It's a lesson in how dangerous it is to let emotions in. Once Lucy is gone, you can bet I won't fall for anyone ever again. It's too distracting. Too painful. The good news is that it seems unlikely I'll ever meet anyone who makes me feel like Lucy does, so I won't have to worry about experiencing heartache again.

She stirs and stretches, then looks up at me. "I fell asleep."

"I hope it's not a sign that I'm boring." My fingers trace along her arm. I can't seem to stop touching her.

Her lips twitch up. "You're many things, Donovan, but boring isn't one of them."

My stomach growls. "I'm hungry. How about we get room service?"

"Sounds good. I'm starving."

Twenty minutes later, we're wrapped in robes, compliments of the hotel, and sitting at a table eating a hearty breakfast of Belgian waffles, eggs, bacon, and fruit.

I watch Lucy, for once looking more relaxed, less on edge.

"Can you tell me about your meeting?" she asks.

My instinct is to be vague, but this impacts her life. She's clearly strong enough to handle the dirty aspects of this life. Plus, she wants in on bringing her parents down.

"Met with Liam, Niko, and a Bratva guy named Igor Peprov." I study her, wondering if the name means anything to her.

"Bratva? Is that through Niko's *consigliere*?"

I nod. "You know Liam came from Bratva?"

She shrugs. "Just the bits and pieces I've overheard."

I smirk at her. "Spying on us?"

Her eyes narrow. "I don't like being in the dark. Not when my or Elena's life is in the balance. Did you have to suffer the black eye before or after getting information?"

I laughed. I'd nearly forgotten about that. "After. We learned that your father is MIA, holed up somewhere like a fucking coward. Your mother, however, she's got balls. She's been seen around Atlantic City."

"That's why we're here?"

I nod.

"Would have been nice if she'd gone to Paris."

"Not liking your honeymoon spot?"

Her cheeks flush. "I like it well enough."

"When this is done, I can take you…" I remember that when this is done, Lucy will be gone. "Well… you can go to Paris."

She stares at me, and I think I see sadness in her eyes.

I clear my throat.

She sips her coffee. "I'm not surprised she's been coming here. She always did enjoy the casinos, more than anything—or anyone—else. My father would try to put her on an allowance. Then she'd concoct some business scheme and—she's a vile woman." Her words are filled with bitterness… no, something deeper. Hatred. Considering the woman planned to sell her daughter in a trafficking business, I can't blame her.

I'm not sure if I should mention the next bit, but then I remember Lucy is a strong woman. "We were given information about two warehouses. It's how we'll pull the business out from under your father." I hesitate, and when I do, she looks up at me. I suck in a breath. "It sounds like one could include… people."

Lucy's eyes darken. "That's what you're taking over?" She jumps up and looks at me with a mixture of disgust and horror.

I rise from my chair as well but keep my distance. "No." I don't mind breaking the law, and I do it every day. But I can't get behind selling women and children. "Liam will handle that through the FBI."

She stares at me like she isn't sure she believes me.

"I didn't have to tell you. You know that, Lucy. I could keep you in the dark, keep you locked up—"

"You think you can—"

"I know I can." This time, my voice is commanding. "I'm being upfront with you, bringing you in because I can see you need to exact your revenge, and I want to help you with that."

It takes a moment, but I see the tension lessen until she sits back down. I move to her then, squatting down in front of her. I take her hand. "If this is too much, you can go—"

"I'm not weak."

I let out a small laugh. "No, Princess, you're not. But if you don't want to be a part of this, you don't have to."

She looks at me then, and I see certainty in her eyes. "I want to ruin my mother."

I nod. "Okay." I watch her for a moment, needing to see the woman who'd been with me in bed. I press my palm to her cheek. "I'm on your side, Lucy. It's my goal in life to hand your mother over to you."

She lets out a sigh and rests her forehead against mine. "Thank you."

"You're welcome." I want to pick her up and carry her back to bed and fuck away all the bad feelings she's experiencing, but my phone rings.

I pick it up. "*Pronto.*"

"It's Igor." He gives his message, rattling off an address.

"Got it." I hang up and turn to Lucy. "How do you feel about having lunch with your mother today?"

Before my eyes, Lucy morphs from a bitter woman feeling no control, to a fierce warrior, to a woman who could lead her own Family if she so wanted. I'm in awe of her. Too fucking bad I can't keep her.

24

LUCY

My breakfast so far has been a rollercoaster ride of emotions. I've gone from riding a high from sexual haze to being pissed off that Donovan would be running my father's business, including trafficking, except no. He said Liam would be dealing with that. And now, he's just asked if I want lunch with my mother. Not as a daughter who wants to see her mother after five years, but as an associate with plans to ruin her. My pulse quickens at the thought. My mother — the woman who should have protected me but instead tried to orchestrate my sale as part of a trafficking business.

"There's a chance to confront your mother. She might know where Giovanni is hiding," Donovan says.

I nod, understanding the situation.

Donovan watches me as he waits for my answer. "You don't have to—"

"I want to," I blurt out.

He sits down at the table, his dark eyes looking into mine. "She'll agree to this thinking it's her chance to hand you back to your father."

"I know." A cold knot forms in my stomach. I imagine sitting across from the woman who gave birth to me but never saw me as more than a commodity.

"It'll be dangerous, Lucy." He takes my hand.

"I know. But you won't let her win."

His smile is sweet. Like I've given him a gift. "I'll protect you with my life. But—"

"You said it yourself, she might know where my father is. We can end his terror once and for all." A wave of sadness flows through me. Once my father is gone, there will be no need for this marriage.

Donovan studies me for a long moment, likely weighing the risks. But I see the decision in his eyes before he nods. "All right, then."

We spend the rest of the morning planning and then putting that plan into motion. At just after noon, I walk into the restaurant where my mother agreed to meet me. To be honest, I was surprised she did. Or maybe I was surprised that after I heard her voice and had flashbacks of all the terror she caused me, I still wanted to follow through.

I'm alone except for all of Donovan's men posted at various tables in the restaurant. I've been in this world long enough to recognize my father's men who are protecting my mother. I'm walking into the lion's den, and if this doesn't go right, I'll be back in my parents' clutches, sold to the next high bidder.

She sees me, her lips pursing as she scans her gaze over me. She looks disapproving, but I know it's jealousy. I was always prettier than her. She used to threaten to scar me, and in those cases, my father threatened her if she did anything to decrease my value.

I sit in the chair across from her.

"Lucia. You look... well." She's terrible at acting friendly.

"Mother," I reply, my lips pressing into a smile that probably looks more like a grimace.

"I understand congratulations are in order. You've married again."

"Word travels fast."

A server brings water and sets a glass of wine in front of my mother. I shake my head when he asks if I want a drink. He leaves us to review the menu.

"Poor Don Conti, barely in his grave and you—"

"Loyalty wasn't something I was raised to understand," I quip.

She purses her lips at me again. "I suppose you didn't have much choice. Had you given Giuseppe a son, you'd have been better protected. I'm not sure this move will help you. A *capo* doesn't carry the weight of a Don."

I let her words flow off me. What I want to do is tell her that Donovan will be the Boss of the Fiori territory in New Jersey, but I hold back.

"Heaven forbid I marry out of love."

My mother scoffs. "You always were soft-headed. Love, Lucia, doesn't exist in our world."

"I know, Mother. I learned that very well from you. Not even parents can love their children." Today, I know that's not true. I saw how Giuseppe loved his son, Luca. I've seen how Niko loves Elena and they both love their unborn twins.

"Love is something we can't afford." She sniffs as if she smells something rotten. "But a *capo*... Lucia, you could do better."

I want to laugh and tell her how Donovan is a million times better than her, but I need to remember the plan.

I look around, as if I'm concerned who might be lurking about. Then I reach across the linen-covered table, my hands trembling as if I'm scared out of my wits. Her hands are cold, just like her, and I want to pull away. But I don't. I stick to the plan.

"Mother," I choke out, moisture welling up in my eyes. "I... I can't bear it any longer. Giuseppe is gone and everything here is just... too much. They forced me into this. I want to go home."

Her eyes narrow, calculating as she holds my hands with a grip that feigns maternal concern.

She leans in. "Lucia, darling, you know you can always come home." The word 'home' is laced with a poison that promises anything but sanctuary.

"Really?" I sniff.

"Of course, my child." Her lips curl into a smile that makes her look sinister, not reassuring.

She rises, towering in her tailored elegance. "Follow me."

I stand and follow her toward the back of the restaurant. My legs shake, and I cross my fingers that everything is going to be all right. We enter the kitchen, heading to the back door. No one seems to notice us as they prepare the afternoon's meals.

"Nearly there, Lucia," she coos, guiding me with a hand pressed firmly against my spine.

Please let this work. The closer I get to the back door, the more I second-guess this scheme. Back in my parents' control, I know I'll experience horrors. I'll be punished for sure. And then I'll be sold again.

The back door swings open, revealing the dim alleyway. Her grip tightens as if she's anticipating her triumph.

A dark sedan sits idling, waiting.

"Quickly, Lucia," she urges, opening the door, gesturing for me to get in.

On a prayer and a hope, I slide in. I don't recognize the driver, and my stomach drops as my heart rate soars. She joins me in the back, and the driver zips out onto the main road. I glance around for Donovan but don't see him. Of course I wouldn't. That isn't the plan. But as we drive along, I'm thinking the plan has failed.

The driver makes a turn, heading into an industrial area of the city.

"Where are we going?" My mother's voice is shrill as she taps the driver on the shoulder.

"Almost there," he says.

My mother's eyes narrow as her gaze darts to the window. I see a crack in her demeanor, and I think maybe the plan is working, after all.

She whips her attention back to me. "What is this?"

I shrug. "I followed you, remember?"

The vehicle slows, turning into an abandoned lot. The car stops, and my mother opens her mouth, surely to make demands, but before she can, her door flies open. Donovan's large hand reaches in and hauls her out. His eyes meet mine for a heartbeat, and a sense of peace washes through me.

"Out," he orders, his tone leaving no room for argument.

My mother struggles and curses at Donovan. "Did you do this, Lucia?"

I exit the car. "I thought you might like to meet my husband."

Donovan and the driver subdue my mother, binding her hands and legs with swift efficiency I know too well from when he'd kidnapped me from the airport when I first arrived back in the States.

"If you settle down, you can ride in the back seat. Otherwise, it's the trunk," Donovan tells her.

"You're a dead man."

"Trunk?"

My mother growls but stops fighting him.

Donovan puts her in the backseat and shuts the door. "See you in a few hours," he says to the driver.

They pull away, and Donovan puts his arm around me. "You were brilliant. You okay?"

"I didn't recognize the driver."

"I'm sorry." His hand cups my cheek. "Were you scared?"

I shrug. "Maybe a little."

He laughs. "My fiercely brave wife."

His use of the word wife fills my chest with warmth I'm too afraid to feel. At the same time, it replenishes my resolve to see this through, to confront my mother for the horrible person she is.

"I'll drive you back to the penthouse and then deal with—"

"I want to go with you. I need to be there."

Donovan studies me and then nods. He guides me to his SUV and helps me in. Then we start on the two-plus hours back to Manhattan. The entire way, I play in my mind what I intend to say and do to my mother. Justice is nearly mine.

The last time I was in the room in the basement of Niko's pizzeria, I was the one tied to the chair and acting defiant. Now it's my mother, and I can't deny the sweet feeling of revenge I'm feeling that she's the one with zero control.

"Even if you whip my skin from my bones, Giovanni will remain a ghost." Her words slither out like the snake she is.

My heart hammers against my ribcage. I lean in until our noses nearly touch. "Maybe death is the only freedom for someone like you. After all, what value are you if you won't talk?" I scan her the same way she would me. "You don't have your beauty, and I doubt you've ever had charm."

Her eyes widen for a split second, the smallest crack in her armor, before they harden. "Lucy, dear, don't be dramatic." The mockery in her tone irks me, but I remind myself that I have the power here.

"Am I?" I step back, glancing over at Niko and Donovan who are standing near the door. Both men have their arms crossed, but Niko seems amused by the situation. Donovan watches me with concern.

"Your threats are empty," my mother hisses, struggling against the ties. "You don't have it in you."

I shrug. "Maybe. Maybe not. There's a lifetime of resentment in here." I press my hand over my heart. "Then there's the fact that Elena and I, and those we care about, will never be safe with you and Dad alive."

She laughs. "You're your father's daughter, after all."

It hits its mark. The last person I want to be like is my father. But I regroup. "How is it that you don't despise him? He treated you as badly as the rest of us. Tell us where he is and you can be rid of him too."

She sneers at me. "Your father knows he'd be dead and buried, his business under the control of some other Boss if not for me. He has the violence down, but not the brains."

I cock my head to the side. "I'll be sure to tell him you said that."

She jerks her head away. She knows that if my father knew she felt she was the brains of the business, he'd kill her. My father won't put up with that sort of disrespect.

I pull up a chair and sit in front of her. "So, all the horrors I went through. They were your idea? I know the trafficking deal was yours, but all the others too? How about killing Dylan and making me watch? Was that your idea?"

She purses her lips. "The killing was your father's idea. In front of you was mine. You had to be punished for what you did. The truth is, the boy died because of you, Lucia."

"Do you know how Giuseppe treated me? Did you care?"

She looks at me like I smell rotten. "He was supposed to kill you."

That takes me aback. A growl escapes from Donovan.

I manage a smile. "Too bad for you, he didn't. In fact, Giuseppe was the first person to show me there could be kindness in the world. He was good to me. He's left me an estate, you know. And money. Freedom."

I hear shifting, and I turn to see Donovan rolling his shoulders, his expression unreadable.

"Then why are you here?"

"Because Dad is a menace. All Elena and I want is to be happy. And it's become painfully obvious that it can't happen as long as Dad is alive. Tell us where he is, and perhaps you can learn about kindness and mercy."

"You always were a problem."

"Always? Even when I was a baby? A child? Did you ever love me?" My breath holds, although I don't know why. I know the answer.

Her lips twitch, almost imperceptibly, as if the word 'love' is foreign to her. "Love is a luxury. There's no room for it in our world. I think I told you that already."

My gaze locks onto hers, searching for a hint of maternal affection but finding only calculation. "So that's a no?"

"Your value was never in who you are but in what you could offer. And the only thing of worth you had was your youth, your beauty."

I know this already, and yet hearing her say it is like a stab to my very soul. It taps into all the times I felt like nothing, like no one.

"No..." Niko says.

I turn to see him putting his hand on Donovan, who appears to be taking a step toward me.

"She's got this," Niko finishes.

For a moment, Donovan's and my eyes lock, and emotion—hope—fills me.

"Where is Dad?" I ask one more time.

"You'll never get me to turn on him."

I let out a breath and rise from the chair.

Her eyes follow, and while I see defiance, I finally also see fear.

I turn to Donovan. He meets my stare unflinchingly. He steps forward, his gun out. I move out of the way, but he extends his hand, offering the gun to me.

"Your choice, Lucy," he murmurs. "Whatever you decide, I'm here."

I look at the gun. Can I do this? Can I kill my mother? Can I become what I've for so long despised?

"Or I'll do it. You can go upstairs. Lou can take you back to the penthouse so you can see Elena."

I glance at my mother. She's the embodiment of evil. But beyond being the source of my pain, she's a threat to all I hold dear. To Elena. To Donovan.

I take the gun from him. The feel of it is empowering, and yet, I know doing this could change me in a way I don't know I can accept.

"Kill them, Lucia. Kill Donovan and Niko. It's our only way out."

I laugh derisively. "You betrayed me and sold me, and now you want me to save you? From the two men who have shown me and Elena kindness?" I lift the gun, pointing the barrel at my mother's head. Elena's face flashes in my mind. Could she forgive this?

A glance at my mother reveals a crack in her veneer. Her breath hitches.

"Did you ever love me?" I ask again.

"Yes, of course, Lucia."

She's lying.

I hold the gun steady despite the storm raging inside me.

"I'm your mother. I tried to protect you."

More lies.

A calm settles over me. She must see it as her eyes widen.

"Goodbye, Mother." I feel nothing as I pull the trigger. The sound is deafening. Her body slumps. Silence envelops me. I've killed my mother. There's no triumph, no satisfaction—only the acknowledgement that from this point forward, I'm free of her.

Across the room, Niko leans against the wall, his arms folded across his chest. The corner of his mouth lifts in what could pass for approval—or maybe it's admiration. He inclines his head, an imperceptible nod that suggests respect. His gesture doesn't fill me with warmth or a sense of accomplishment. Instead, it's a reminder of the violent world we inhabit.

Donovan approaches me. There's no smile on his lips, no glimmer of pride in his eye. For a moment, I wonder if this changes things for him. But when I look carefully, I see understanding.

"Lucy." He takes the gun from me, holstering it. "Let's go home." He extends his hand. It feels like a lifeline, so I take it.

"I'll deal with this," Niko says.

"Thank you." I meet Niko's eyes, and for the first time, I feel like he doesn't look at me with suspicion. For the first time, I don't look at him that way, either.

Donovan leads me to the stairs, and a cold chill runs through me. As if he knows, Donovan's grip on my hand tightens just slightly, reminding me that I'm not alone. The question now is, will Elena forgive me for what I've done?

25

DONOVAN

I escort Lucy out of the basement and up the stairs. My mind is whirling as I replay Lucy's taking her life back by confronting her mother and then killing her. I glance at her, wondering how this will impact her. The protective part of me wishes I'd done it so Lucy didn't have to deal with the ramifications of taking a life.

We make our way through the back of the pizzeria. Lou sees us and stands ready.

"Let's go," I say.

With a nod, he precedes us out the back door into the alley where a car waits. I help Lucy into the back seat before sliding in beside her.

"Take us back to the penthouse," I tell Lou, who's in the front seat, ready to drive.

My gaze latches onto Lucy. She's quiet. Distant. Did she ever pull a trigger before tonight? If so, was it out of protection or like tonight, justice? Based on her reaction now, I suspect that she's never pulled a trigger, but I remember that she's seen it. Her father killed a man in front of her as punishment.

"Lucy."

She turns her head slightly, acknowledging me without really seeing me.

"You're fucking awesome. You faced the devil and didn't flinch." I take her hand, lifting and pressing my lips to her knuckles. "You took back control tonight."

I squeeze her hand, offering up all the reassurance I can muster, hoping she feels the truth behind my words—that I'm proud of her, that she's not alone in this fight.

"What will Niko do with her?" Lucy asks.

I study her profile. "Niko will arrange everything. It won't be tied to you."

She swallows hard. "But where?"

"He'll probably leave her at the house. It's empty now that Giovanni is hiding, but she'll be discovered eventually, and word will get back to him." My words are measured, wanting to be honest but not wanting to say something to add to what she's grappling with.

"A message."

I nod. "A message."

"It won't be linked to me, so he won't know I did it."

My brow furrows as I consider that I'm misreading her. "Do you want him to know you did it?"

"I want him to know he doesn't own me anymore."

I'm amazed by this woman. Her parents mistreated her, didn't honor the beautiful daughter they had. In her survival, she became cool and aloof, untrusting of others, but now I see a fierce woman coming into her own power.

"I'll make sure he knows that," I promise.

WE ARRIVE BACK at the penthouse, and I guide Lucy toward the staircase. "Why don't you go see Elena? Rest."

She stops and glares up at me. "Do you think I can't handle this? You think I'm weak—"

"Lucy." I press a finger to her lips.

Her eyes flame with irritation as she jerks back.

I smile and take her hand, holding it tight when she tries to pull away. "You're one of the strongest people I know. But unlike your

Family, the Leone Family recognizes that sometimes, people need time and space." I trace the back of her hand with my thumb, willing her to feel the sincerity behind my words. "You should be with Elena. Tell her whatever you need to. Blame it on Niko or me if it makes it easier."

A steel edge hardens her jaw. "No. Elena deserves the truth. I won't hide behind lies."

"All right." I nod, respecting her resolve.

She squares her shoulders and heads up the staircase. I watch her go, my heart a mixture of aching to make the world easy and beautiful for her and being in awe of her strength.

Turning away, I make my way to Niko's office. Lou sits on the couch, scrolling on his phone.

"Any news on Giovanni?" I ask, going to the bar in Niko's office for a drink.

Lou glances up, shoving his phone in his pocket like a child caught with his hand in the cookie jar. He's probably watching porn.

"Nothing solid. But he can't hide forever."

"We need to find him. End this thing. It's drawing out far too long." With Giovanni gone, Lucy will finally be free. Safe. Gone.

"Any ideas that we haven't tried?"

I think of how Niko is likely arranging to send Giovanni's wife to him as a message. "Perhaps."

Before Lou can ask me my thoughts, the door opens and Liam strides in. "Where's Niko?"

"Taking care of business." I take a sip of my drink.

"Something I should know about?"

"Mrs. Fiori won't be causing us any more problems."

"Dead?"

"Very." The image of Lucy deliberately, confidently pulling the trigger plays in my mind.

He nods. "Got something on Giovanni." He hands me a piece of paper from his jacket pocket.

I unfold the note, my heart rate ticking up a notch. There, in neat print, an address stares back at me. "He's here?"

"Solid intel from the Bratva. They say Giovanni's been using it as a safehouse." Liam goes to Niko's bar and pours a drink.

"Is it his?" I was sure we'd scouted all of Giovanni's properties.

"That's unclear at this time."

"Are we sure he's there?" I ask.

"Enough to bet on it."

I pull out my phone and call Niko. It rings once before the line clicks.

"*Talk to me,*" Niko's voice cuts through.

"Got a lead on Giovanni. Sending you coordinates now." I text him the address knowing it will be encrypted.

"*From whom?*"

"Liam. Says it's a Bratva tip."

"*I'll let the guys know to bring his wife to him there.*"

"That's what I thought too."

"*I'll be back shortly. See if Liam can't hang around until I get there. We need to figure out how to end this now.*"

"Will do."

The line goes dead, and I pocket the phone. Liam leans against the desk, his expression carved from stone, as usual. I wonder if the guy ever cracks a smile.

"Niko wants you to stay. He'll be back shortly."

He nods and sips his drink.

"What about Elena's friend?" Lou asks.

It takes me a minute to figure out who he's talking about.

Liam's eyes narrow. "What do you know about it?"

Lou looks at me, surprise in his expression at Liam's dark tone. Lou shrugs. "Just that the Boss was hoping Elena could have her friend back."

"Since when are you so invested in the woman?" I ask. Lou is always about the job. He once told me women were for fucking, not making a life with. They're too demanding and distracting.

He shrugs. "I just know it was something the Boss wanted."

Liam's jaw tightens. Before he responds, a sudden sound shatters the silence—a woman's voice echoing through the hall.

We all hurry to exit the office, hands instinctively moving to the guns holstered on our sides.

We immediately drop our hands as Aria Leone, Niko's little sister and only surviving family member, turns to us.

"Hey, there you are." Her tone carries a playful lilt. She was always the opposite of Niko's serious personality. Perhaps it's because she was the baby of the family. Or maybe it's because she's always been pampered and protected.

"Little sister doesn't knock?" I quip.

"Since when does family need to knock?" She jumps into my arms. "Don't tell me you're a grump now too, Uncle Donovan."

I laugh and give her a hug. "Never. Does Niko know you're here?"

She steps away. "It's a surprise." She turns to Liam. "Will you arrest me if I hug you too?"

"Maybe."

She laughs. "I'll risk it." She gives Liam a hug, which he reciprocates.

Then she turns to us. "I'm really peeved at my brother. I hear he got married and is going to be a father. He never said a word."

"Donovan's hitched too," Lou says, earning him a glare. My marriage isn't like Niko's. At least it's not supposed to be. My heart says what I feel for Lucy is as strong as what he feels for Elena.

Aria stares at me with wide eyes. "And you never said a word."

I shrug. "We've been preoccupied." It's a lousy excuse, and I wonder why Niko hasn't told her about his marriage and impending fatherhood. Then again, he's in the middle of a war with Giovanni Fiori, and Aria is supposed to be in Europe for her safety. Niko has to know she'd want to come home if he told her about Elena.

"Where is Niko?" she asks.

"Handling business," Liam answers

"Anything I should know about?" Despite Niko's attempt to keep her out of the loop, Aria is no stranger to the life we lead.

"No. And I suspect Niko isn't going to be too happy about your surprise visit."

She rolls her eyes like a teenager despite the fact that she's twenty-four. Or is it twenty-five? "Isn't that always the case?" There's a hint of rebellion in her tone.

Lou clears his throat. "I'm heading out. Got to check in with the uptown club."

I nod, letting him know he's free to go.

"Well, I'm going up to my room. Then I'm going to hunt down my new sisters." Aria grabs her suitcase and heads to the staircase.

Liam and I exchange glances.

"Something tells me we're in for quite a ride," Liam murmurs once she's out of earshot.

"More like a storm."

26

LUCIA

I'd felt numb as I left Donovan and headed up the stairs in the penthouse. It seemed like I should have felt relief that my mother is gone or horror that I killed her. Perhaps the two offset each other and that's why I felt nothing.

After taking a shower, I'm now making my way to Elena's room where Maria told me she was resting. But as I approach her door, nerves skitter along my skin. What will she think of me now that I killed our mother? A part of me considers taking Donovan up on the offer for him to take credit for it, but I quickly dismiss it. I can't demand to have control of my life and then not take responsibility for what I do.

I take a breath and knock on the door, opening it when she calls for me to come in. She sits in the window seat with a book and smiles when she sees me.

She stands and comes to give me a hug. "How was your honeymoon?"

The memory of Donovan touching me, making me feel whole and wanted, comes back, and I smile because it's a sweet memory.

She smirks. "I knew you and Donovan would get along."

I quickly push the image of me and Donovan and anything

beyond this arranged marriage away. "It's not like that, Elena. We had a lovely time, but we don't have anything like you and Niko have."

She rolls her eyes. "I wish you could let yourself be happy. I understand why you always had to be on your guard with Mom and Dad around. But it sounds like you didn't need to be like that in Italy, and you don't need to be like that here. Niko and Donovan are going to keep you safe."

I let out a sigh and take Elena's hand, tugging her over to the window seat where we both sit down.

"There's something I need to tell you."

Immediately, her expression turns to worry. "Are you all right? Is Donovan all right?"

"Yes, everything is fine. But you know that they are on a mission to kill Dad, right?"

She nods, and I study her face carefully, wanting to see if there's any hint that she is against the idea that our father needs to die.

Her hand rubs her belly, and I wonder if she's thinking about the car accident that could have hurt her babies. Our father had arranged the accident to kidnap us. Then he handed Elena over to Romeo Abate, a man with a violent reputation. A man she had to kill to save herself and her babies. So no, I don't think there is any love lost between her and my father.

"The problem is that he's in hiding. Finding him is proving more difficult than I think Niko and Donovan expected. But Mom, on the other hand, has been spending time in Atlantic City."

"She always did like to gamble." Elena's tone is hesitant, like she knows big news is coming and is trying to prepare.

"So we came up with a scheme to take her and find out where Dad is."

Her head tilts to the side. "By *we* do you mean you were involved?"

"Yes. I invited her to lunch and pretended that Niko and Donovan had kidnapped me and forced me into the marriage. But it was a ruse. We took her and brought her back to New York."

Elena's eyes watch mine, and I can see that she suspects that

Mom is no longer with us, but she doesn't know that I'm the cause of it.

"She wouldn't give up Dad." I look down as the memory of the way she talked to me, even though she was tied up, came back. The way I was nothing to her.

When I look up, I stare directly into Elena's eyes. "I suspect you know that she's dead now, and I need you to know, and hopefully, you won't hate me for it, but I'm the one who killed her."

Elena sucks in a breath. My own breath stalls as I wait to see how she's going to react.

She squeezes my hands. "I had to kill Romeo. It does something to you to kill somebody. Are you all right?"

I blink because that isn't what I was expecting. "My biggest concern is how you would take it. If you would be upset at me or maybe look at me differently."

She shakes her head. "I couldn't imagine that Niko would be able to exact his revenge without taking Mom as well. You're the most important person to me in our family. Mom and Dad... they weren't real parents. If you are okay, then I'm okay too. I know she was so much worse to you. And now, she's gone."

Elena wipes tears from my cheeks that I didn't realize I'm shedding.

The door flies open, and a woman about my age breezes into the room. I jump up and guard my sister.

"Okay, I'm here to meet the women who have stolen my brother and Uncle Donovan's hearts."

Did she say brother?

Elena stands, her expression looking delighted. "Are you Aria?"

"I am."

Elena rushes to her, giving her a hug. "I'm Elena."

When she pulls away, Aria looks at Elena's belly and shakes her head. "I was sure my brother wouldn't ever find his heart. Not only has he found it, but he's going to be a father." She turns to me. "And you must be Uncle Donovan's wife."

I'm not as gregarious as Elena or Aria, but I muster a smile and accept her hug. "I'm Lucia."

Aria tugs us both over to Elena's bed. "I'm so excited to meet you, even though I'm so mad at my brother for not telling me about you. How'd you meet?"

Elena's cheeks flush. I can't blame her. Does she really want to tell her new sister-in-law that she sold her virginity to Niko?

"Niko kidnapped her from her wedding," I say.

Aria's eyes widen. "No! Really?"

"I didn't want to marry the man I was supposed to marry," Elena quickly adds.

"And you? Did Donovan kidnap you too?" Her tone is teasing.

"As a matter of fact, he did," I answer.

She laughs. "Oh, my God, this is even better than I thought."

"What the fuck, Aria?"

We all turn to Niko bounding in the room with a scowl.

"Hello, Big Brother." Aria cheerfully rises and gives him a hug. He's irked, but I can see in his eyes that his concern for his sister is genuine.

"You're supposed to be in Europe."

"And you're supposed to tell me important news like... hmm... let's see... oh, I know. Like you're married and having twins." She pouts. "I didn't even get invited to the wedding."

He stares at her with pursed lips, clearly not caring that he upset her. "It's not safe to be here now."

"Fine. But if it's not safe for me, then it's not safe for them. They should come with me." She turns toward us. "I have a beautiful flat in Paris. Or, we could go to Marbella. Have you been to Spain?"

"They're not leaving," Niko says through gritted teeth.

Aria turns back to him. "Then neither am I." She smiles and pats his cheek. "Now, tell me why you kidnapped Elena from the altar?"

He grimaces.

I decide to give Elena and her new family some space. "I'll go get some refreshments."

"Oh, yes," Aria says with enthusiasm. "We have a lot to cover."

I leave the room and head down to the kitchen. I glance around looking for Donovan but don't see him. When I step into the kitchen, I'm surprised to see Liam. He's hunched over his phone looking bleak, although he always seems that way.

He lets out a low growl. "Fuck. Where is she?"

He's in the FBI, so he could be talking about anyone. But I suspect he's talking about Kate, especially since I know Niko asked if Kate could come out of Witness Protection for Elena.

"Is everything okay?" I ask. "Kate's all right?"

Liam looks up at me, and his expression is… pained is the only word that comes to mind. Maybe tortured is better.

"I've got to go," he says, leaving the kitchen.

I don't know what to make of Liam's behavior, but I shrug and set about getting drinks and snacks. Admittedly, I'm out of practice when it comes to girl talk. Elena and I used to stay up late and dream about a life away from our parents. But that ended when my father sent me to Giuseppe. I had a few female friends in Italy, but I was never close to them.

But I can see Aria and Elena are already fast friends, and I'm happy about that. My plan is to stay close to Elena from now on, but I also know that once my father is dead and Donovan annuls our marriage, there could be limits to when I can see her, so I'm glad that she'll have a woman like Aria around to help her.

My heart pinches at the idea of Aria being the sister I want to be, but that's life, right? I know firsthand that in the Mafia, personal hopes take a backseat to the orders of the Bosses.

As I approach Elena's room, I muster a smile to hide the sadness of realizing I'll be alone again.

27

LUCY

It's been two days since Aria arrived home. Two days since I killed my mother. To be honest, I'm a little surprised I don't feel different. I'm a murderer. I've become what I despised. I mentioned this to Elena, and she said she too thought that when she killed Romeo but knows now that it's not true. My situation is different, of course. Romeo was killed in physical self-defense. I was killed in mental and emotional self-defense. Or maybe it was physical too. Had the situation been reversed, my mother would have handed me over to my father and sold me to the highest bidder no matter how depraved the man was.

Today, I'm curled up on the plush sofa, reading a book. I read a lot in Italy when I wasn't caring for Giuseppe. It's nice to lose myself in fiction for once. I have the time because Elena is resting and Donovan is off plotting and preparing to kill my father while also managing business.

The sound of footsteps approaches, and I don't need to look up to know it's Donovan. The air shifts, turns electric with his presence. My irritation flares briefly at my reaction to him. It's a coping mechanism that I try to control now.

"They say truth is stranger than fiction." His voice is light, but I hear the undercurrent of concern. I resist the urge to smile, keeping my eyes locked on the page, pretending to be engrossed.

"You should know."

He chuckles, moving to sit opposite me, ankle crossing over knee. I peer at him over the top of my book, feigning annoyance yet secretly savoring the attention. And the view. Donovan is a good-looking man... strong, handsome, and sexy.

"You're not hiding, are you?" Again, his tone is light, but I know he's worried about me.

"No. Just taking a breath. Living a regular life."

I see a flash of something that almost looks like pain, but it vanishes before I decipher it. "You deserve a regular life after all you've been through. It won't be long now before you can be regular twenty-four, seven."

This time, I'm the one feeling pain because my regular life will be without Donovan. "Speaking of a regular life," I say, closing my book. "Elena has been telling me about all the plans Niko has for the twins. He seems quite eager to be a father."

"Ah, yes." His face softens, a smile tugging at his lips. "I wouldn't have believed Niko would fall in love and want kids if I hadn't watched it happen. I'm happy for him. And I know he'll make a good father."

I wonder if he says that to assure me that he won't be like my father. Niko has issues, but he's not a monster like my father.

"Elena won't let him be otherwise," I say.

Donovan laughs. "The Fiori women are a force, that's for sure."

I study Donovan, realizing I don't know his thoughts on marriage and children. Had he planned to be a bachelor forever? Does he believe in love?

"Have you ever thought about having children?" The question escapes before I can consider the wisdom of it.

Donovan blinks like I caught him off guard. The silence stretches between us, and it makes me feel vulnerable. Like I've revealed too much, especially since Donovan's expression is unreadable. I regret asking the question and get ready to take it back, but Maria appears, and behind her, Luca barges in.

"What the fuck, Donovan?"

I'm taken aback by Luca's anger.

Donovan slowly rises. "Careful, Luca."

"You married her?" Luca glances at me and then back at him. "Why wasn't I informed?"

"It's none of your business." Donovan's tone is flat, dismissive.

"It is my business. Lucia is my business." Luca strides into the room, not afraid of Donovan. Why should he be? He's a Boss in his own right. His story is no different from Donovan's or Niko's where crime and violence are concerned. "She's a Conti—"

"Now she's a Ricci."

"You know that I'm in the room." I'm getting irritated that they're talking about me like they own me.

Donovan's jaw tenses. It's a reminder that he's bent over backward to go against his instinct when it comes to me. He's told me more than once that he can force me to do whatever he wants. I hate it, but until my father's dead, he's right. The only power I have is what Donovan allows, and I have to admit, he allows a fair amount.

I rise from the couch. A moment ago, it was a quiet sanctuary. Now, I'm in the middle of a war. "Luca, I'm sorry you weren't informed."

"I promised my father I'd look out for you."

"I know, and I appreciate how much you honor your vow."

"We did what we had to do so that Lucy could stay here with her sister. You knew that's what she wanted," Donovan says. His words are a reminder that our marriage is one of convenience. All so I could be with my sister and hopefully take away my value to my father.

Luka's hands clench into fists. "I should have been informed."

"I'm sorry you weren't," I say again, and I look to Donovan, hoping he reads in my expression that he needs to tone it down.

A sudden movement catches my eye, and Aria enters the living room. "It sounds like World War Three in here."

Luca glances at her and then does a double-take.

She smiles and holds out her hand. "I'm Aria Leone."

He takes it, his gaze going to their entwined hands and then to her face. "Luca Conti. *Piacere di conoscerti.*"

"Oh, a true Italian." Her eyes light up in delight. "I'm sorry to say my Italian isn't very good."

"Then I will speak English."

She continues to smile as she looks from him to me while extricating her hand from his. "What's going on?"

"Luca is the son of my deceased husband," I explain.

She turns to him. "She's married to Uncle Donovan now. You can't take her."

"It's my duty to honor my father's wishes to look after her." Luca's tone has changed. It's gentler, friendlier. I note how his eyes have softened and are zeroed in on Aria. He's captivated by her. I hope it passes, because I'm not sure Niko is ready for his sister to be involved with a man.

"That's sweet. But she's with us now." Her phone rings. "Oh, I've got to get this. *Ciao.*" She's practically out the door when Luca responds with *Ciao.*

His gaze stays on the entryway long after she's passed through it. I glance at Donovan, wondering if he's noticed.

"She's off limits." Donovan answers my question.

Luca turns back to us. A hint of pink shades his cheeks at being caught.

"Now, if we've settled everything—"

"Can you be sure Lucia is safe? I can see how Niko's wife is safe as Niko is the Boss. But you... will he think Lucia is untouchable married to you?"

Donovan's eyes narrow. "Let him try and take what's mine and he'll find just how untouchable she is."

The woman in me enjoys hearing the fierceness in his voice. The feminist in me is annoyed that I'm again a thing.

"You can rest assured, Luca, that Lucy will be protected by me for as long as she needs or wants it."

Luca looks at me. "You're okay with this?"

I nod.

He puts his hands on his hips and turns away as if he's thinking. Finally, he looks back at us. "All right, then." He pauses for a moment. "But I wouldn't underestimate Giovanni. And I did promise my father that I'd make sure you were all right—"

"She's not your responsibility anymore," Donovan asserts.

"A vow is a vow." Luca's tone suggests he's not going to budge. "I assume your goal is to remove the threat."

"Of course."

"I can help. I must help to fulfill my father's wishes. The last thing he wanted was for Lucia to end up under her father's control again."

I look at Donovan. "You can't have too much help when it comes to my father."

Donovan's eyes are hard. He doesn't want to accept Luca's help. But he's also smart and practical. "All right. I'm sure Niko will appreciate any help you can offer."

Luca shifts, studying me. "And when the threat is gone, what will you do, Lucia?"

I swallow because I know the answer is to stay with Elena until the twins are born and then likely return to Italy.

"One thing at a time, Luca," Donovan says, looking at me with that expression I can't decipher.

"Just remember, you have a home in Italy."

"Thank you." I smile, but deep down, I know my home is here.

28

DONOVAN

Luca makes his exit, and it's not a moment too soon. All I can see is him with his arms around Lucy. Is that why he's pissed? Because I married her instead of him? Doesn't he see how creepy it is to want his stepmother? Or maybe it's not desire. Perhaps it's duty. He did take a long look at Aria. God, if Niko were here, we'd be figuring out how to dispose of Luca's body.

"You keep forgetting you don't own me." Lucy pulls me from my tangled thoughts.

"You keep forgetting that I do until your father is dead. Then if you want to go to Luca, you can." My chest is caving in at that idea. I can hardly breathe.

She lets out an exasperated breath. "I want to stay… with Elena."

With Elena. Right. Not with me. Not with the man she calls a toady. It reminds me of what a fool I was to think her question about having babies was code for she wanted them with me. "Then you have to live by the rules. You know that."

I hate how her eyes dim. "I do. I guess I should thank you."

"Why? You wouldn't mean it." I'd come to find her today needing to see her. Why is this conversation devolving into a pissing contest?

She looks down. "I do mean it. I know I'm only here because of you."

I study her, wishing I could read her mind. "I meant what I said to Luca. As long as you need or want me, I'm here." Protecting her isn't just a duty anymore. It's a need that's as important as breath.

She looks at me, and I really wish I knew what was going on in that stubborn head of hers. For long moments, we stand like that. Slowly, the air between us charges and my irritation morphs into desire.

I reach out my hand. Relief washes through me when she takes it. I tug her close and look into those dark eyes that I want to lose myself in. "Are you all right? I don't mean about Luca. I mean about your mother."

She nods. "Surprisingly so. I should feel guilt or—"

"Why? You may not have died, but she killed you, parts of you, most of your life."

Lucy looks at me in a way that makes me feel like I'm her hero, which is odd because she's clear she doesn't need one. I dip my head and kiss her. It's fifty-fifty whether she'll allow it. Her fingers clutch my shirt as she opens for me, letting me take the kiss deeper.

When I pull back, I take her hand and lead her to my room, shutting and locking the door behind us.

"I know you hate this, but whatever it takes, I'm here. With you." It's as close as I can get to telling her the feelings that are overflowing my heart. "For as long as you want."

"Donovan, I—"

"Shh." I stop her because I don't want to hear her protests or to be reminded that this will all be over as soon as her father is dead. I kiss her to stop any further attempt to talk. My hands undress her, taking in the smooth silkiness of her skin, her sweet, spicy scent.

Heat sears through my veins as need explodes. Her hands find their way into my hair, tugging me closer as if she could pull me inside her soul. If only she would. I'd willingly go.

There's nothing tame about the way she kisses back, nothing

hesitant. Not anymore. Now, she's all fire and need, matching my own desperation.

I shift, wrapping an arm around her waist to draw her flush against me, feeling the rapid beat of her heart against my chest. It syncs with mine, and it drives me crazy that we're so perfect and yet can't ever be. Not in the long run, anyway. But I push those thoughts aside. She's here now, and so now, I'll savor the moment.

A low moan rises from deep within her, fueling my hunger. The tether on my control loosens. Need drives me mad as I push her back on the bed and frantically remove our clothes. I'm not gentle. I'm not tender. I'm a man who desperately wants to claim this woman. I want to make sure she never forgets me.

I push her legs apart and drive into her. Into what's mine.

She cries out, arches into me, and something inside me snaps. I still. My breath comes in pants as I look down at her. Fucking hell, how I love her.

She looks up at me, her eyes clouded by passion. The words I want to say to her hang on the tip of my tongue. But I swallow them. Instead, I kiss her and take my time to love her with my body. Slow caresses. Hot kisses. Does she feel it? Can she feel my love?

"Donovan." My name comes out in a sigh. It's the most I'll ever hear of her feelings for me.

I withdraw and sink in, only then realizing I don't have a condom on. Fuck.

I stop moving and close my eyes. It takes all my strength to not make love to her, to empty my soul into her. And if she became pregnant, well then, she'd have to stay, right? But if I've learned one thing from Lucy, it's that she hates life being dictated to her.

"Lucy... fuck..." I start to pull away. Her eyes look at me in confusion as her legs hold my hips to her. "I don't have a condom on, baby." I let out a frustrated growl as need claws at me.

"Oh... right." She releases me.

"I do want kids someday." The words tumble out without warning.

"You do?"

I take a hard look into her eyes, wanting to know, to understand what she's thinking and feeling. I swear to God, I see myself in their depths. *It's time*, I tell myself. It's time to tell her that I love her. That I don't want her to go. That I want to fuck her, and if we make a baby, my life will be complete.

The moment is shattered by the shrill ring of my phone.

"Fuck." I look down at her, for the first time in my life, hating my job. "I'm sorry, baby." I disentangle from Lucy. My dick shrivels as I hunt my phone out of my pants pocket. "Yeah."

There's a pause. *"Everything all right?"* Niko asks.

Fuck, no. "Fine. What's up?"

"Giovanni. It's time. Let's go get him." Niko's voice is tinged with excitement. Lucy isn't the only one who seeks vengeance through Giovanni's death.

I glance at Lucy, my heart aching. I have to go. I have to finish this for Niko and her. But when I do, the reason she's bound to me ceases to exist.

"Understood," I say once I get the details. I hang up and begin to dress.

"Is everything okay?" Lucy's voice is laced with concern, her eyes searching mine for answers I don't want to give.

"Yep."

"Tell me," she insists, sitting up. Her beautiful, naked body is exposed, and all I want to do is bury myself in her. Forever.

"Nothing you need to worry about," I lie smoothly, hating my cowardice.

But maybe it's not too late. Maybe when Giovanni is dead, I can tell her the truth. I can ask her to stay. Her choice, just like she'd want. "Stay here. I'll be back."

I kiss her one last time, a promise, a goodbye—I'm not sure which since it will be up to her.

29

LUCIA

The memory of our bodies entwined lingers. Donovan's touch had been urgent, his gaze searing into me with an intensity that seemed more than just desire. Or that's what I hope I saw.

This aching is unbearable, and I've decided I need to tell him how I'm feeling. It's possible he'll still want the annulment. But maybe he won't. As much as I'm terrified to find out, I have to know.

But after hours of waiting for him to return, worry grows. The bedside clock reads 2:37 AM. I've only managed to snatch moments of restless sleep as Donovan's face haunts my dreams. I have no doubt there are times he works late, but even so, he or Niko always manages a call or a text. Tonight? Nothing. I've called, but no answer and no return call after leaving a voicemail. Nearly an hour ago, I texted, and still no response.

"Lucy?" Elena's soft voice pulls me away from the screen.

I set the phone on the nightstand. "Hey, is something wrong? It's late." I force a smile, not wanting her to know about my concern.

"Have you heard from Donovan?" She sits on the bed tentatively, like she's in discomfort.

"No. But I know he and Niko are off doing something."

"Dad?"

"Probably. I don't know." But because I think it involves my father, I'm extra worried. The last time Donovan ran into my father, he'd been shot.

I work to hide my fears so as not to concern Elena. "I'm sure they'll be back or in touch soon."

Her face crumples, and at first I think it's worry. But then I realize she's in pain.

"Elena. What's wrong?" I clamber out of bed.

"It's cramps."

"That's not normal, is it?" I wish I had paid more attention at the doctor's office.

"I don't think so." The pain seems to have subsided, but now her tears fall. "I don't know what to do, and Niko isn't picking up when I call."

I'm on my feet, slipping on the first clothes I reach. Then I'm on the phone, using the system to intercom Maria's room. When she answers, I tell her to come up to my room. I don't give her a reason, but I know she'll come. It's her job.

Moments later, she's in a house-dress and shoes. I wonder if she keeps clothes by her bed, like firemen do.

"Elena is having cramps."

Maria immediately understands the crisis.

"We need to take her to the hospital, but Niko and Donovan are working. I need you to help us arrange whatever security we need," I tell her.

"Why don't I call Doc? He can—"

"I don't want to risk that something serious is going on. The twins aren't due for months. She needs all the resources from the hospital."

"I'll call down." Maria picks up the phone to contact Niko's men in the garage to prepare a car.

Elena lets out a moan and lies on my bed, curling into a fetal position. Her face contorts into pain.

I sit by her. "Can you get up? We're going to the hospital." I brush damp strands of hair from her forehead as I make a silent prayer that she and her twins will be okay.

"What's going on?" Aria stands at the threshold of my room, concern showing in her dark eyes.

"Help me get her to the car." My words come out as a command rather than a plea. I imagine Niko wouldn't like me bossing his sister around, but right now, I don't have time to be polite.

"Of course. What's wrong?" Aria steps forward, and we help Elena sit up, and then, each taking a side, we help Elena stand.

"She's not well."

"Where's Niko? Or Donovan?" Aria asks.

"Working."

"They've been gone a long time without a word," Elena says, her body hunched over, making it difficult to help her.

"Don't worry about my brother. He's invincible." I'm not sure if Aria is trying to lessen the seriousness of the situation or if she truly believes Niko is Superman.

"Let me call again." I let Elena go and grab my phone off the table.

"Let me call," Aria says. "Maria, can you help Elena get downstairs?"

I wrap my arm around Elena and hand the phone to Aria. "If you don't get Donovan or Niko, call Liam," I say, and then Maria and I assist Elena out of the bedroom and slowly descend the stairs.

It seems to take forever, but finally, we reach the foyer. From here it's the elevator down to the garage where hopefully, a car awaits.

Elena's hand is cold in mine. It sends a chill down my spine. I've killed my mother. My father is next. Elena is all I have left.

A click from the elevator door sends my hopes soaring that Niko or Donovan is returning home. I make a mental note to give them hell for not calling or checking their phone for calls or texts after Elena is at the hospital.

The elevator doors slide open and Lou steps out. Not who I want to see, but he'll do. He's Donovan's trusted friend. Maybe he has news of what Niko and Donovan are up to.

He stops short, as if he isn't expecting to see us. Of course he isn't. It's past two in the morning.

"Elena needs to go to the hospital. Do you know where Niko is?" I ask.

He stares at me blankly, and my relief at seeing him quickly morphs into concern. Something isn't right. He looks disheveled and confused. Terror shoots through me that perhaps he's a lone survivor and Niko and Donovan are dead.

"Lou!" I bark out to get his attention. "Where are Niko and Donovan?"

His eyes narrow at me. In them, I see a menace that has me holding Elena and Maria back.

"Is Niko with you?" Elena's voice trembles, and I'm not sure if she can see how off Lou seems or if it's from her fear about the babies.

Time slows as his hand moves, drawing out a gun. My breath stalls as I contemplate what's happening. Lou holds up the gun, the barrel pointed at my head.

My pulse hammers. I've been scared a lot in my life, but this time, I'm truly terrified. Lou's dark eyes are devoid of any hint that he is loyal to the Leone Family, that he's a trusted friend to Donovan.

The air between us crackles with anticipation as I wait for what's coming. Maria is praying. Elena is crying, and by the way she bends forward, she's also having another cramp.

"What's going on, Lou?" Is he on drugs? Has he been brainwashed? Or is he a traitor?

He says nothing, and I decide that the latter option is the more likely answer. And if he's a traitor, it has to mean he's in with my father. If I'm right about that, then he wants me.

"Are you working for my dad?"

He sneers, and I wonder why he's not talking.

"Then take me. I'm what he wants, right? Take me and let Elena and Maria go." I realize that Aria hasn't come downstairs yet, and I hope that means she's reached Niko or Donovan. I also hope it means she stays put.

I nod my head up and down, as if that will get his agreement. "Let them go, okay? I'll stay right here."

Upstairs, I hear movement. "Lucy?" Aria's voice echoes down the stairs.

Lou's attention snaps upstairs. I'm dead anyway, so I use the distraction to my advantage. I spring, using my weight and hopefully the element of surprise to tackle him. He turns to me, but it's too late. My hands are already on him, pushing, unbalancing him. He takes a step back, but his center of gravity is off. He falls back. I fall with him, landing hard, my chin hitting the bone of his chest, making my teeth rattle. I hear what I hope is the gun skittering along the floor.

He pushes at me, but I grab on, wondering how I'll ever overpower him. I won't. I'm thrown like a ragdoll, landing on my side, a blast of pain radiating through my shoulder.

"Get back, motherfucker," Aria's voice bellows through the room.

I shake my head of the stars floating around and see her standing over him, holding the gun in shaking hands. She had to have flown down the stairs to reach us.

I stand, wobble a moment.

"Oh, God, Luce, are you okay?" Elena cries out to me.

"Yes." I go to Aria. "Let me have the gun. I'll deal with this." I look at her, hoping she sees in my eyes what needs to be done and that I'm willing to do it.

Her head nods, and she hands me the gun.

Lou moves to stand, but I kick him where it counts.

"You fucking cunt!" he yells, grabbing at his dick.

"I'll blow it off if you move again."

I turn to Maria and Elena. "Get in the elevator. Now. Aria, help them."

Aria pokes the button and waves Elena and Maria toward them. Maria nods, her face ashen, while Elena's lips press into a thin line. It occurs to me that my father wanted to raise docile, subservient women, but Elena and I are strong.

I turn my attention to Lou. "You know I'm not afraid to use this, right? Donovan told you what I did to my mother."

"Go fuck yourself."

"Where are Donovan and Niko?"

He sneers at me. "I hope your father sells you to someone who loves S-and-M."

"Maybe he will. Where is he?" If Donovan and Niko are in trouble, chances are it's because of my father.

"I'm not telling you nothing."

I look at him in disgust. "Fine." I fire a bullet into his head. I wait a moment, to make sure he's dead, and then I stride toward the elevator. Aria is holding the door while Elena and Maria stand in the back.

I poke the button for the garage. "Is everyone okay?"

"Thanks to you," Aria says.

"And you, Ari." Elena puts her hand on Aria's arm. "The way you got that gun."

I nod. "Thank God you did."

When the doors open again, we spill into the underground garage. I go first because I don't know whether Lou has accomplices.

One of Niko's men steps into our path. We gasp, and I hold up the gun.

He raises his hands in surrender. "Is there a problem, Mrs. Ricci?"

"Who do you work for?" I demand.

He looks at me like I've grown a horn on my head. "Don Leone."

"Did you let Lou up?"

He nods. "He said he was sent to protect you."

"He tried to kill me."

"What the fuck?" Another of Niko's men steps into the light.

"Do you know where Niko and Donovan are?" I ask, hoping the adrenaline keeps pumping because it's the only thing keeping me from losing it.

"Somewhere in New Jersey, but we don't have the details."

"Is our car ready? I've got to get Elena to the hospital."

"Yes. I'll drive—"

I wave the gun at him. "I'll drive. We go alone. I can't trust anyone right now."

"Niko won't like it."

"Yeah, well, Niko isn't here."

He nods to an SUV running and waiting for us.

"Get in, Ladies."

Maria helps Elena get in the back seat. Aria climbs into the passenger seat. As I slide into the vehicle, I catch the men's eyes in the rearview mirror. They're watching us, looking uncertain.

Elena moans and bends over again. That's my cue to get going.

"Won't be long now, Elena." I doubt I sound reassuring. The car glides forward, and my eyes dart everywhere. Every sense is heightened, looking for potential threats.

As I come up toward the reinforced metal door, it starts to rise. A flicker of movement on the other side of it catches my eye. The gate ascends, revealing a man standing in the drive, his gun pointed at us. My pulse spikes as a new threat descends on us. I slam my foot down on the accelerator, not sure we have the headroom to exit the garage without hitting the bottom of the gate. The SUV lurches forward.

"Hold on," I call out.

A shot rings out, followed by the sickening thud of the vehicle hitting his body. The left wheels rise as I roll over him.

My passengers let out a scream.

"It's okay," I say even though I'm not sure it is. Maybe leaving without more protection is unwise. But it's too late now. I press harder on the gas, and we burst out of the garage and into the streets.

It's true that New York is a city that doesn't sleep, but at nearly three in the morning, it's quieter than during the day. I'm able to navigate through the streets toward the hospital with few cars in the way.

Elena's breathing hitches.

"Hold on, Elena. Do you hear me?"

"I'm okay." But her voice is weak. Whether it's from the cramping or fear, I don't know. At this point, all that matters is getting her to a doctor. My grip on the wheel tightens, my knuckles white as I navigate the city.

"Almost there—" The words are cut off by the sound of crumpling metal as another vehicle rams into us. I hold tight to the steering wheel as the SUV lurches. Screams fill the interior of the car. I work to steady us, pressing on the gas, but we're hit again. I counter steer, praying to regain control as the SUV jerks and rocks.

Just as I'm about to make a right turn that I hope will give us some breathing room, we're hit again. The SUV skids. The steering wheel rips from my grip. We're jostled as the SUV bounces up, likely on the curb. Then it comes to an abrupt stop, but my body keeps moving, my head hitting the steering wheel, dazing me.

All I can think is that we're all going to die. To be honest, maybe it will be nice to be dead. No more grief and chaos. I only wish I'd saved Elena and told Donovan that I love him.

30

DONOVAN

Awareness creeps in. My eyes open and a dim, dark room greets me. I blink, trying to scrub the darkness from my vision. My head pounds, but it's from the inside, like a headache, not the outside like a hit on the head.

Where the fuck am I, and how did I get here? I try to rise from the chair I'm in, only to find my wrists bound behind me, the bite of zipties cutting into skin.

With effort, my focus sharpens. To my left, Niko sits slumped in his chair, his eyes closed. I watch and note his chest rising and falling with a steady rhythm.

"Niko," I whisper harshly. No response. He's out cold.

I scan the room further. On the other side of Niko sits Liam. His eyes are wide open. Being tied up, I knew something was up, but the fact that the three of us, Niko's highest-ranking soldiers, are in a bind, so to speak, is a whole different thing. It suggests we got sloppy.

"You all right?" Liam asks.

"I'm alive. Which is more than I can say for the motherfucker who put us here when I get my hands on him." I want to rub my temple as it feels like the dull pain is preventing me from remembering what happened. "What's going on? Last thing I remember, we were driving to meet with one of Giovanni's men. Lou was at the wheel." I look around. "Where is Lou?" A memory flitters into my consciousness about Liam. "You called... warned us of a trap."

"Igor is going after Lucy," Liam says.

"What?" My heart stalls.

"I didn't know, Donovan. He's got Kate too." With that, Liam thrashes like a wild animal.

Me? I'm thinking it's time to get the fuck out of here. No one is touching Lucy. Not as long as I have breath.

"What the fuck?" Niko's head shakes as he winces.

"Welcome back, Brother," I say.

We sit quietly, listening, regrouping.

"What do we know?" Niko finally asks.

I repeat that he and I were going to Jersey to deal with Giovanni after a call from Igor who said his guys were raiding Giovanni's location. I also mention that Lou is missing.

"If he's not here, he's likely dead." Fucking shame. Lou was a good friend.

"Or in on it," Liam quips.

"Lou?" I lean forward to look at him, wondering why he'd say that.

"You asked about Kate coming out of Witpro, so I started the process, but someone beat me to it." Liam lets out a growl. "Or I led them to her. Fuck." He starts jerking around frantically, trying to free himself again.

I glance at Niko, thinking Liam's distress over Kate seems a bit more than losing a witness.

Liam settles for a moment. "She dropped off the radar. I've been looking for her, but in the meantime, a cousin of mine let me know there's turmoil in Bratva."

"Where do you suppose we are?" Niko asks.

"Could it be the warehouse?" I offer. "Maybe Giovanni wants to kill us where we dumped his wife on his doorstep. Or could be

Bratva. Sounds like Igor is a fucking traitor if he's after Lucy and Kate."

"So, does that mean Giovanni has us, or Igor?" Niko asks.

"Could be both." Liam thrashes again.

"Fuck!" Niko barks. "I should have gone full-out war, not this stealthy shit. We don't have backup."

"We shouldn't have walked into their trap." I don't say it, but it's the second time this has happened. But how?

Or Lou is in on it. Liam's words come back to me. I close my eyes as I'm forced to consider that my friend, the man I brought into the Family, is a traitor. Lou was the one who was supposed to check Ugly Eddy for tracking devices the night Giovanni ambushed us and I got shot. The other day, Lou asked about Kate during a meeting with Liam, which seemed odd at the time. Lou was with us when we first met with Igor.

A new memory filters through. An image of Lou putting on a mask in the car as we arrived. Him twisting a small canister open, and a scent, sweet and cloying, filling the car. Then everything went dark.

"Son of a bitch." My voice comes out a growl as betrayal burns in my gut.

"Who?" Niko asks.

"Lou. He was in on it." I'm pissed that I didn't see it. Then a new fear jolts through me. "Fucking hell."

"What?" Niko asks.

"Lou can get into the penthouse."

"What are you saying?" Niko's voice goes cold.

"Igor and Giovanni want Lucy. Lou can walk right into the penthouse and get her." Terror like I've never felt before fills me. Followed by guilt at not having told her how I really feel. "If he hurts her, I'll chop him up, inch by inch, while he's alive. Goddammit." Lucy. She won't ever know that she is loved. That she is seen and respected.

"Lucy's strong," Liam says. The words are meant to reassure, but they don't.

"Strong doesn't mean invincible." Did I leave her a gun? "Fuck. If I fail her—"

"You won't." Niko's eyes narrow at me. "Do you suppose you'll ever admit that you're in love with your wife?"

I glare at him. "Now? I have more important things to do than discuss my love life. Are you going to ask Liam about Kate?"

"What are you talking about? That gas must have fogged your brain." Liam doth protest too much.

"I'm just saying that if you and Lucia are in love, I'm happy for you, Donovan."

Yeah, well, that doesn't mean that if I survive and take out Giovanni, she'll stay. But if I do survive, I will lay it all on the line for her.

"This is all nice and well, but there's no happily ever after for you two lovesick puppies if we don't get out of here." Liam tugs at his restraints again.

We sit in silence for a moment. My hands test the bonds once more. I realize they're zip-ties. I can get out of these.

"Tonight, it ends, one way or another," I say as I get ready to stand and snap the ties that hold my wrists together.

A sound comes from the other side of the door.

"Did you hear that?" Liam hisses.

Niko and I cock our heads to listen further.

The door opens, and a man enters, stopping just beyond the reach of the dim light. The only thing I can see clearly is the semi-automatic pistol in his hand.

Finally, he steps into the light. Igor.

He steps in front of Liam and sneers. "Not such a big shot now, are you, comrade?"

"You think you are a big shot?" Liam laughs. "*Ti nikto.* You're nothing, *comrade.*"

Igor's eyes narrow, clearly not liking being called nothing. He collects himself and shakes his head. "I don't understand you. You could have been the Boss, but you joined the FBI? I thought that made you untouchable, but then you go to work for the Mafia? I don't care that others want you back in Bratva. You're a traitor."

"I'm a traitor? Really?" Liam scoffs. "You're Bratva working for Giovanni Fiori. What does that make you?"

"It's an alliance," Igor hisses. "Your Boss asked for one, if I remember correctly."

Liam shrugs. "Does Dimitri know about it?"

"Shut up." Igor hits Liam with the butt of his gun.

"Just tell us what the fuck you want," Niko barks out.

Igor turns his attention to Niko. "Nothing from you. I'm just babysitting until Giovanni is finished with Liam's little friend. She'll make a pretty penny on the—"

"If you touch her, I will guarantee you a long and painful death," Liam hisses.

"How does Lou fit in?" I ask, needing to know whether he was a part of this betrayal for sure.

Igor moves to me, his sneer filled with too much victory for my taste. I want to punch it off his face. "I'm sorry to say that Lou is with us. And by now, he's killed the Fiori women."

Fury like I'd never felt before rushes through me, making me feel invincible. I stand. Bending over, I lift my arms off my back and bring them down hard, breaking the restraint. Igor points his gun at me, but I don't stop. I rush him, tackling him as the gun goes off. If he hit me, I don't feel it.

I'm vaguely aware that Liam and Niko have broken free, and just in time as Igor's men rush in. I wrench Igor's gun from his hand, making sure I break his wrist as I do so. I lift it and shoot at the men coming in. Chaos erupts. Niko and Liam grab guns from the men I've shot, and then we're all shooting and swinging fists until none of Igor's men have breath.

When the dust settles, we're scraped and bruised, Niko has a superficial wound where a bullet grazed him, but overall, we're okay. Certainly, much better than the dead men at our feet. Except for Igor, who is writhing in pain.

Liam hauls him up. "I will make sure Bratva knows of your gallant cowardice." Then, stepping behind Igor, Liam takes Igor's head in his hands and torques it hard. A crunch sounds, and Igor drops to the floor boneless, dead.

"Elena," Niko says as he picks up a second gun and rushes to the door.

I grab another gun as well and follow him. I'm not a good Catholic, but I pray that when I see Lucy again, she'll be alive.

31

LUCIA

I can't afford to panic. We've run into a traffic light, but I think I'm okay. I whip my head around. "Are you okay?"

Elena, Aria, and Maria are rattled, but unharmed. Well, except for Elena, who seems to be having another cramp.

A movement outside the car snags my attention. Through the side rearview mirror, a man strides toward us with a gun in his hand.

"Shh," I command, my gaze never leaving the approaching threat. "Get down."

My fingers fumble beneath the seat as I give a silent prayer for Lou's gun to be where I left it. My hand wraps around it just as the door flies open. Instinctively, I turn in my seat, the gun pointing at the man, and I fire.

His shoulder jerks back, a pained grunt escaping him as his gun clatters to the ground. I push the door open hard, hitting him and making him stumble back.

I exit the car and hold the gun on him. "Stay back."

He growls at me as he holds his shoulder. "Bitch!"

"Why are you after us?"

He glances at the gun on the ground.

"Don't think about it," I warn.

Aria comes around the SUV and snatches his gun from the ground. She points it at the man. "He won't fuck with us now."

I'm beginning to think Aria and I make quite the team tonight.

"Who are you? Where's Donovan?"

He chuckles, a sick sound that makes me want to shoot it off his face. "I'm not afraid of a woman." He spits out the words in a Russian accent. I think back to Donovan saying they were aligning with the Bratva. Did something go wrong?

"That's because you're an idiot." My finger itches against the trigger, but I don't fire as I think he could be the key to finding out where Niko and Donovan are.

"Don't need to be smart to know women are pussies."

"Women *have* pussies. A real man would know the difference. Clearly, you've never had one or you'd know that." I aim my gun lower to his groin. "Maybe I'll make sure you never have one."

Instinctively, his hand covers his dick, as if that would stop a bullet. "You don't scare me."

"I should. I killed my own mother just the other day. And your buddy Lou? Well, as you can see, he failed. He's dead in the foyer."

He glares at me, but I see a flash of reality hitting his brain.

"Where's Don Leone?" Maybe using Niko's status will instill the gravity of the situation into him.

He shrugs.

"Wrong answer." I step closer, raising the gun to head level.

Aria moves closer to me, holding the gun steady on our Russian attacker. "Lucy, Elena needs—"

"Check this asshole's car for something to tie him up." I can't waste any more time. Elena needs a hospital.

Aria nods and dashes away. She returns moments later, zip-ties in hand.

"Maria, come help," I command. I don't want to give this guy any opportunity to overpower me and take the gun. "Use two or three so he can't break free." Maria and Aria secure his hands while I hold the gun in front of his face.

Once he's restrained, we force him into his car and I strap him in the seat belt, making it harder for him to move.

It occurs to me that with cameras everywhere, police should be arriving soon. I'm not sure whether that would be problematic. It could help Elena get the care she needs. But then I decide that it will prevent me from finding out what's going on with Donovan and Niko.

"Is the SUV still drivable?" I ask Aria, watching Elena clutch at her side.

"Let me check." Aria slips into the driver's seat. She's surprisingly calm for a woman whom Niko has sheltered for so long. The engine coughs then comes alive. She puts it in gear and backs away from the traffic light. "Yes, it'll move."

"Take Elena to the hospital. Maria will help you."

"What are you going to do?" Aria asks.

"I'm going make this asshole take me to Donovan." Because I know that's a dumb idea that could lead to my demise, I go to the back of the SUV and open the door where Elena is sitting. She's trying to be strong, but I see the fear. "I'm going to find Niko and Donovan, okay?"

Elena reaches for me, her fingers trembling. "It's too dangerous."

"Hey." I take her hand and squeeze it. "It's time to be strong. For Niko, for the babies. I love you. I know whatever happens, you and the babies will be well loved and cared for."

Her eyes brim with tears, and she nods, understanding the weight of my goodbye.

Turning to Aria, I see steely resolve that makes me feel okay to entrust her with Elena. "Be good to her, Aria. If something happens to me, be the sister I can't."

"I will," Aria promises. She jumps out of the driver's seat and gives me a hug. "Please find my brother and Uncle Donovan."

I hug her back. "I plan on it."

With one last glance at my sister, I turn back to the man's SUV, getting in the driver's seat. I press the muzzle of my gun against his temple. "Where is my husband?"

He shrugs. I put the gun to his knee and fire.

He cries out, followed by a string of curses. Or I think they're curses. I don't speak Russian.

"Let's try this again. Where is my husband? Oh... and you only have two more chances. The third shot will be in your brain."

He's breathing hard and staring at me with murderous hate. "Jersey."

"Jersey's a big state. Lots of territory," I say, referring to organized crime sections, not the land itself.

He tells me the location, and I put the car in gear, heading to the Holland Tunnel. We have a drive ahead of us. At least two hours. I drive with my right hand, holding the gun in my left, which isn't my dominant hand, but it's further away from him if he tries anything.

Hours later, on the outskirts of Atlantic City, I pull into a lone warehouse parking lot. The area is dark since the sun won't be up for another hour or so.

"He's here?" Nerves have me darting my gaze around. The place is quiet. It appears empty.

"The girl is here."

Confusion lances through me. "What girl?" My mind races, trying to piece together this puzzle.

He shrugs.

Perhaps it's related to my father's trafficking business. But Donovan told me Liam was going to shut it down. Did he lie? Was Donovan here running my father's business? Had he negotiated with Bratva to partner in it?

"Where's your phone?" I ask.

He looks away. I take the gun and point it at his other knee.

"Fuck you. The console."

I flip up the lid and turn on the phone. I hold it up to his face to unlock it and then scroll through his list of contacts searching for any clue as to who this man works for. I'm relieved when I don't see Donovan's name, followed by guilt for questioning him.

I stare at him. "Who are you really working for?"

"Go to hell."

I consider shooting him, but on the off chance I still need him, I whap him with the butt of the gun, twice, before he slumps in the seat.

I'm going to die. Even so, I exit the car and stride into the warehouse. At first, I note that it's mostly empty. But then I see them and I stop short.

My father stands over Kate, who's tied to a chair and sobbing.

"You're not as valuable as my Lucia was, but she's dead now. You'll do as compensation." Giovanni sneers. His back is to me, oblivious to my approach. "You'll fetch a nice price."

"Father." My voice echoes through the building.

He whirls around. The shock on his face morphs quickly into rage. "Lucia? You're supposed to be dead."

"Sorry to disappoint you again."

His gun turns on me, but I fire first. The sound ricochets off the warehouse walls. He stumbles backward, his face contorted with shock. But he quickly recovers, lifting his gun toward me. I fire again, and he falls to the ground, his hand on his chest as blood oozes through his fingers.

I move to him, picking up his gun. Then I turn to Kate, who's gone quiet and is pale. "Give me a minute and I'll untie you."

Her head bobs up and down.

I stand over my father. "How does it feel to have no control? To have your life in someone else's hands?"

"You won't kill me."

"Haven't you heard? I'm the one who killed Mother."

His eyes widen in surprise. Then he laughs. "You're like her, you know. Bloodthirsty. Power hungry."

I shake my head. "I'm willing to kill, yes, but I'm not bloodthirsty. I have a heart. I'm capable of love." Of all the things I've learned about myself since returning to the States, it's that. I can love. I love Donovan.

"Where are Niko and Donovan?"

He shakes his head. "I'll never tell."

Dammit. But I don't let him see my frustration. "Funny. That's what Mom said right before I killed her."

I point my gun at my father's head and I pull the trigger. Giovanni Fiori, the man who gave me life only to shackle it, lies still.

I'm free.

I savor the feeling for a moment and then go to Kate. My fingers work fast, breaking through the ties.

Her breaths come out in hurried gasps, and I'm concerned she'll hyperventilate.

"Kate, look at me," I urge softly, cupping her face to get her attention. "Are you hurt?"

She shakes her head. "It's Liam... he's—"

"He's what?" Did Liam betray Niko?

Her eyes, wide and glistening with tears, latch onto mine. "A Russian man—he took me from where I was staying."

"Liam?" He's Russian. I know he has ties to Bratva.

She shakes her head. "No... another man. He said Liam had to die."

"What about Donovan and Niko?" Does she remember them? She'd only met them briefly when she'd come to the penthouse to say goodbye to Elena before going into Witness Protection.

"I don't know." She takes in a steadying breath. "I just... I heard them say something about a building behind the warehouse. That's where the Russian guy went."

The building behind the warehouse—could they be there? I need to check. I think about sending Kate to the car, but I don't know if anyone else is lurking about. It's better that we stay together.

I hold out my father's gun to her. "Just in case."

She shakes her head. "I don't know how to use it."

"Your father didn't teach you?" I know her father was a police captain.

She shrugs.

"Just hold it and stay close to me, okay?"

She takes it, holding it with her thumb and forefinger like it's hot. I figure if the shit hits the fan, she'll either use it or drop it.

We move toward the rear exit. I open the back door and look out, seeing a smaller office building. My fingers tighten around the gun as I move toward it. Kate keeps pace beside me.

We approach the building. My pulse thrums in my ears. Am I close to finding Donovan, and if I am, is he alive?

I open the door and step inside. Two small offices flank the entry, and just past that to the right is a hallway. We silently turn right and start down the corridor. We nearly make it to the end when the sound of gunfire explodes.

Kate cries out and drops to the floor. I look around, finding a door to somewhere just a few feet ahead of us.

"Come on." I grip Kate's arm and tug her to the door. I open it, holding my gun up as I look around. It's a basic office with a desk. Better yet, it's empty. "In here."

We go in, and I shut the door. We crouch behind the desk, listening as the gunfire continues. Then it slows down until finally, it stops. I have no clue who is fighting or who won, but I want to think it's Niko, Donovan, and maybe Liam if Kate is right.

"You stay here under the desk." I start to rise.

"No. Don't leave me."

"I'm going to see what that was about."

She bites her lip. I can see she's weighing the risks. Finally, she says, "I want to stay with you."

We stand up. "Don't forget the gun," I say when I see it on the floor.

She picks it up and we move to the door. I look out in the hallway. No one.

I step out, and we continue down the hall. At the end is a left-hand turn down another hall. This one seems darker, but I can make out more rooms and a couple more hallways.

I turn left and hear movement. I wait for a moment and then start to move again.

"What if that's the bad guys?" Kate asks.

"Then—"

"Fucking hell... that's Kate."

I stop as I recognize Liam's voice.

"Liam?" Kate asks.

"Come on." I hurry down the hall. Before we reach the end, Niko steps out, gun drawn.

"No!" Donovan grabs Niko's arm. "It's Lucy. Holy hell, it's Lucy."

Relief washes through me like a tsunami. I run to Donovan and throw my arms around him. "It's over. I killed my father. It's over." The adrenaline drops, and I start to shake.

"Lucy." Donovan says it over and over again as he holds me.

"Elena?" Niko asks.

I work to pull myself together. "She's fine… well… she was having cramps, so Aria and Marie took her to the hospital. I think it saved us. We were up when…" I turn to Donovan. "Lou tried to kill us. I killed him first."

Donovan grabs me and holds me again. It feels like a forever hold, but I don't know. Right now, it's enough.

"We need to go." Niko continues toward the exit.

Liam passes me, going to Kate. He presses a palm to her cheek but then quickly pulls it away. "Are you okay?"

She nods, and I feel like he should hug her. She needs his strength. I don't know if there's something between them, but I do know she's looking at him like he's a superhero. For that alone, he should comfort her. Instead, he takes the gun I gave her from her.

Donovan's arms wrap around me again. "I don't know how you did this. I'm in fucking awe of you."

"Donovan!" Niko barks.

"Let's go home." Donovan guides me down the hall.

Home. The word settles in my chest. It sounds warm and loving and permanent. But now that my father is dead, will Donovan follow through on the annulment and send me on my way?

32

LUCIA

"How'd you get here?" Donovan asks as we exit the building.

"I took the car of the Russian who drove me off the road."

The men look at me with surprise. Except Donovan. He's grinning like he's in awe.

"It's an SUV. In front of the warehouse," I finish.

"Ours is up the street a bit," Donovan says.

"I need to get Kate to a safe location." Liam is so tense, I'm worried something will explode. Isn't he relieved that we're all okay?

"Take Lucia's car. It should get past any Bratva looking for you," Niko says.

"The Russian is in it. Zip-tied and belted in. He might still be unconscious. Oh, and he has a gunshot to the shoulder and one to the knee."

Again, the men look at me. I shrug. "You guys didn't answer your phones."

Donovan laughs and kisses my head. "My warrior queen."

Queen. Not princess. Not ice queen.

"I'll deal with it," Liam says, guiding Kate into the warehouse.

"Keys are in the car," I say as he makes a beeline toward the front door.

Donovan and Niko stop over my father's body.

"Three shots," Niko states.

"One kill shot." This time, Donovan hugs me as if he's wanting to comfort me. Or maybe in acknowledgement that the horror in my life is over. "Do you wish it were you who took the shot?" he asks Niko.

Niko shakes his head. "He killed my mother and brother. I'm just glad he's dead. In fact, I take some satisfaction in knowing that his own daughter did it."

"I'll arrange for cleanup," Donovan says as we move to exit the warehouse. A few minutes later, we're in Donovan's SUV. Donovan's hands grip the steering wheel as we peel away from the curb to rush back to Manhattan.

Niko is beside him, phone pressed to his ear as he calls the hospital.

"They let you keep your phones?" I ask from the back.

"Nah, we took them off their corpses." Donovan glances at me through the rearview mirror. In that one look, I see something that brings me hope. It makes me want to stop the car and talk to him, but Elena's health is on the line. My future can wait.

"Keep her safe," Niko murmurs into the device, the strain evident even in his tone.

Donovan uses his phone making calls to clean up the warehouse and building behind it, and he follows that with a call to deal with Lou's body. I feel a sense of triumph that Lou will soon be erased as if he never existed. I watch Donovan, knowing the betrayal from his friend must cut deep.

Exhaustion finally hits me, and I fall asleep. I wake when I hear the familiar sound of the tires on the bridge from New Jersey into Manhattan. The sun is rising, and I have a sense of today being the first day of my new life. What I don't know is whether it will include Donovan.

"Almost there," he says, glancing again through the rearview mirror.

Niko ends another call, his thumb rubbing circles on his temple, a telltale sign of his unease.

"Is it Elena?" I ask, my own unease growing.

"I won't feel right until I see her."

"Stay alert," Donovan says as we enter the city. He's right. Our ordeal may not be over.

We arrive at the hospital, and Niko is out of the vehicle and rushing in before Donovan puts it in park. Donovan takes my hand, and we hurry in after him.

"Where is she?" Niko demands.

A nurse with tired eyes and a gentle smile points us down the corridor. "Room 204. She's—"

We don't wait for more. We hurry down the corridor to Elena's room. The door swings open, and there she lies, looking peaceful. Like an angel.

Niko steps forward, his hand trembling as he brushes a stray lock of hair from Elena's face. The vulnerability in his gesture tells me just how much he loves Elena.

Her eyes flutter open. "Niko!" She grabs for him and tears well in her eyes.

"I'm sorry, baby," he murmurs against her cheek.

Elena's eyes dart around until they land on me. "You're okay? You saved them."

I laugh, pretty sure that Donovan and Niko wouldn't want anyone to think a woman saved them.

"She sure did." Donovan loops his arm around me.

"I didn't. They'd saved themselves when I found them." I step to the other side of the bed from Niko and take her hand. "Dad was there, I—"

"He's out of our lives now." She looks at me with knowing eyes. She's okay with what I've done.

I nod.

She gives me a wan smile. "I'm glad."

"Enough about us, what did the doctor say?" I ask.

She shrugs. "He says it's ligaments or something."

"Or something?" Niko's tone suggest he doesn't like that answer.

"From the uterus growing, especially with twins."

"She's right." The doctor appears behind us. "The fetuses are fine. I recommend more rest and less stress for Mom, here."

"I'll put her to bed for the rest of the time." Niko's tone says he won't take any objection from Elena.

"Full bedrest isn't necessary. Light exercise, walking, can help. I think we'll be able to discharge her in a few hours."

"I'm staying." Niko says it like he's staking a claim.

"I can stay—"

"No." Elena interrupts me. "You look exhausted. And... you saved me, Elena." Tears form again. "You saved me, Aria, and Maria."

"Yeah, well, Aria was a big help."

"What does that mean?" Niko's gaze narrows on me.

"It means you have a brave sister."

"Please, Luce. Go home and rest. I'll be fine." Elena turns her attention to Niko, her eyes filled with relief and love.

"Let's go, Lucy." Donovan takes my arm, leading me out of the hospital and to the SUV. It seems like a million years have passed when I take the elevator up to the penthouse. My breath catches as the door opens and I expect to see Lou. But he's gone. There's no blood or anything to suggest he was ever there threatening to kill us. I'm safe. Elena's safe. For the first time ever in our lives.

"I need to check on a few things," Donovan says as we exit the elevator. "Lou is... I need to—"

I press my hand to his cheek. "I know. I'm sorry he betrayed you."

He shakes his head. "How did I miss it? Fuck!" He sucks in a breath, and his anger dissipates as he kisses my palm. "Go rest. Okay?"

For a moment, we stare at each other. There are so many words to say, but they're stuck in my throat.

He gives me a kiss. "Thank God you're okay." Then he heads to Niko's office.

I intend to lie down, but when I get to the room, I feel dirty. I want to wash away the horror of the day. I enter the bathroom, turning on the shower and peeling away my clothes. I think I'll burn them.

Water trails down my body, the heat and steam penetrating my muscles, my bones, easing my tension. I'm no longer under the thumb of a man who saw me as nothing more than a commodity to be traded. I'm free.

But I no longer want to be free. That's not to say I want to be controlled. But I don't want to be alone. I have to tell Donovan that. I laugh at the courage I had to tackle Lou, but I'm not sure I'm brave enough to tell Donovan that I love him.

I turn off the shower, stepping onto the bath mat. I reach for a towel, wrapping it around myself. I dry off and put on a robe. Opening the door, I pause when my gaze lands on Donovan. He perches on the edge of the bed, his jaw clenched like he's having a silent war with his thoughts.

"Is everything all right?" I ask.

He looks up, and at first, I see sadness. But his expression morphs into frustration. Immediately, my defenses go up as I wait so see why he's upset with me.

"Lucy." His voice is a low rumble. "You belong with me." The words are delivered with command, a fact I'm not allowed to contradict. No choice given.

A shudder of conflicting emotions courses through me.

His gaze holds mine. "It's within my rights, as your husband, to make you stay."

My breath catches. I don't like the tone, and yet, is he saying he wants to make me stay? "I—"

"But your happiness means more to me. So, if you want to go, if you want the annulment, I'll grant it."

I stare at him, wondering if the hit on my head earlier is causing me to hallucinate. "Is that what you want?"

"Fuck, no!" he roars and stands up, his muscles flexing and bunching as he fists his hands. "I want to claim you." His fingers thread through his hair as he lets out a breath. "I'm fucking this up." He stops, takes a breath. "I love you, Lucy."

The declaration crashes into me, shocking me into silence.

"I love you, and I know this isn't the life you want—"

I throw myself into his body, my arms wrapping around his neck. "I love you."

He studies me like he thinks he heard me wrong.

"I love you, Donovan. I want to stay."

His arms wrap around me, drawing me closer until there's no air between us. I bury my face in the crook of his neck, inhaling the scent that is undeniably Donovan.

"Thank fuck," he murmurs.

A laugh bubbles up from deep within me, a sound of pure joy that I don't know I've ever made. I've definitely never felt it.

His smile is wide as he watches me. "You're fucking beautiful." He lifts me and carries me to the bed, his lips already consuming mine before he sets me down again. I let go and open fully to him, amazed by how different things feel now.

He removes my robe and then undresses himself, lying over me. "I hope I don't stink."

"I like how you smell." I rise up to kiss the scar on his chest.

"You smell sweet and spicy, just like you." His nose rubs along my jaw, and then he kisses me again. His hands roam, and I close my eyes, taking in each touch and caress that makes my blood hum.

He settles his hips between my thighs. "Lucy."

I open my eyes. "Donovan."

"I want kids." His cheeks blush. "You asked earlier, and well... that ship may have sailed."

"Oh?" I don't know what he means.

"Earlier when we were like this... well, I was inside you. I didn't have a condom on."

"I remember." It had felt different. More intense. Like he was a part of me.

"I didn't come in you, but there's always a little bit there... you know... so I can fit."

It takes me a moment to figure out what he's saying. "You think I'm pregnant?"

"I don't know. But... you could be."

I'm still stuck on what he's trying to tell me. "Are you okay with that?"

"Hell, yeah. I hope you are."

To be honest, I haven't thought much of marriage and family. But the idea of having it with Donovan fills me with a joy I've never felt.

"I'm okay with that."

His lips twitch up. "Of course, maybe you aren't. And if you want to wait, I need to get a condom."

All of a sudden, I understand what he's saying. "Are you asking whether you need a condom or not?"

"Yes."

I run my fingers through his hair. "I'm okay with whatever you want."

"I want to be inside your sweet pussy bare, Lucy. My dick aches with it."

I spread my legs wider. "Well, then."

He kisses me, full and thorough, making my head spin. When he lifts his head, his gaze holds mine as the head of his dick presses inside me. He takes his time, and it's excruciating and sweet at the same time.

"Tell me you love me again," he says.

"I love you."

He rewards me by sliding all the way in. "I so fucking love you." He surprises me by levering back on his knees and hauling me up to straddle his thighs. He settles me over him, and I sink, taking him deeper.

His hands slide up my back and then down to my backside, squeezing and kneading as his head dips and he suckles on a nipple.

"Oh!" My hands hold him tight as pleasure floods to every cell of my body. I close my eyes and lose myself in the sensation. My hips rock over him, and he groans, the sound reverberating through my body.

"Mine." His lips slide up my neck until he finds my mouth. His tongue dances with mine in the same rhythm of our bodies as we move together. "Do you trust me?"

"Yes." That doesn't mean I'm not nervous about what he has in mind. I'm still new to sex.

He stops moving, lifting me like I weigh nothing and turning me so that my back is to him. He settles me over his thighs and enters me again. A long sigh of relief escapes me as he fills me again.

His hands move from my hips to my breasts, where he teases my nipples. His mouth suckles my neck. "You okay, baby?"

"Yes. More..."

One of his hands slides down my stomach and between my legs. He flicks a finger over my nub... clit. He likes it when I use his words. He does it again and again as his dick slides in and out of me. My entire body is on fire.

"Donovan... Oh, God..." My world spins away in the sweetest pleasure.

He grunts and buries his face against my neck. "All fours, baby." He moves me forward until I'm on my hands and knees. He grips my hips and drives in. I gasp.

"You okay?"

"Yes. Don't stop." I've already come, but I feel the tingles that suggest there could be more. He thrusts in, withdraws, repeats, faster, faster until we're both panting.

"Fuck..." He pulls out, and I think maybe he's changed his mind about the condom.

He flips me over on my back and lies over me, lifting my leg as he slides in again. "Look at me, Lucy. Look at me while I plant my seed in you. Be sure, because I will claim you. You won't be able to leave me."

It's funny how those words a little while ago would incense me. Now I want them.

"I'm sure. Claim me, Donovan."

A wild fire flashes in his eyes. He takes my wrists and holds them over my head as he plunges in, grinding against me. Our gazes hold, and I'm lost in his dark eyes, filled with passion and love. Again, he moves, picking up speed until he's rocking in and out of me at a wild pace.

"Fuck... I'm coming..." He throws back his head as he drives in and groans. Liquid warmth floods my womb. With it, emotion overwhelms me at the idea of making a child. The image of him emptying inside me, impregnating me, turns erotic, and soon, I'm coming again.

"Yes... come on me, Lucy... so fucking good."

We move until depleted of strength. He collapses on me, his weight on his forearms as he kisses me.

"Mine," he whispers in my ear.

"Have you ever considered that maybe you're mine?"

His smile is radiant. "It's true. You claimed my heart from the very start."

That can't be true, but I don't argue.

His expression turns serious. "When Igor said you were dead, something inside me died. I hated myself for not telling you I loved you when we were like this earlier."

I brush his hair from his temple. "I felt the same. I'm glad you said it. I'm afraid I might not have been brave enough."

"You're the bravest person I've ever met."

I laugh. "I think you're mistaking bravery for bravado."

"Is there a difference?"

"I talked a big talk to keep others away."

He rolls us until I'm on top and he's holding me close. "You don't have to keep me away. I won't hurt you. And I won't let anyone else hurt you."

I think about where I was when I met him. I didn't want this life of crime and violence. But I realize now that it's not the life that was the problem. It was the lack of love and respect and choice. I look into Donovan's eyes, and I can see everything I've ever wanted.

I smirk, hoping it mirrors the one he so often gives me. "My Toady."

He laughs. "Forever, my queen. Forever."

33

DONOVAN

Two days later, and I'm still the luckiest motherfucker alive. I confirm it every morning by waking next to Lucy. Turns out, her telling me she loved me wasn't a dream. I'm obsessed with my wife and would be happy to spend life in bed showing her how much I love her. I wonder if a life is growing inside her, a life I made with her.

But time spent naked in my wife's arms has to wait as I get back to work. Especially since Elena is home and Niko is preoccupied with making sure she and the babies are fine.

"You're driving her nuts," Lucy says when she shoos him out of the bedroom so Elena can rest.

He's reluctant to leave but heads downstairs. "Donovan. Lucia. My office."

She looks at me, and for a moment, I'm dazzled again. It's crazy how easily she can distract me.

"Me?" she asks.

I shrug. "Come on. Let's see what he wants. Then we can talk about getting our own place."

She smiles and again... dazzle.

Once inside the office, Niko stands behind his desk. "No word from Liam."

I lean against the edge of the desk. "You sound worried. It's not like he doesn't have a legit job."

"He's never MIA this long."

"He said he wanted to hide Kate. Maybe he has to hide too for that to happen," Lucy offers.

"Maybe. Or maybe his cousins don't like what happened to Igor."

I think about that but dismiss it. "His cousins were the ones who told him to look out for Igor."

Niko lets out a humorless laugh. "A little too late. We were already in Igor's clutches."

Next to me, Lucy shudders. I tug her close, reminding her that we're safe. "Liam's a survivor."

"Yeah," he agrees, but the worry doesn't leave his eyes. I see a man whose concern is about his lifelong friend, not a soldier in his business.

"Is there a thing between Kate and Liam?" Lucy asks. "He seemed different around her."

"I wondered that too. Did you see how he was ready to gnaw off his own hand to get free and help her?" I say.

Niko shrugs. "Hard to tell with Liam. If you're right and he has feelings for her, I hope it doesn't cloud his judgment. Something tells me he's between a rock and hard place. I wish he'd let me know."

"If he needs you, he'll call," I say.

"Right. Well, on to other business. Giovanni, thanks to you, Lucia, is gone."

"Good riddance," I murmur, rubbing Lucy's back.

"That means his Jersey territory is yours for the taking, Donovan. Just like we discussed." Niko glances at Lucy, and I wonder if he thinks she's hearing this for the first time.

"I've already been working on it." My men and I have been doing what needed to be done to make Giovanni's men bend a knee or die.

"The thing is, there's been a lot of talk about Lucia," Niko says.

"Talk?" Lucy looks at me, but I shrug because I don't know what he's talking about. Well, I know there's talk of her bravery and fierceness, but I don't know what Niko is getting at.

"Of your... exploits. Taking out your parents and Lou." His eyes flicker to me, and the guilt at not knowing Lou was a traitor burns in my gut. But Niko's look isn't condemnation. It's sympathy.

"And the way you handled the Russian who drove you off the road. Quick thinking. Efficient. Brutal." Niko laughs. "My men you met in the garage admitted to being afraid you were going to kill them."

"It's no easy thing to put fear in Niko's men." I beam at Lucy with pride. She has fire and ice coursing through her veins. She's as dangerous as any of us. "Thank fuck you love me." I wink.

Niko's lips twitch upwards. "Yes, I'm glad you're on our side."

Her brow arches, and a laugh breaks free from her. It's a rare sound until the last few days. Each time I hear it, it sends my heart soaring.

"Don't forget it, boys."

"What do you think?" Niko asks her, and I realize he's suggesting that she take over. If it were anyone else, I'd have a problem. But Lucia taking over her father's business makes sense. She's a Fiori. It will be easier to garner loyalty from the men we don't end up killing.

"About what?" She glances at me again.

"He's asking what you think about running your father's old territory?" I grin. "I could become your toady."

She laughs again, and I really wish Niko weren't here because I want to kiss her senseless. "Well, that is appealing." She turns to me, looking up at me. "I think I'd rather have a partnership."

How my heart is still in my chest after swelling with love, I don't know. I trace the line of Lucy's jaw with my finger, the closest I can get right now to kissing her. "My queen."

The sudden piercing ring of Niko's phone slices through the moment. He snatches it from his desk. The frown as he glances at the number tells me he doesn't know the caller. "Leone."

Lucy and I exchange a look, both sensing a shift in the air as

Niko's face drains of color. He turns his back to us, blocking us from whatever news he's getting on the other end of the line.

"Understood." Niko ends the call, turning back to us.

"Trouble?" I ask.

"Liam's cover is blown."

I cock my head. "You mean the FBI?"

He nods. "They know he's working with us."

That could explain why he's MIA. "Was he arrested?"

"No. He is on the wanted list, though."

"Is Kate still with him?" Lucy asks.

"That I don't know."

My mind is already working on what we can do for Liam. "We can help him—"

"There's more," Niko interrupts.

"What?"

"Liam isn't just wanted by the FBI."

"Okay…" I let my comment hang as Lucy and I wait for whatever shoe that's going to drop to hit the floor.

Niko's gaze pierces us both. "Liam has taken over the Bratva."

LOVED LUCIA AND DONOVAN? *Great News!* **Prince of Darkness** - Kate and Liam's story, will be available soon. Meanwhile, don't forget to **check out Soldier of Death - Niko and Elena's story here.**

a dark
mafia romance
Soldier OF
DEATH
SHADOWS OF REDEMPTION
BOOK ONE
AJME WILLIAMS

WANT MORE AJME WILLIAMS?

Join my no spam mailing list here.

You'll only be sent emails about my new releases, extended epilogues, deleted scenes and occasional FREE books.